Oh, baby!

For the first time in her life, adventure reporter Miranda Wilde has a plan that doesn't involve scaling mountains or swimming with sharks. Miranda is about to do something scarier—she's about to become a mother. Determined to deliver the news to her unborn baby's father, Miranda arrives in Swift River to find the rugged resort owner with whom she shared an unexpectedly sexy weekend. Except Carson Swift is out of town—on his honeymoon—leaving his twin brother in charge. It's all Miranda can do not to fall apart in Cody Swift's strong arms....

Miranda is the only woman who ever tempted Cody to settle down, which is exactly why he doesn't reveal that he's the twin who shared those soul-searing nights with her. Cody knows Miranda needs more than a rough-edged river guide to give her the life she deserves. Then he learns Miranda is carrying a baby—his baby—and he's ready to stake his claim. But can he prove his heart is in the right place—and that this is one adventure they're meant to have together, for a lifetime?

Books by Kristina Mathews

More Than A Game Series
Better Than Perfect
Worth the Trade
Making A Comeback
Earning A Ring

Swift River Romance series
Swept Away
In Too Deep

Published by Kensington Publishing Corporation

In Too Deep

A Swift River Romance

Kristina Mathews

LYRICAL PRESS
Kensington Publishing Corp.
www.kensingtonbooks.com

First Electronic Edition: December 2016
eISBN-13: 978-1-60183-923-7
eISBN-10: 1-60183-923-5

First Print Edition: December 2016
ISBN-13: 978-1-60183-926-8
ISBN-10: 1-60183-926-X

Printed in the United States of America

To my mother, because she's my mom. The most important thing I learned from her is to never let anyone tell me I can't do something that is really important to me.

Chapter 1

Standing at the top of the driveway, Miranda Wilde tried to calm her nerves. All she had to do was take a few more steps, knock on the door, and tell a man she barely knew that he was going to be a father.

She'd jumped out of airplanes, climbed mountains, and explored underwater caves. But it was her latest excursion, a scenic rafting trip down the Yampa River, that had turned out to be a life-changing experience.

There were two paths leading from the long driveway. A river-stone-lined walkway meandering toward the front of the house, and a short wooden staircase leading to an expansive deck and glass doors overlooking the river.

Friends probably approached from the deck, not the formal front entry. Yet, she couldn't quite consider herself a friend. They'd spent less than a week together. Hardly more than a one-night stand.

She'd been seduced by the scenery, the solitude, and the sexy stud who guided her and the other passengers through the secluded sandstone canyon. A few sunset swims, moonlit walks, and predawn hanky-panky, and she'd made her own private memories to tuck away like a wildflower pressed between the pages of her journal.

Miranda decided to take the longer path to the front door. As if those few extra steps would help her figure out just what she expected from this reunion. She had the cover of doing an article for the magazine. That would give her a chance to ask questions, get to know a little more about her child's father. And then? Hopefully they could at least form a friendship, a solid base on which they could build a coparenting strategy.

As she walked toward the door, a figure appeared in the window. Tall, blonde, and female. She was singing or humming or perhaps even whistling while she worked at the kitchen sink. She was wearing a blue satin dress and seemed very happy this morning.

Great, Miranda hadn't counted on Cinderella.

The chances of her being Carson's sister were probably pretty slim. Of course, he had a new girlfriend, lover, or whatever. They hadn't made any promises to each other or even plans to see each other again. He'd clearly moved on.

If only Miranda had that luxury.

A part of her wanted to turn around. Head back to her car and the rest of her life. But then she thought of having a conversation with her child years down the road. A daughter, perhaps, asking her why she'd never known her father. And Miranda would have to explain that she'd tried to contact him. Once. But there had been a woman in his kitchen. Then her daughter would ask why that woman had been more important than her.

Good question.

Most likely Cinderella was just another one of Carson's flings. If she was in a relationship with him, wouldn't she have brought a change of clothes? It was a little early in the day, and late in the year, for prom. Not to mention the fact that he'd been out of high school for at least a decade.

So Miranda wasn't going to worry about who the woman was or where Carson had picked her up.

Miranda looked down at her T-shirt and shorts—she was dressed for a day on the river—and wondered if she should have dressed up for this meeting. Tried to present herself as a sophisticated urban journalist. But who was she kidding? If she even owned business casual outfits, she'd feel like she was heading to court, not on assignment. No. This was an occasion that called for the familiar. She needed to be herself, the woman he would hopefully remember.

With one, last, deep breath, she approached the front door. Her original plan was a good one. Pretend she was here on assignment. Her readers would want to know all about him, the company, his life on the river. She would make sure he was comfortable, at ease, before she would turn his life upside down.

Then she'd let Carson worry about the other woman.

* * * *

Was that the dish fairy in his kitchen?

Cody Swift expected to face a huge mess the morning after his brother's wedding. Instead, he found a woman dressed in blue satin and yellow rubber gloves.

Fisher.

She'd stayed over to help. Damn her. Or bless her. He couldn't make up his mind. That was part of the problem. She'd worked for him for three years. Why had things gotten weird between them lately? They'd always been friends. She was one of the guys. She had to be, working at Swift River Adventure Company. And Resort. He couldn't forget the Resort. Especially now that he was temporarily in charge.

He'd always been the relaxed one. The easygoing one. His brother would have called him the irresponsible one. But it was just as much Carson's fault as it was his. Carson took care of everyone and everything. But now he had Lily. She took care of Carson.

Cody was surprised by how much he envied his brother. Not just because Lily had chosen his twin over him. He envied the fact that Carson had someone to come home to each night. Someone soft and warm and...

Fisher hinted that she could be that kind of someone.

And last night could have been... It could have been a huge mistake.

What was it about weddings that got women all crazy? Fisher was a bridesmaid. Between the champagne and the flowers and the dress, she'd been transformed into a very feminine—and he had to admit—very sexy woman.

"Good morning, sunshine." She turned and smiled at him. That's right, she was one of those morning people. "I made you coffee, since I know you haven't quite gotten used to Carson not being here."

"Thanks." He offered up a half-smile. He didn't want to encourage her. Thank God he hadn't encouraged her last night. It was bad enough waking up to her in his kitchen. If she'd been in his bed...

"So, I hope you don't mind I started cleaning up." Fisher was still wearing her bridesmaid dress but she'd ditched the heels. Not that she needed them.

"You don't have to do that." Cody felt like he was taking advantage of her. "I can manage."

"Yeah, right." Fisher laughed. She was a great gal. They had a lot in common. Too much, maybe. But unfortunately she wasn't...she wasn't *her*.

A knock on the door startled him out of the fog his quick, and cold, shower hadn't quite cleared up. Who could be here this early on a Sunday?

"I'll get it." Fisher beat him to the door. "Hi, can I help you?"

A stranger. Maybe a guest who'd left something behind after the wedding.

"Hi, I'm Miranda Wilde from *Adventure Chix* magazine." He knew that voice. Had been haunted by that voice for almost two months. "I'm looking for Carson Swift."

"Oh, you're a day late," Fisher said. "He's on his honeymoon."

Shit.

"Hi, Miranda." Cody stepped forward, his heart hammering in his chest. "I'm Cody, Carson's brother. Is there something I can do for you?"

She looked flustered. Confused. A little surprised by his appearance. Of course, she didn't recognize him. Or rather, she didn't realize that they had met. They'd more than just met. They'd had the time of their lives.

And boy, did he now regret pretending to be Carson at the time.

"Oh, you must be twins." Something else he hadn't mentioned. Miranda recovered herself a little. But she wasn't the woman he remembered. The woman he couldn't forget. It wasn't just her long, lean legs, her toned and tan skin, or her glossy, dark hair. There was something about her he just couldn't shake. "I hadn't realized..."

"Please, come in. Would you like some coffee?" Cody led her to the kitchen. He still couldn't believe she'd tracked him down. Tracked Carson down. Oh boy. This could be interesting.

"No, thank you." Miranda looked at him and then looked at Fisher. "Am I interrupting?"

"No." Fisher pulled her gloves off. "We were just cleaning up after the wedding last night. I'll be going."

Miranda must think that Fisher had spent the night with him. She had, but in the spare room. Carson's old room. Damn. He missed his brother already. He'd know what to do. He'd be able to figure a way out of this mess. Except he was too busy being in love and getting ready to have a kid.

"Are you sure I can't get you anything?" Cody wanted to make Miranda feel at home. Hell, he wanted to feel her.

"Maybe a glass of water." She looked up at him, confusion and disappointment in those deep green eyes of hers. Those eyes he'd spent five days and four nights getting lost in.

He turned to the sink and poured her a glass of water. They'd met on the Yampa River, in eastern Utah. At the time, he was filling in for his brother, working the river as Carson. He'd been angry about Carson planning to leave him, so he'd gone in Carson's place. It had seemed like a good idea at the time.

Then he'd met Miranda. Watching her walk away from him had been the hardest thing he'd ever done. But they'd agreed. Keep it casual, keep it fun, keep it within the time frame of the five-day trip. She never knew where she'd be sent on her next assignment, and Cody would go back to being himself once he got off the river for the last time.

Only he hadn't quite been himself since he'd met her.

* * * *

"Thank you." Miranda took the glass from Carson's brother. His twin. Hopefully he hadn't noticed her hands shaking. It was hard enough coming to face a man she barely knew and telling him he was going to be a father. But to find out that he was now somebody else's husband?

"My pleasure." Cody smiled at her. He was cute. Of course he was. He looked just like his brother. Only his beard was a little longer. Not shaggy, but more than a few days' stubble. The crooked smile, the dazzling blue eyes, the tall, muscular frame—exactly the same. "So, I'm sure I can help you. With your story. You are here to do a story on Swift River Adventures Company, right?"

"Yes. That's why I'm here." Miranda swallowed. It had to be the only reason now. "I'm a writer."

"I remember." Cody's eyes softened into a warm smile. "I mean, I figured that, since you said you were from the magazine."

"Yes, *Adventure Chix* magazine." Oh, she must sound like she was from *Adventure Ditz* magazine instead. She did not get flustered. Not like this. But the combination of finding out she was carrying a married man's child, and having that man's twin stare at her like he wanted to have her for breakfast was enough to rattle anyone's nerves.

"I apologize for not making a reservation." She hadn't been able to even bring herself to open up the website. She'd had to just get in her car and drive. "I had a last minute cancellation, and got the idea of doing a piece on adventures you could do on the spur-of-the-moment. Within a few hours' drive of San Francisco. I've traveled halfway around the world, with months of planning. But sometimes you don't want to make reservations six to twelve months in advance. You don't want to spend twelve hundred dollars on one night's stay in a famous lodge. Sometimes you just need to get away for the weekend, find a nice spot, and lose yourself in your surroundings."

"That's one of the things we pride ourselves in." Cody was smooth, a real operator. Just like his brother. "We offer once-in-a-lifetime experiences that you can do every day."

"Yes, that's what I'm looking for." Miranda took a sip of water. Thank goodness the morning sickness wasn't too bad today. She'd left extra early to allow for having to pull over on the way here, but she'd been fine. Just fine. Physically. "I'm looking for a way to satisfy our readers' craving for excitement, without having to leave the country or break the bank."

"Well, I can satisfy your cravings." Oh God, he was definitely hitting on her. "All of them."

Would he be interested if he knew her cravings for the next several months would run toward ice cream and pickles? She shuddered at the thought.

"Look, I'm sure you're a nice man." Miranda needed to nip this flirtation in the bud. She was starting to fall for it. Damn hormones. "But I am only here in a professional capacity. I don't get involved with men on assignment."

"Really?" He eyed her with suspicion. As if he knew she'd made an exception only once. And that was the real reason she was here. "That's too bad."

"So, should we get started on the interview or should I come back when your brother returns?" She hoped she sounded professional. It had never been a problem before. She'd climbed Kilimanjaro, rafted down the Zambezi. She'd even swum with sharks. So why did this man make her so nervous?

"Carson and Lily will be gone for two weeks. Maybe longer." Cody stared at her, as if he had all kinds of ways to keep her entertained until their return. Most of them naked. "I can take care of everything while they're gone. I can take care of you."

Hoo boy. Her traitorous hormones had her thinking she should take her chances while she could. Before she got too big, before she was up all night with a new baby. Alone. She'd have to do this parenting thing on her own. She wasn't a home wrecker. Even if she had a good reason for it.

She felt so stupid. Of course he'd been more than happy to keep it casual. When she'd told him she wasn't looking for a relationship, he'd agreed. Sure, he wasn't looking for a relationship. He had one. While his bride-to-be had been off interviewing photographers and sampling wedding cakes, he'd been interviewed by Miranda and had been sampling her.

Maybe he wasn't the kind of guy she'd want her child calling "Daddy." Obviously, he wasn't exactly the reliable type, not if he could sleep around a mere six weeks before his wedding.

She wanted to get out of there. Get back in her car and just drive. Anywhere. But she had a job to do. And running away wouldn't solve anything.

"Tell you what, I think we'll both be more comfortable on the river." Cody leaned against the counter, a picture of ease. He smiled as if he knew a secret. "I could tell you about what we do here at Swift River Adventures, or I could show you."

"Sure." Miranda relaxed a little, now that he'd dialed down the charm a notch. Besides, she needed information. To find out more about the man she'd met, about his business, and his family. "Do you have room for me on one of your trips?"

"Actually we didn't schedule any trips today, because of the wedding," He pushed off the counter. "But I wouldn't mind taking a ride down the river with a pretty reporter."

Just when she thought he was giving up on the flirting. And the staring. Yet this man seemed to look at her in a way that made her think he knew everything about her. And he wanted to know more.

He was definitely going to be a challenge. But she'd stood up to bigger challenges before. Soon, she'd be facing the biggest challenge of her life. Parenthood.

"So tell me something, Miranda." He said her name like a caress. "How did you learn of Swift River Adventures? Why did you decide to come here for your last minute escapade?"

"Word of mouth." She felt her skin flush. "I took a trip with Epic Adventures on the Yampa, and they spoke highly of your company."

A slow, knowing smile spread over his handsome face.

She gulped down her water. "Could I use your restroom?" If she was going to spend a few hours with this man, she needed a minute to compose herself.

He directed her to the powder room. She closed the door, took care of business, and then splashed cool water on her face. Reaching for the towel, she was surprised by how soft the terry cloth felt. And when she held it against her face, she noticed a hint of lavender. She wondered about the woman who'd answered the door. What was her relationship with Cody? And why did she care?

With an exhale, Miranda carefully folded the towel and looked into the mirror. She didn't belong here. But then again, she'd never felt she'd belonged anywhere. She'd traveled the world looking to find a place where she fit in, but so far she'd never felt at home. Not even in this small, yet homey powder room. The little details of the room stood out, especially in a man's house. The granite vanity was expected, but the color was more gray than brown, almost as if it had been quarried from the nearby Sierras. The floor was slate, instead of tile, and the backsplash was made of small river rock, not glass mosaic. The gray of all the stone was offset by a warm, mossy green color on the walls, and the repurposed fishing reel made a clever and unexpected holder for the necessary toilet paper.

A nice place to visit, but who was she kidding? She wouldn't stay. She couldn't. Not when the man she'd come to see was married. The room started to close in on her, and she flung the door open. She needed air.

"So, are you ready to hit the river?" Cody was waiting for her, that sexy smile still on his face. He looked at her as if he could see right through her. Not just her clothes, but inside. Into her heart. Like he could see her deepest desires and darkest fears.

At the moment they were one and the same. So yeah, the sooner they got on the river, the better.

"Sounds great. I really appreciate you altering your plans for your day off."

"For you, anytime." There was something in his voice that made her feel like he was giving her more than his standard charm. Obviously, he was a player. Like his brother. Or at least, like his brother had been until last night. But somehow, the way Cody looked at her, the way he spoke to her, made her feel special. Cherished. But that was ridiculous. They'd just met. And it wasn't like his brother would have told him to take care of her, since neither of them had ever expected to see each other again.

That's what they'd agreed upon. And if she hadn't been knocked up she'd have had no reason to go back on her word.

Sure they'd had a good time. The sex was great. But it was just a vacation fling. Nothing more. Or it shouldn't have been. Until she'd returned home to find her birth control pills had been recalled. It seemed several batches had been mispackaged, with the placebo pills switched with the active pills. She'd been unprotected against pregnancy for a month or more. And somehow the condoms they'd used had also failed.

So she didn't need any more complications, like getting involved with the brother of the last guy she'd slept with. Her child's uncle.

She swallowed the big lump in her throat and pasted on a fake smile and said, "Let's do this."

Chapter 2

He could do this. Get her on the river, show her a good time, and somehow find a way to bring up the fact that he was the guy she was looking for, not his brother, Carson. Cody had been kicking himself for not making plans to meet up with her again after their little adventure in the desert. But they'd both made it very clear that a continued relationship was not possible. She lived in San Francisco, but traveled a lot for work, so it would be difficult to connect.

And Cody? He'd never had a relationship that lasted longer than a weekend. And by Sunday he'd felt trapped. So he'd been surprised at how disappointed he was to watch her drive away after five days together. He knew the name of the magazine she worked for and she knew he had his own company in California, but they hadn't exchanged numbers or any means of communication.

So now he wondered what had made her change her mind. Or was it just coincidence that brought her to his river? His company? Didn't matter. She wanted a story. He'd give her a story. Hopefully one with a happy ending. Maybe a love scene or two.

"So, Miranda." Just saying her name brought back memories. How her skin held the day's warmth like the sandstone. How her smile brightened his nights like the full moon. And her touch? Her touch was like an oasis. "You've been on the Yampa. What other rivers have you run?"

"The Salmon, the Pacuare, the Zambezi." She rattled off the rivers in Idaho, Costa Rica, and Africa as casually as someone might list roadside attractions.

"I haven't traveled outside of California much." Cody hoped he didn't sound too much like a stick in the mud. "I've got pretty much everything

I need right here. I've got my river to run, trails to hike or bike, beautiful women to entertain."

He flashed his trademark grin, hoping she'd fall for it, like she had back in Utah. They'd been like a couple of teenagers away at summer camp, sneaking off from camp late at night, or early in the morning, snatching kisses—and more—whenever they could.

"And when I want to hit the slopes in the winter, I can grab my skis and hop in my truck…"

"And land a ski bunny?" Miranda teased.

"You ski?" He could picture her swooshing down the mountain, in form-fitting powder pants, her long, dark hair whipping behind her.

"A little. For work."

"Let me guess," Cody knew he was outclassed by her. "Aspen, Whistler, St. Moritz?"

"Actually, the last time I skied was in Sochi," Miranda informed him. "I did a story on Maddie Bowman, Jamie Anderson, and Hannah Teter."

"They're from around here." There had been a viewing party down at the Argo to cheer them on in the 2014 Olympics. "Well, Tahoe, but close enough. We were all pretty proud of them."

"They made all Americans pretty proud." She flashed a bright smile that went straight to his heart. "It was a fun story to work on."

"You must get a lot of fun stories to work on." Cody might not be an Olympic athlete, but he had talents of his own. "That take you all over the world. But there's something here in Prospector Springs that you won't find in Russia, Africa, or Costa Rica."

"What's that?"

"Me." Cody offered his cockiest grin. "I'm going to show you the time of your life."

"Oh really?" She tilted her head to the side and smirked, as if she was trying to hold in a laugh. "You're that good?"

"Why don't we find out?" Cody grinned. "Let's start by packing a lunch. You're going to work up quite an appetite."

He started pulling food out of the refrigerator. "We've got some leftovers from the wedding. The best tri-tip you've ever tasted, sliced thin, on sourdough… It's not quite San Francisco sourdough, but it's pretty tasty, made just up the road at a small, artisan bakery. We've also got a nice kale salad made with locally grown olive oil."

"Sounds delicious. What would I get if it wasn't the day after a wedding?" There was a bit of a challenge in her voice. "If it was a regular Sunday trip?"

"Same bread. With a choice of whole wheat or buttermilk as well. Deli meats, cheeses from the little shop downtown. Fresh berries in season. We try to feature as many local farmers and restaurants as much as possible."

"And do you use raisins dried from local grapes in your GORP?"

"Nah, we get the big bags of trail mix from Costco."

"And is there a Costco in Prospector Springs?"

"No. We don't even have a Starbucks. But I still wouldn't want to live anywhere else."

"Really? Where else have you lived?"

"Across town. Our grandparents had a small place down the street from the elementary school." Selling that little house had been harder than he'd imagined, even if it had allowed them to build their current home. His current home. It still seemed unreal that his brother had moved out. Moved on. "But you didn't come here to do a story on growing up in a small town. You're looking for adventure. The kind you can have on a moment's notice, right?"

"Right. Let's get on the river." Miranda grabbed the lunch he'd packed. "Just let me know what I can do to help prepare for the trip. I want to know all that's involved."

"Certainly. I'd love to show you everything." No, that didn't sound cheesy or desperate. "Everything about life on the American River. Sure, it's not the most secluded or wild river out there, but that's part of its appeal. You don't need a passport or tons of experience to enjoy it."

"Sounds perfect." Miranda sighed. "I mean, that's what my readers are looking for. My editor, and many of our subscribers who've been with us since the beginning, are starting families, establishing careers that might not allow them to take a two-week trek to South America. Yet they still crave excitement. Adventure. Getting away from it all, even if it is only for the weekend."

"We do accommodate kids as young as eight. And I anticipate encouraging more family-friendly trips in the near future." With Carson becoming a father soon, he imagined there would be a lot of changes around here. As long as they didn't turn it into some daycare center.

They made the short drive across the river from the house to the boat barn. He'd grabbed a couple of energy bars to eat on the way since he hadn't had time for breakfast. Cody hopped out of the truck and was around to open Miranda's door and help her out.

"This is where we keep all our equipment." He punched in the code to unlock the overhead door and lifted it open. "These three boats are brand new. We'll take this one."

Cody patted one of the rolled up rafts and tried to lift it from the slightly raised platform, but he dropped it on his foot. He held back the curse word as tears stung his eyes. Hopefully nothing was broken.

"Let me help you," Miranda was at his side. "It seems like a two-person job."

He nodded, still swallowing his pain. And his pride.

"Take my hands." He grabbed both her hands, ignoring the charge the contact sent through his body, and cradled the raft, rocking it onto their outstretched arms. "Now lift. Steady."

Cody kept most of the weight on his end, and she just helped provide balance in getting the raft to his truck and dropping it carefully on the tailgate. Cody shoved it toward the cab.

"Thanks." He still felt like an idiot for even trying to be all macho and do it himself.

"No problem." Miranda smiled. "We make a good team."

"Yeah." Wasn't that what he was trying to convince her of?

* * * *

"Is there anything else I can do to help?" They'd managed to get the heavy raft into the back of his truck and he was heading back into the large warehouse for the paddles. Miranda tried not to stare as his muscles flexed when he carried three paddles over his shoulder. One of them was several inches longer than the other two.

"No. I got it. By the time I showed you where everything is, I could have it loaded myself." He flashed a brief smile before tossing the paddles into the back of his pickup.

"Are you sure?" Miranda felt like she was intruding. "I mean I did sort of force myself on you. And you probably had plans for your day off. Like spending time with your girlfriend."

"Who? Fisher?" He laughed. "She's just a friend. Really. And she works for me. She just stayed over to help with the wedding cleanup."

He was almost a little too dismissive.

"Look, if you really are bored watching me gather up all the gear, you could check out the store." Cody pointed in the direction of a log building with a wide porch. "You could pick out some snacks. We have sodas, sport drinks, juice. Beer or wine?"

"Are you in need of a little hair of the dog?" She didn't want to encourage him. Much. "After the wedding celebration?"

"Nah. I had a good time, but I didn't celebrate too hard." He took a step closer. "It's too bad you didn't arrive yesterday. I would have saved you a dance."

"I'm not much of a wedding crasher." Especially when she was carrying the groom's child. "I think I will take a look around the store. Want anything?"

He gave her a look, a half smile, cocked eyebrow, eyes lowered just enough for her to think that in other circumstances he might have said, "*Just you*." But he just sighed and instead informed her, "It shouldn't take me more than ten, fifteen minutes to have everything loaded and ready to go."

"Okay. I'll be back in ten minutes." That should give her plenty of time to catch her breath. It was weird how much he looked just like the man she'd met in Utah. Okay, maybe not weird, since they were obviously identical twins and all. But she was flustered by the attraction she felt for this man. The wrong man. But then, the right man was wrong for so many other reasons.

Maybe she should just pack it up and skip the rafting trip. She could come up with another story for her editor. But Cody had already gone to the trouble of loading the boat and the paddles. Who knew what else he'd have tossed in the back of his truck by the time she got back?

She'd get through this day, and then she'd take some time to think about what to do next. She had nine months. Well, less than that, but it wasn't like the old days when an unwed mother was all that unusual. And it wasn't like she had family to be scandalized by her situation.

Miranda pushed open the door to the store and a bell tinkled overhead. A young man, about twenty-two, smiled when she entered. She gave him a polite nod and headed toward the back of the store, to where the cold beverages lined the coolers. There were sodas, sports drinks, and beer. Your standard American big names, but also six packs of craft beers, mostly from California breweries, like Sierra Nevada, 21st Amendment, and Bear Republic. What she wouldn't give for a nice hoppy IPA. But that would have to wait.

Instead she found herself checking out the varieties of apple cider. There was the standard fresh cider, flash pasteurized for safety and maximum taste. They also had apple-cranberry, apple-raspberry, and a special blend of wild berries and apple juice that was probably amazing, but sounded a little too much for her at the moment. She selected the straight cider and then grabbed some trail mix.

"Are you checking in to the campground?" the clerk asked. "Because I would be more than happy to show you around. You know, help you get settled."

"No. I'm actually here to do a story on Swift River Adventures." Miranda didn't want to encourage the boy. "I'm from *Adventure Chix* magazine."

"Oh. Cool." He smiled, as if embarrassed he'd never heard of the magazine. "I'm Tyler, and if there's anything you need…anything at all… just let me know."

"Thanks. But I've got Cody Swift taking care of me."

"Oh." The young man seemed to deflate just a little. "Cody's great. He'll show you a real good time. I mean, he's practically a god on the river. And he's a good boss, too. He's pretty chill, but knows what he's doing and all."

"Good to know." Miranda handed over the cash to pay for her purchases. "How late are you here? In case I have further questions?"

"The store is open until seven." He leaned on the counter. "But you could come find me any time. I live in the guide house right behind the barn. With three other guys and Fisher and Brooke. We sometimes get rent-a-guides who crash in the loft if there isn't room in the campgrounds. We're kind of like one big happy family here."

"Thank you." The words happy and family suddenly made her stomach lurch. She stepped outside and twisted the top off the apple cider and took a long swig. It did taste just like a fresh, crisp apple. Sweet, but not too sweet. With just the hint of tartness. She gulped down half the bottle and suddenly felt the porch sway. Oh crap. She shouldn't have done that. She knew better than to drink so much, so fast. She leaned against the railing, closing her eyes and taking slow, deep breaths.

Please. Oh, please, don't let it come back up.

After a moment, the nausea passed and she put the cap back on the bottle. If Cody had a cooler, she'd save it for later. If not, she'd toss it, and stick to the much safer water.

She rounded the corner just as he was slamming the tailgate shut. His T-shirt stretched across broad shoulders. And his board shorts were just snug enough to let her appreciate a finely sculpted ass. He was a fine specimen of the male species, that was for sure. Tall, strong, with a body carved by the river.

Just like his brother.

"Oh, hey, there you are." Cody turned around and lit up with a bright smile. "I'm all packed up. The only thing left is to fit you for a life jacket."

"Sure." She knew the drill. Fortunately, she wasn't one of those women who had trouble fitting into life jackets, wetsuits, or skydiving harnesses. Her breasts were fairly average, not too big, not too small. They would probably get a little bigger in the next few months, but she wasn't going to think about that now.

Cody looked her over, and even though he was wearing sunglasses, she was confident that he liked what he saw. "I'd say a small/medium would suit you just fine."

He walked back into the warehouse with a little bit of swagger, returning shortly with a bright orange vest in one hand and a smaller, black and pink vest in the other.

"This is the standard we've used for years." Cody held up the orange one. It had the familiar floatation collar and was about as stylish as a traffic cone. "But recent advancements in PFD technology have made this model pretty popular among my female guides."

He slipped the black vest over her shoulders, his fingertips barely brushing her arms, sending currents of electricity through her entire body. He pulled the zipper up and tugged gently on the straps. "This isn't too tight, is it?"

"No." It wasn't the snugness of the jacket that had sucked her breath out of her lungs. It was the attention of the man. And the attraction between the two of them. He trailed his fingertips across her collarbone as he reached for the shoulder straps and gave a quick lift.

"Seems to be a perfect fit." He said the words as if he was talking about more than the life jacket. He didn't have to say it, but she could tell he thought they would fit together quite nicely.

Sure, until her belly became rounded with the baby. And wouldn't he be surprised when she gave birth to a child that looked just like his brother?

No. A guy like him wouldn't stick around long enough for her pregnancy to show. And she wasn't sure if that was a good thing or not. Hell, she wasn't sure of much since coming here and finding out she was carrying a married man's child. Especially a newlywed.

But if there was one thing her mother had taught her was that life never promised an easy road. And there were always detours along the way. Sometimes they were rough and bumpy, yet sometimes they led to hidden wonders.

She wasn't sure where this detour was going to take her. She knew she could handle the journey of motherhood on her own. But was that really fair to her child? Or her baby's father? Oh, she wouldn't keep him from her child forever. Just long enough for him to get settled with his new wife. The last thing she wanted was to break up a happy home.

There were so few of them around.

Chapter 3

"Oh hey, Fisher, thanks for coming down." Cody had called her, asking her to ride with them to put-in, so she could drive his truck back to camp. On a commercial trip, they had drivers. A bus would take the passengers upriver, and someone would drive the equipment trucks back to camp. Since he only had one passenger—one very special passenger—he didn't need the bus. But he would need his truck later. Especially if he could convince Miranda to have dinner with him.

"Hey, what are friends for?" Fisher shrugged and reached for the door behind the passenger seat.

"You have been a good friend." He appreciated her. Really. "But you're more than that. You're practically family."

"Yeah. Sure." Fisher ducked her head and leaped into the backseat. "One big, happy family. You should put that in your article, Miranda. Swift River Adventure Company and Resort is not just a company. We're a family."

Oh hell. She was upset. With him. Because he saw her as more of a sister than anything else. Even if Miranda hadn't shown up like she did, she would still come between him and Fisher. Or any other woman for that matter. Miranda had somehow captured his heart.

Who knew he had one? He sure as hell didn't. At least not until he'd met Miranda. And now he had to figure out how to let her know that he'd been her vacation fling. And he wanted more.

"So, how long have you worked here?" Miranda turned around so she could question Fisher. Oh boy, this could get interesting.

"Three years." Fisher sounded cheerful. Almost too cheerful. Yeah. She was pissed at him.

"So, tell me more about your business." Miranda turned toward him. "Did you grow up here? Is whitewater rafting in your blood?"

"It is now." Cody tried to think back to what it was like before he'd found the river. "But we actually stumbled upon the business by accident. Literally."

"Oooh, do tell." Miranda sounded excited by the juicy bit of information.

"It's kind of a long story." Cody hesitated to give too many details about that night that had changed his life—and Carson's.

"I think that's what she's looking for." Fisher piped up from the backseat. "The long story."

"Yeah. Right. So I was in high school. A senior." Cody was embarrassed about that night, yet grateful for the way things had turned out. "There was a spot upriver, where kids would gather. You know, build a campfire, tell stories…"

"Drink beer?" Miranda was no dummy. "Make out?"

"Yeah. Something like that." Cody could still remember the way his heart hammered and his life flashed before him as his car slid off the road and into the fence. "Anyway, I was leaving the gathering. Okay, party. I thought I was fine, but I took the curve a little too fast. Next thing I knew, I was trying to unhook my bumper from the fence just up the road. This old guy—old to me, he was in his fifties—he comes out, and after determining I was okay, let me call home, instead of him calling the cops."

"You're lucky." Miranda said.

"You have no idea." Cody put the truck into drive and headed toward the main road. The fence was in good shape. For now. They usually had to repair it at least once a year, usually in the late spring, when the high school kids were getting restless and stupid. "When it was my brother who showed up, instead of our dad, Travis made us an offer we couldn't refuse."

From the backseat, he could hear Fisher humming the music from *The Godfather*.

"Anyway…" Cody stopped at the end of the driveway. "Travis offered to let us make up for my mistake. He offered us a job. We started with the fence, right there."

He pointed to the section just before the entrance. The start of a whole new life.

"Then we stayed on, doing odd jobs around the campground. Picking up trash, cleaning out fire pits, keeping the bathrooms clean and well stocked."

"The glamorous life." Miranda teased.

"Yeah." He didn't mention how much he'd hated the work at first. How he'd resented spending his weekends doing slave labor, when his friends were still screwing around, chasing girls and drinking beer on the banks of the river. Not scrubbing toilets, picking up beer cans, and hauling trash to the dump.

"So how did you end up owning the company?"

"Well, we eventually worked our way onto the river. Travis trained us himself." Cody drove to the state highway that would take them upriver to put-in. "Started out as assistant guides, which meant we got to haul the gear and make the lunches, and learn from the head guides how to read the river."

"Is that how you started, too?" Miranda turned toward Fisher.

"I went to guide school, then worked my way up." Fisher said. "I didn't do as much of the dirty work, though. I work in the store sometimes when they need an extra hand."

"Fisher is one of our best guides. She's recently been promoted to Assistant Manager." Cody was certainly grateful to have her help, especially with Carson gone for two weeks.

"Congratulations." Miranda said.

"Thanks." Fisher leaned forward to participate in the conversation. "I think it was Lily's idea. To take some of the pressure off Carson."

"Lily?"

"My brother's wife. And our bookkeeper."

"Oh." Miranda sounded a little disappointed, maybe.

"See, it is one big, happy family." Fisher said. "Who would have thought wedding planning would be part of the job?"

"And cleaning up, afterward?"

"Nah, I did that just because." Fisher said. "But I could put it on my timecard."

"You're salary now." Cody reminded her. "No overtime, but you get other benefits."

"Not *those* kind of benefits." Fisher jumped in. "We're just friends. Really."

"Uh-huh." Miranda sounded like she wasn't quite buying it.

"He meant benefits like health care." Cody glanced in the rear view mirror and noticed Fisher was blushing. Just a little. "But all the full-time employees get health care. Which is a good thing, really because Lily's going to need it."

"Oh, is your sister-in-law . . . sick?" Miranda asked, concern in her voice.

"No. She's expecting."

"Oh. I see." Miranda looked out the window, as if the news was something unexpected. "So, the picture I'm getting is that this is a family business. And the two brothers and one wife are all equal partners?"

"Well, Carson and I are partners in the business." Cody was going to have to explain this to her, but not in front of Fisher. He didn't need both women judging him for what he'd done. Fisher had been pretty steamed at him for leaving so suddenly, not telling anyone where he was going. He and Carson had had a fight. A knock-down, drag-out fist fight. Lily and Fisher had witnessed the whole thing. And he didn't know how to explain his complicated relationship with his brother to Miranda. Why he'd needed to walk in Carson's sandals for a while. "Lily and Carson are partners in everything else. She's also our office manager."

* * * *

So Carson's wife was pregnant. And also his bookkeeper. Miranda's news could potentially break up a not just a family, but also a family business.

Great. She was the worst person ever. No. Make that the guy who gets two women pregnant at the same time. He's the worst person ever.

Except he seemed like a really good guy. And his brother seemed like a good guy. Who was she to come up here and disrupt their happy family?

She supposed her child would be their family.

Family. What a concept. Something she'd never had. Her mother, Elizabeth, had been disowned after Miranda was conceived.

She looked out the window, watching the pine and oak trees as they wove along the winding two lane highway to the start of the river. So different than the desert landscape of the eastern Utah river where she'd met Carson. Yet both settings were beautiful in their own ways.

Along the banks of the Yampa River, there were plenty of sandstone cliffs, wide open spaces, and solitude. It was almost as if she had left all her worries behind once she'd stepped onto that raft. Her troubles had not been welcome on the isolated river.

Here, in the foothills of the Sierra Nevada, she didn't feel quite so disconnected from civilization. Along the way, they'd passed orchards, vineyards, and a couple of small farms, with goats, horses, even a few head of cattle.

Split-rail fences, stacked-stone walls, and a few brick-and-wrought-iron gates marked the private properties out here in the country. She saw rambling Victorian farmhouses with sprawling porches, two-story log homes, and small stone cabins that looked like they could have housed miners back in the 1850s.

As they wound their way closer to Placerville, more modern neighborhoods came into view. Modern, being anything from the 1920s bungalows to 1970s era ranch houses and even a small development of more recent construction. They took a sharp turn off Highway 49 to 193. After a quick view of the American River Canyon, they made several hairpin turns through more moss-covered oaks, towering pines, and tangles of lush blackberries.

The closer they got to the river, the lighter her burdens seemed to feel. It was so green here, even late into the summer, when some of the grasses along the valley had started to dry up. The oaks were still green and the pines were evergreen, having bounced back from several years of drought.

It was hard to believe she was only a few hours out of the city. But wasn't that the angle she was going for with this piece? How to get away from it all, and still get back home in time for dinner. Or at least work on Monday.

Right, she was working here. She needed to keep that her main focus. Not let her emotions get in the way.

"Tell me more about how you bought the company." Miranda had figured they had inherited it, since they were still pretty young, maybe thirty. "Does cleaning out fire pits and working your way up to head guide make a lot of money?"

A stifled laugh came from the back seat.

"At first, the main benefit of the job was not involving the cops." Cody took a particularly sharp turn with care. "Or our father."

She wanted to ask, but held off, wondering what the deal was. But also feeling that familiar combination of envy and sadness. At least he had a father to resent.

"Anyway, once we turned twenty-one and were on track to graduate college..." Cody let out a small sigh. Regret? No. It was something else. An emotion she had no experience with. "Travis made us the offer to buy the place. All of it. His own kids had gone off and pursued different careers. Followed their women out of state. So Travis felt like he was getting older, missing out on grandkids. He realized he wasn't going to pass along the family business to his sons. So he offered it to us."

More mention of family. More salt in her own wounds.

"But how did two college kids manage to make that kind of investment?" From what she'd gathered so far, they hadn't had much. If they'd been rich kids, surely their father would have paid their way rather than make them work for practically nothing.

"We sold our granny's house." Cody's voice held just a tinge of sadness. "It was in our name, not our father's, when she passed. He only came to stay with us because we were too young to live on our own."

Miranda got a chill down her spine at the way he spoke of his father. Normally, she'd be able to draw out the full story. Especially the juicy details. But for some reason, she didn't want to pry. Not when it was so personal.

"But we really couldn't have done it without the money from the settlement." Cody slowed down as they came to a bridge. They were at the river finally.

"What settlement?" She almost didn't want to ask.

"From the hospital." Cody took a turn upriver once they'd crossed the small bridge. She could see a small dam about a quarter mile upstream. "See, our mother died in childbirth. But it was a mistake on the hospital's part."

Miranda's heart just broke a little. For him. His brother. Their mother. And her thoughts drifted to her own unborn child. No words could escape her lips.

"Anyway, our dad freaked out and took off. Couldn't deal with all of it, I guess." He sounded so matter-of-fact about it. Like he was telling her about a pet he'd lost as a child. "Our grandparents, on my mom's side, they took us in. Made sure the hospital paid for their mistake. We couldn't touch the money—well, except what we needed to get by after they passed—we had to wait until we were twenty-one to access the rest of it."

"And you used the money to buy the company? The resort?"

"Yeah. It seemed like the best way for us to build a career. A life." Cody pulled into a wide spot on the road near the river. There were other rafting operations setting up for a day on the river. "I mean, if you can make a living doing something you love, you've pretty much got it made, right?"

"Yeah." She thought about how traveling had always been like that for her. She'd always enjoyed going to new places. Seeing new things. New people. But lately she'd wondered if she truly loved it or if it was all she'd ever known.

* * * *

Cody was glad they made it to put-in before he could ramble on too much about how they'd been able to buy the business. He didn't like talking about money. Especially the money from the lawsuit. Sure, he was grateful that his grandparents hadn't had to bear the financial burden of raising him and his brother, but the whole idea of having the cash instead of his mother never sat right with him. So he pretended like it was no big deal. If he didn't think about where the money came from or where it went, he wouldn't have to think about what it had cost him.

He put the truck in park and jumped out, ready to get to work. Miranda insisted on helping unload the smaller gear, while he and Fisher pulled the heavy raft out of the back of the truck. Once everything was unloaded, Cody started unrolling the raft to prepare for inflation.

"Hey Cody, I don't see the pump?" Fisher went back to the truck, looking for the necessary piece of equipment. "Is it over there?"

He looked around, but didn't see it. He had the hand pump, but that would be a lot more work than simply plugging in the electric pump and inflating the raft in a matter of minutes.

"What does it look like?" Miranda started turning over smaller pieces of gear, trying to be helpful.

"It's red." Cody could picture it. Sitting on the shelf of the gear shed. "Looks kind of like a smaller version of a leaf blower."

"Could it be on one of the dry bags?" Miranda suggested. "With the lunch maybe?"

"No." Cody sat back on his heels. How many times had he packed for a trip? Hundreds? Maybe more. The process had become automatic. Something he didn't even have to think about.

Except now that he'd thought about it, he'd completely forgotten to pack the electric pump.

"I'll go see if we can borrow one." Fisher just smiled and shook her head. She knew he'd been distracted by Miranda and instead of making things worse, she simply went off to solve the problem.

Worst case scenario, he'd have to pump up the raft by hand. While he wouldn't mind showing off his muscles, he didn't want Miranda to get bored before the trip even began.

"Is there anything I can do to help?" Miranda offered.

"I think we're pretty much set, once we get the raft inflated." Cody felt like a complete idiot. "There's not much we can do until we get that part accomplished."

"Oh, okay." She wiped her palms on her board shorts. The mossy green fabric clung to her hips just right. Not too loose. Not too tight. Her T-shirt hung just below the waistline of her shorts, and he could see the darker green string of her bikini peeking out the top.

Cody pulled his gaze away from her before he could picture her sliding out of the board shorts and diving into the water. He rifled through his gear bag and pulled out the sunscreen.

Slowly, he tugged his shirt over his head and started rubbing lotion on his arms and chest. He was glad he had sunglasses on so he could secretly watch Miranda secretly watch him.

Her little sigh told him she liked what she saw.

"Would you mind?" Cody held out the bottle. "I can't reach my back."

Another sigh accompanied her movement toward him. "Do you always have your passengers apply sunscreen for you?" A small smile crept across her lips as she grabbed the bottle.

"Consider it a late booking fee." Cody tried not to sound too pleased with himself as he anticipated her hands gliding over his skin.

"Oh. Right. I have my company card from the magazine. I guess we should have taken care of the fee before we left."

"Nah. I'll write it off as advertising and promotion." He now knew they did have a budget for such things. Lily had taken the time to go over the bookkeeping with him so she could enjoy her honeymoon without worrying about the bills being paid.

"I guess I could send you a few extra copies. Once the article is published." She squirted lotion into her palms and started rubbing his back and shoulders. All thoughts of bookkeeping, advertising, and pretty much everything else drifted from his mind. Her hands were like magic. He'd started to wonder if he'd only imagined how good she'd felt, but nope. It was real.

He let out a small groan and she dropped the bottle of sunscreen.

"Well. I think you're covered." She stepped back, sounding just a little flustered.

"Would you like me to return the favor?"

"Um. No. I already applied." She avoided his gaze. Even behind the safety of two sets of sunglasses, it was obvious she didn't want to get too close. She bent to pick up the sunscreen and handed it back to him.

He'd have to keep an eye on her. Make sure she didn't get burned.

"I found a loaner." Fisher stepped up, with the borrowed pump in her hands. She glanced from Cody to Miranda and sighed. She'd picked up on the tension between them and tried to fake a smile. "I just hope you didn't forget anything else, because I'm not going to try to cover for you again."

"No. We have everything else we need." Cody plugged in the small portable pump and inserted it into the first valve on the raft.

"Well, if there isn't anything else, I'll go ahead and drive your truck back." He could feel Fisher's glare, even behind her dark sunglasses. "I'll leave the keys in the store. Behind the register?"

"That would be great." Cody gave her his most charming smile but he knew she wasn't buying it. She was pissed at him. And he had a feeling it wasn't because he'd asked her to run shuttle for him on her day off. He just hoped she'd be professional enough to not let it get in the way of them working together. She was a valuable member of the team and he'd hate to lose her simply because he'd fallen for Miranda instead.

Once the boat was inflated, it didn't take long to get the rest of the preparations underway.

"Anything you want to throw in the ammo can? Personal items you don't want to get wet or crushed, like your phone?"

"Oh, I have a waterproof pouch for my phone. That way I can take pictures." She held up the strap around her neck and glanced at the screen. "Oh, I don't seem to have service."

"Yeah, you probably won't have much of a signal until we get back to camp." Cody explained. "But the way I see it, you have a chance to unplug completely, even if it is just for a few hours."

"I kind of like that idea."

"Is there someone who will worry if they can't get a hold of you? A boyfriend?" After almost two months, it was possible she'd entered a relationship since they'd parted ways.

"No. No boyfriend." She said it like she thought the idea was ridiculous. "And my editor isn't expecting my submission for a few days. So I guess I will relax and enjoy being off the grid."

"Well, you'll be in good hands."

Chapter 4

After a quick, yet thorough, safety talk, they were finally underway. Cody was an excellent guide, showing her points of interest along the way. They'd barely been on the water when they'd passed a slate quarry that had been in operation since 1886.

They'd had a little time to practice the simple commands—*forward, back paddle, right back, left back*—before they encountered their first rapid.

"This first rapid is about a quarter mile, a lot of little rocks, some big waves, and I'll make sure to steer us away from that hidden boulder near the bottom." Cody explained while maneuvering the raft from his perch on the rear of the boat. Miranda sat near the middle of the raft, with her paddle extended out over the left side. "We like to give you your money's worth right off the bat."

Sure enough, the raft pitched and swayed down the rapid, splashing cold water and sending just enough of an adrenaline jolt through her to let her forget about her troubles. Mostly. She still had a child to think about and she was pretty sure that she'd never think only of herself again.

But the scenery and the calming, yet exhilarating, feeling of being on the river let her relax somewhat. She didn't have to have everything figured out right away. There was a reason it took nine months. She'd have time to work out a few details.

For now, she'd sit back, enjoy the ride, and think about what angle she wanted to present on this article.

As they made their way down the canyon, Cody did an excellent job of infusing humor with his extensive knowledge of the history of the area. He pointed out remnants of the gold rush era, from rock walls and roads built by Chinese immigrants to rusted remains of cable-operated trams. He informed her they would pass by the original site of Sutter's Mill, where James Marshall made his famous discovery.

"I didn't realize there was so much history around here." Miranda liked to live in the moment for the most part, maybe because her own history was so uncertain. But for some reason she was drawn to the significance of the gold discovery. Would her current hometown of San Francisco be what it was today if not for the rush of the forty-niners seeking their fortunes?

"Yeah. It definitely made it more interesting in the fourth grade. Not like living in, say, Bakersfield." He paused. "You're not from Bakersfield are you? Not that there's anything wrong with it. I've never been there, actually."

"No." She couldn't help but smile at how quickly he'd backtracked, so as not to offend. "I'm not from Bakersfield."

"So where are you from?" He asked, innocently enough.

"Oh, all over, I guess."

"Parents in the military?"

"No. My mom…" What could she say? That her mom was like Juliette Binoche's character in *Chocolat*, dragging her daughter from place to place, only without the community Johnny Depp's gypsy character relied on. While every other woman was drooling over Depp or applauding Binoche's character for defying the rigid social mores of the time, Miranda had identified most with the daughter, who created an imaginary friend to follow her from town to town. "My mom just never liked to stay rooted in one place for very long."

"I never knew my mother." Cody's voice got all serious, and a little sad. "And my dad… Well, he wasn't exactly worth knowing."

"Yeah, well…" Sometimes she would make up stories about why she'd never spent more than a year in any one school. In any one town. She would tell her newest friends that she and her mother were in a witness protection program, or royalty from a small country that had been overthrown by insurgents and she would return when it was safe. Or that maybe she was the daughter of a famous athlete or movie star and they'd move from place to place to keep his wife from finding out about her.

The truth wasn't nearly as interesting. Her mother had been kicked out of the house—or run away, Miranda had heard different versions over the years—after getting pregnant. And asking questions about her father never amounted to much more than upsetting her mother to the point where they would start packing for the next spot on the map.

"So this next rapid is pretty straightforward." Cody positioned himself to navigate through the current. "We just want to head to the left of that—"

They hit the small rock dead center, and Cody flipped out of the boat. Miranda's first instinct was to stand up and head toward the rear of the raft, but she quickly realized her mistake as she pitched backward. She managed to steady herself against the center tube, and tried to think about her best course of action when finding herself up a creek without a guide.

She knew she wouldn't be able to paddle upstream so she grabbed her paddle and managed to sit down again, facing forward, just in time to bounce off another small rock. This time, the raft lurched toward the right side of the river and she managed to get caught in an eddy. The current flowed backward, basically keeping the raft at a standstill long enough for Cody to swim toward her.

"Here, grab my paddle and pull me toward you." He'd somehow managed to hold onto his paddle and she was able to latch on and reel him in.

Once he'd reached the raft, he tossed the paddle on board and tried to heave himself over the side, but he couldn't quite make it.

"Grab the shoulders of my life jacket." Cody instructed. "I'll kick off as you pull me over the side."

Miranda reached for him, but worried that the effort would be wasted. She was pretty strong, but the man had to be about six-two or six-three and must weigh at least two hundred pounds of solid muscle. No way she'd be able to haul him up out of the river. But she couldn't just stand there doing nothing, so she grabbed his shoulder straps and yanked. Hard. She almost toppled backward as he slid over the side of the boat.

Once she had her guide safely back on board, Miranda's legs gave way. She slumped against the center tube, her hands shaking. Everything was shaking.

"Great job." Cody took off his sunglasses, held in place by a strap with the Swift River Adventures logo printed on the side. He raked his hands through his hair and then positioned himself at the rear of the craft. "So where did you do guide school?"

She shivered, even though the temperature was in the high eighties and climbing.

"I've never..." She bit her lip to keep it from quivering.

"Well, the way you caught that eddy, I figured you had more than just casual experience." Cody started to back paddle, maneuvering the boat into the current.

"No. Just luck." Even her voice sounded shaky. "I almost fell out, too."

"What do you say we break for lunch?" He reached his paddle out over the water, steering the boat toward a small island, not much more than a sandbar in the middle of the river. "I know the perfect spot."

"Yeah. I guess I could eat." Maybe he'd think low blood sugar was the reason for her sudden trembling.

"Me, too." He paddled a few strokes and the next thing she knew, they were gliding straight into a perfect beach. "Could you grab the bow line? Just slide it out of the loop. That's it. Now hop on out."

Miranda froze. She'd managed to untie the nylon webbing, but she couldn't make her legs move.

With amazing swiftness, Cody was at the front of the boat, hopping over the side and securing the rope to a sturdy branch of what looked like some sort of willow.

"Take my hand." He reached out and pulled her up so she could step out of the boat.

Miranda was surprised at how warm his hand was, considering he'd just been in the water.

* * * *

Miranda was trembling, and since they weren't naked, Cody didn't see that as a good thing. He'd scared her. Scared her good.

What an idiot. He'd been so busy trying to impress her that he'd made several rookie mistakes. Forgetting the electric pump was just the beginning.

For too long, he'd kept his eyes on his passenger and ended up dumping himself into the river on a fairly straightforward rapid. Without anyone else in the boat to help her, Miranda had been left alone on the raft. And it had freaked her out.

"Miranda, look at me." He reached up and removed her sunglasses and saw fear in her green eyes. "It's okay. Really. I need to take an unintentional swim every ten years, or so, just to stay fresh."

She barely cracked a smile, but her eyes lost some of that terror.

"What do you say we tear into those sandwiches?" It was a little early for lunch, but he knew she wasn't ready to get back on the river.

"Great." She broke their gaze. "I'm starving. The oatmeal and juice I had this morning has worn off, so let's eat."

Miranda dropped his hands and a small part of him missed the connection. But if he'd kept holding her hands there was another part that would become larger. Uncomfortably so.

Cody took out the sandwiches and offered Miranda a bottle of water.

After a few bites, she started to perk up.

"This is really good." She moaned as she ate her tri-tip sandwich. "I mean, *really* good."

"Yeah. I think our friends at the Argo might find themselves branching out into the catering business." They had done the wedding as a special favor, since the event had been rushed and the Swift brothers had sent a lot of business their way from recommendations and their own patronage.

"What's the Argo?" Miranda asked, her reporter's curiosity showing.

"The American River Grill. It's a restaurant and bar, but everyone calls it the Argo for short. It's kind of a reference to Argonauts, you know, those who came here during the gold rush."

"I thought they were called forty-niners."

"Yeah, that's another name for the gold rushers. Wait, is that a word?"

Miranda laughed. The sound was richer than any pay dirt found since James Marshall's big discovery.

"I'm afraid I don't know much California history. I didn't move here until I was in my twenties." She took her last bite of her sandwich. "I know a little about the gold rush. The great earthquake in 1906, and the other one in 1989 that canceled the World Series."

"Postponed it. The World Series," Cody said, remembering to finish chewing first. "I was only two at the time, but Granddad was there that day. He never heard the end of it. It was the last time he ever went to a Giants game without Granny."

Miranda looked at him kind of funny, and he realized she didn't know that he'd been raised by a couple of rabid fans. It's too bad they'd never gotten to catch a game at the new ballpark. At least they'd all been able to say goodbye to Candlestick together.

"So. You ready to get back on the river?"

"Yeah. I think so." Miranda dug through the dry bag where she'd stashed her personal belongings. "Let me just check my phone."

She looked at it and shrugged. "Still no signal."

"Yeah. But you might find that being disconnected from your phone just makes it that much easier to get away from it all." It was one of the lines he'd perfected to reassure passengers that they would not, in fact, die without access to their phones at all times.

"Just as long as my guide doesn't get away from me again." Her voice held just enough of a playful note for him to realize she was teasing him.

"I wouldn't dare get away from you again." He teased back, but hoped he was dead serious.

"Yeah, sure." She started packing up the lunch items. Acting like she had zero faith in him.

"Hey." He took two steps closer to her. "Would it help if I told you that the only reason I fell out is because I've fallen head over heels for you?"

She snorted. "Does that kind of line usually work for you?"

"No." Cody laughed with her.

"Good. Because I'd hate for you to confess your undying love only to get shot down."

"Ouch." Cody feigned a deep wound to the chest. "Shot down so early in the day. Well, just so you know, I don't give up easily."

"I'm not interested in any kind of relationship."

"And here I was getting ready to propose." Cody pretended to drop to one knee. "Just ignore the skywriting in about ten minutes."

"Skywriting?" Miranda cracked a smile. "Isn't that a little over the top?"

"Well, it's not dark enough for fireworks. And they're illegal in this county." Cody sat down on a rock, stretching out like he hadn't a care in the world. "I could arrange for a surprise rainstorm, but that's more effective in a rowboat on a lake, with dozens of swans."

"Don't forget the lily pads and a frog choir."

"How about hundreds of rose petals strewn along a path that leads to a secluded hot spring?"

"With a candlelight dinner and a string quartet playing just for us?"

"No string quartet." Cody leaned toward her. "The hot spring I have in mind would require privacy."

"Bathing suits optional?"

"That would be entirely up to you." But Cody looked her over, knowing how beautiful she was without her bathing suit.

"Well, if you're going to propose, then I'd have to be dressed." She played along. He liked that about her. "I think naked proposals are tacky."

"You like baseball?"

She shook her head briefly, as if the question came too far out of left field. "I guess so, why?"

"Because I think scoreboard proposals are tacky." Cody stood and took a step toward her. "I mean, people are there to watch the game. And then some guy interrupts the whole thing, throwing off the timing of the batter and the pitcher."

"That is rude." Miranda smiled. "Almost as rude as bringing a beach ball to a game."

"You are a baseball fan." Cody was secretly pleased by this revelation.

"Well, living in San Francisco, it's hard to not enjoy watching the Giants."

"How long have you been a Giants fan?"

"Since I moved there, in 2008."

"2008, huh? Where did you live before that?"

Before she could answer, a raft full of passengers drifted by.

"Hey, Cody," Todd from a rival company called out. "Looks like you're no longer feeling flat."

"No. I was able to get pumped up with a little help from a friend." Cody knew it was Todd's pump that Fisher borrowed. "Thanks, man."

"Can't leave a brother deflated." Todd laughed. "Besides, you and Carson have bailed me out more than once."

Todd then turned to address his passengers. "But this is the first time I've had to return the favor. The Swift brothers are legends around here. Both on and off the river."

With a wave, Todd gave the command to his crew to move forward, paddling downstream.

Cody had always been proud of his and Carson's reputation on and around the river.

"Legends, huh?" Miranda finished cleaning up the lunch. "Both on and *off* the river? I take it you're known for your volunteer work around the community?"

Damn. He'd finally met someone he truly wanted to impress. And she was merely amused.

"We do our share of charity events. We donate trips to the major fundraisers, like for the Rotary Club, Soroptimists, and Boys and Girls Club."

"But that's not what he meant, is it?" Miranda wasn't one to be fooled. "You guys are players, aren't you?"

"We both played ball in high school. Until we fell in love with the river."

She tossed the last of the sandwich wrappers in the dry bag and approached him. She put her hand on his chest and looked up at him, but her eyes were shaded by her sunglasses. "You know that's not what I'm asking."

"Hey. What can I say?" His heart thudded uncomfortably in his chest. "Yeah, two young single guys had our share of fun."

"Had?"

"Well, my brother's married." Cody knew he was on a slippery slope here. "He's all Lily's now."

"And you?" Miranda asked. "Are you going to have to have all the fun for both of you?"

"I'm all the fun you'll need."

"Too bad I'm here to work." She took a step back, pulled her phone out of her pocket, and started snapping pictures of the river.

"Why didn't they send a photographer with you?" Cody closed up the dry bag and tossed it into the raft. "Couldn't find one who works on Sundays?"

"I like to take my own pictures. Just to enhance the story." She slipped her phone into the waterproof pouch and then tucked it between her breasts inside her life jacket. "I prefer to paint pictures with my words."

"If your words are half as beautiful as the rest of you—"

"Please. Let me stop you before you get yourself all worked up." Miranda held her hand out. "This is the absolute worst time for flirting or anything else. It's not you. But I'm in a place right now where I can't even consider a relationship. Even a temporary, less than twenty-four-hour one."

He wondered if she'd had her heart broken recently. And more importantly, if he'd been the one to break it. Only...oh hell. How did he even begin to explain that he was the guy she'd met on the Yampa? Not Carson. That the guy she'd connected with wasn't, in fact, married, but available, to her, right now.

"Are you ready to get back on the river?" When all else failed, he stuck with what he knew.

"Yeah. That would be great." Miranda hopped into the raft, picking up her paddle and holding it almost as a shield.

Chapter 5

It felt good to get back on the river. Miranda could concentrate on dipping her paddle, completing the stroke, and even though she knew Cody was doing most of the work, she had at least a sense that she was contributing to the navigation of the raft.

The rest of her life felt as out of control as when Cody had fallen overboard and she was completely at the mercy of the forces of nature. The river. Her hormones. The automated machine that dispensed the wrong pills combined with the failure of one or more condoms due to desert heat, improper storage, manufacturing error—take your pick. The results were the same.

She was pregnant. And that changed everything.

If she wasn't, she could enjoy the obvious and over-the-top flirtations of her guide. The whole outrageous proposal suggestions—they were cute, corny, and completely clichéd. But that was his whole point. And under different circumstances—why not? He was quite charming. Fun. Sexy.

And the twin brother of the last guy she'd slept with.

The part of her brain that could spin stories, come up with plot twists, and ask "what if?" started spinning, wondering if she could just sleep with the guy, and then a few months down the road spring the news she'd been planning on springing on his brother.

As far as she knew, there would be no way to tell from a DNA test whether a child was his or his twin's. She could always claim a premature birth, but with the father being such a big, strong guy, it wouldn't be unrealistic for the child to catch up in weight after a few months.

But no. She couldn't do that. To him or to her child. She couldn't live the lie. Couldn't sit there at Thanksgiving dinner knowing that the man her child called "Daddy" was really "Uncle" and vice versa. She couldn't stand side by side with Aunt Lily doing the dishes all the while knowing the cousins running around together were really half-siblings.

Miranda couldn't think about all that right now. She had a tendency to overthink things, and while her contemplations would make for an interesting family drama—if she ever got around to finishing a novel—it wasn't good for keeping her attention where it needed to be, on the river.

Dipping her paddle into the deep, dark water, she put her energy into something she could control. The river. She watched as the water swirled around the paddle, making interesting patterns in the somewhat calm surface and just below.

"It helps if you only paddle when I give the command." Her guide's voice brought her back to the present. "You'd be surprised at how much one or two strokes can alter our course."

"Oh. Sorry. I guess I got caught up in my own head." She lifted the paddle and set it across her lap. "I thought maybe I'd missed your directions."

"No big deal, I can make the necessary corrections." He dug his longer guide's paddle into the current and with one strong stroke, got them back on course.

They took on a series of fun, but not too challenging rapids. The kind that made a splash, getting her wet, but not soaked. That were exciting without being frightening. Exactly the kind of ride she'd expected from this trip. More like a roller coaster than a high speed chase.

But then they glanced off a small boulder, spinning the raft into an unexpected turn. They went over a moderately sized rapid backward, yet Cody seemed confident, in control. He used his paddle to steer the craft around so that they bounced off the next rock and were facing downstream once again.

"The boat is a little lighter than I'm used to, I hope you didn't get dizzy."

"No. I'm fine." Except for the way the whole experience made her think of that scene in *The Little Mermaid*, where the rowboat spun around, and the creatures started singing "Kiss the Girl."

Maybe it was Cody's earlier mention of rowboats and romantic clichés that had her thinking about a scene from a movie she hadn't seen since she was seven. Or maybe it was the fact that, if circumstances were different—if she wasn't pregnant—she would want him to kiss this girl.

But she couldn't think about what she wanted. Not for the next nine months—make that eighteen years. She had to focus on what her baby needed.

She needs a father.

No. That wasn't possible. Not at this time.

But when would be a good time to spring the news on a married man that his one last—hopefully, it was his last—fling had resulted in a child? A year? Two years down the road? Did she subscribe to the local paper to see if his name showed up under pending divorces? Stalk him on Facebook to see if he changed his relationship status? Or just take her chances that her news wouldn't destroy the man's marriage?

Cody's voice penetrated her thoughts. "Get ready for Troublemaker."

She whipped her head around. Was he reading her mind? Or did he know why she was really here?

"The next rapid." Cody must have sensed her confusion. "It's called Troublemaker. It's kind of the signature rapid on this stretch of the river."

"Was it named after you?" Miranda reverted to teasing—okay, flirting—to keep from going crazy.

"You want to know if I'm trouble?" He dipped his paddle into the water, steering them toward the approaching rapid. "Have dinner with me and find out."

Dinner. A necessary part of her day, yet too complex to even think about.

"We could get a reservation at The Majestic." Cody continued with the flirtation, obviously unaware of her connection with his twin. "It's been named the most romantic restaurant in town by the readers of the *Prospector Springs Sentinel.*"

"Not the best place to propose?" Why? Why was she even thinking about that train wreck?

"No. That would be the river." His grin spread slow, and sexy. "At sunset. Who needs a string quartet, when we've got the soothing sounds of the water sliding over granite, night critters calling out to their mates..."

"So how many women have you propositioned?" She couldn't stand how smooth he was. How damn sexy. "Not marriage, of course, but a more temporary arrangement?"

He stroked his beard, as if he was giving the matter some thought. "Seriously? I can't remember a single woman I've met since I laid eyes on you."

Whoa. Not at all the answer she expected. She didn't have the first clue as to how to respond to such a line.

"Forward paddle." He switched into river guide mode. "Here we go."

Miranda dug her paddle into the water, somehow she managed to keep up with his commands and they hit the big rapid dead on. The drop off was more than any of the rapids on the last river she'd run, but not too terrifying.

Exhilarating, was more like it.

The raft dipped and lurched and sped down the big rapid. Water splashed up over the sides and several photo companies caught the moment on camera from the rocks just below.

* * * *

They made it through the last few rapids without any trouble. Cody managed to keep himself and his passenger in the raft the rest of the way, so he considered that a successful trip.

What he hadn't managed was to get Miranda to agree to dinner. Oh, they'd gone back and forth with playful flirtation, but she hadn't really committed one way or another. Sure she'd dropped the usual lines about not looking for a relationship. But they all said that. Only a psychopath would truly expect a long-term commitment to a woman he'd just met. Which is why he joked about proposing. It fell flat.

He'd been able to borrow a pump to inflate the raft. How was he going to pump up his chances with getting Miranda to spend more time with him? Enough time for him to come clean about their previous encounter?

The only thing he knew for sure was that he was not going to watch her drive away. Not this time. Not without finding a way to see her again.

They approached the campground where they would take out of the river. He could ask her out again while they were still on the boat, but he decided to wait until they were on solid ground. Maybe he could get her alone in the boat barn and she would fall for him over rolled up rafts and spare paddles.

Although the way his day had been going, she'd probably fall over the rolled up rafts. Or he would. No, he had to be smoother than that. He had to be sincere. It was time to tell her the truth.

Cody rowed the boat ashore, hopped out, and secured the bow line. He extended a hand to Miranda, well aware of the electricity between them. How could she miss it? How could she fight it?

With a tentative smile, she stepped onto the river bank. She held his hand just a moment longer than necessary, giving him hope.

But then she sighed, and stepped aside, unzipping her life jacket and reaching for her phone.

Cody started for the raft, but stopped when he noticed the expression on her face. She stared at her phone with a look of concern. Bewilderment. Most people were surprised at how they could go from zero signal on the river to a strong, clear signal once they reached the camp. But this was something different.

"Is everything okay?" He took a step toward her as she held the phone up to her ear.

She listened to a message, then stared at her phone and touched the screen again. Shaking her head, she listened to another message. Or the same one, he couldn't be sure. All he could tell was that it was bad news of some sort.

She looked up at him when the message ended, a look of shock on her face. "What's wrong?"

"That was my downstairs neighbor." She shook her head. "There was a fire. Everything's gone."

"I'm so sorry." He couldn't help it; he reached for her. Putting his arms gently around her shoulders. "Was anyone hurt?"

"No." She buried her head into his chest. "But it's completely burned down. The whole building."

She let him hold her briefly before pulling away. "I have to go. I have to see what's left. What I can salvage."

"I'll drive you."

"No. You don't have to do that." She shook her head. "It's three hours away."

"I can't let you go alone." He touched her shoulder, she was trembling. "I can't let you drive when you're upset."

She sat down on the side of the raft.

"Yeah. Okay." She looked up at him. Dazed, she took a few quick, panicked breaths. "Wait. We have to put everything away."

She reached for the gear bag, but it was still tied down.

"I'll get my keys. Someone else can take care of all this." He offered what he hoped was an encouraging smile and jogged off to the store.

"Hey, Tyler." Cody went around behind the cash register to retrieve his truck keys. "I need you to close down shop for a bit. Get anyone who's available to help you put away the gear from my trip."

"Yeah. Sure." Tyler looked surprised by the request. Of course he was. He'd been trained to always put everything away, right away. And he'd also observed his bosses pulling their own weight after every trip. "What's up?"

"Emergency. I have to go to San Francisco." Cody could tell that Tyler was curious, but wasn't going to pry. "I'm not sure if I'll be back tomorrow or not. Fisher is in charge until I get back."

"Does she know what's going on?"

"No. And there's no time for me to talk to her. Will you let her know?" Cody started for the door, then thought of something. He grabbed a woman's sweatshirt off the rack. Miranda could find her clothes destroyed, and San Francisco nights could be chilly, even in summer. "I'll worry about inventory when I get back."

"Yeah, sure. No problem." Tyler grabbed the keys to lock up the store. He pulled his phone from his pocket and started texting, probably to round up some help.

"Hey, thanks." Cody gave a nod as he headed out the door. "It's nice to know I can count on my crew."

Cody found Miranda pacing by the side of the river. She'd piled the paddles and loose items from the raft neatly on the soft sandy bank.

"Let's go." He held his keys out. "My truck is right over here."

"But what about all this?" She pointed to the raft.

"My crew will take care of it." He led her to the parking lot behind the store. "I trust them completely."

He hoped she trusted him. He hadn't been at his best on the river today, and he had a feeling she didn't completely buy the "we're just friends" thing with Fisher.

Fisher was going to be pissed at him. But there was no time to talk to her directly. He'd deal with her later. Right now he had to get Miranda to San Francisco so she could salvage whatever was left of her home. He had to do what he could to make her feel safe.

Chapter 6

It had taken under two and a half hours to get to Prospector Springs this morning. But she'd left San Francisco before seven, so there hadn't been much traffic. The trip home was another story. They hit traffic before Sacramento. It was a Sunday afternoon. All the people who'd spent the weekend in the mountains and the foothills were now heading back home.

She tried not to think about the possibility that she might not have a home to go back to. Mrs. Moreno had been upset over the phone. But she did have a tendency to exaggerate. And sometimes when she was agitated, her English wasn't always accurate. Maybe she'd misunderstood when the older woman had said the whole house was gone.

Miranda tried to focus on that idea. And the fact that her neighbor was okay. She was able to call and tell her what had happened.

Of course, she was fine. And the house was probably fine. Mrs. Moreno was the kind of person who still kept all her phone numbers handwritten in a little black book. Actually, it was olive green. Mrs. Moreno kept it in her kitchen, next to the wall phone and the notepad where she jotted down her grocery list, her grandchildren's birthdays, and a bible quote of the day. She never would have known how to reach Miranda if her kitchen had burned up.

Still, she wouldn't know for sure for at least three hours, probably more. And sitting in traffic on Interstate 80 wasn't much fun in the best of situations.

"I don't think I thanked you for driving me." And for taking her down the river when he'd been expecting a day off.

"I was hoping to spend more time with you." He did sound sincere. "This is not exactly what I had in mind. I had been hoping for something a little more romantic. You know, a candlelight dinner, maybe some wine. But if I can help you salvage any of your belongings, then I'm okay with being your hero."

He was something else. She noticed a slight smile on his face, even though he kept his eyes on the road.

"Thanks. Since I was on the river with you all day, and I know you didn't have cell coverage, I'm pretty sure you didn't arrange the fire just to spend more time with me."

"Yeah, I've never really found arson all that effective in getting a date."

"Keep making me laugh," she suggested. "That way I won't be able to cry."

"I'll do my best." He reached out and gave her hand a squeeze.

"At least I have my laptop." She looked into the backseat. "Well, it's in my car, anyways. So, I can write the article."

"Yes. The article." He glanced her way briefly. "Are you going to mention the part about me forgetting the pump and falling out?"

"Absolutely." That was what she needed, to focus on the story. To get to work, even if her laptop was back in Prospector Springs. "But I'd also like to write about how your fellow guides, and even your rivals, stepped up and helped you out."

"We are a pretty close-knit community on the river." Cody smiled once again. "Yeah, we might be rivals in that we compete for passengers, but when it comes down to it, we stick together. Especially in a business that is somewhat dependent on nature, we kind of have to work with each other. In the good times, we all benefit from increased flows, great weather, and if one of us is overbooked, we are more than happy to recommend a neighbor. Or there are times when we get a big group and don't have enough personnel, so we need to rent-a-guide."

"Rent-a-guide?"

"I guess in your business it would be like freelancing." He gave a little shrug. "It doesn't happen all that often. Like I was saying, when business is good, it's usually good for all of us, but on occasion, we help each other out."

"That's cool. In a lot of industries, you'd expect people to try to take the client away from the other company, rather than offer up their trained employees."

"Just another reason why this life is the best life there is." Cody laughed. "I've often said that a day's work for us is a vacation for most people. But that doesn't mean this is an easy life."

"Yeah, must be rough having all those bikini-clad women in a boat with you."

"Well, we also get guys in Speedos," he deadpanned. "And most of them are not Olympic athletes, or even close to being built like them."

"Yeah, and a lot of the competitive swimmers wear those full-body suits; they're more aerodynamic. Or would that be aquadynamic? You know, they wax everything so they can shave hundredths of a second off their times."

"Is that so? I guess I'm glad my job isn't about speed." He glanced over at her as he pulled to a stop in the heavy traffic just before Davis. "I mean, yeah, we have moments of exhilaration on a big rapid, but it's balanced out by the calm stretches. By the moments where you can just be."

"I can see what you mean." Miranda leaned back against the seat. "I'm all for adventure, getting the adrenaline rush, but I also like being able to just chill afterward. To sit back and reflect on the day's events. To replay the highlights in my mind."

That was one of the things she'd enjoyed most about her trip on the Yampa. There were plenty of serene moments where she could just kick back and enjoy the moment. She had been able to soak up the last rays of sunlight, listen to the soft sounds of the night, and wonder about how her excellent guide would tuck her in each night.

She glanced at Cody. The sunlight glinting off the hood of his red truck reminded her a little of the sunsets in the sandstone canyon. He looked so much like the man she'd spent those few memorable nights with. And he'd been so great to her today, a part of her wished he'd been the man she'd met nearly two months ago. Because, despite his playful attitude, in the last hour he'd shown her a man who would step up when needed.

But no. She did not need this man. She couldn't afford to need this man. She definitely couldn't afford to want this man. She had to look away, to focus on the road. A tow truck was clearing a fender bender from the side of the road. Hopefully, that had been the reason for the backup and they would start moving shortly.

Sure enough, once they got past the wreck, traffic picked up. The steady whir of the tires, the hum of the engine, and the postgame talk radio combined to lull her into a relaxed state. She closed her eyes, focusing on the voice coming from the speakers. Larry or Marty somebody was discussing the afternoon's ballgame. The Giants had won, so it was mostly praise for the home team talent. Besides praising the boys in orange and black, the host had a way with words. His tone was soothing, his knowledge and passion for the game almost poetic. Miranda closed her eyes, just briefly, as the miles slipped away.

* * * *

Somewhere between Davis and Fairfield, Miranda had fallen asleep. Under different circumstances, Cody might have taken it personally. Thought he was boring her. But she hadn't had the best day. And it was entirely his fault. He'd given her quite a scare when he'd fallen out and she'd been left alone in the raft, floating down an unfamiliar river with just a paddle.

But the worst thing he'd done today had been to let Fisher answer the door. If he'd been the one to let Miranda in, he could have cleared things up. She'd come looking for the man she'd met on the Yampa. Sure, she had a story to do, but there was a reason she'd chosen Swift River Adventures. He was the reason. Only she'd believed his name was Carson, not Cody. So when Fisher had informed her that Carson was on his honeymoon, the lie continued.

Yet the lie was the least of her problems today. Cody drove on not knowing what they would find when they got to Miranda's apartment. All he knew was that there had been a fire. No one was hurt, but the building had been damaged. How much? They would find out once they made it into the city.

He'd tapped in her address to the map app on his phone, so there was no need to wake her. Hopefully he could drive by and assess the situation before she woke. That way he could prepare her should it be as bad as he feared.

Several fire trucks had the streets blocked off. Water ran down the gutters in streams. There was no way they could get any closer, so he turned down a side street and looked for a parking space. He circled the block three times before he finally found a spot.

"Where are we?" Miranda woke up as he was engaging the parking brake.

"We're around the corner from your place. The street is blocked off."

"Oh, I guess I fell asleep." She stretched her neck, which had to be stiff after sleeping for so long. "Sorry about that."

"No problem. I sometimes fall asleep in the car when I'm not driving." He could tell she was a little embarrassed, but there was no need. "So are you ready to take a walk up the block?"

"I need to see Mrs. Moreno, and see for myself that she's okay."

"Of course. And we can use my truck to carry anything that isn't damaged."

"Sure. Good idea." She unhooked her seatbelt and climbed out of the truck. She stretched her back, legs, and shoulders. "But I'm not sure where to take it. I guess if my apartment is uninhabitable, then I'll have to find a new place to live."

She held her head high, but Cody could sense that she was rattled. Who wouldn't be upon getting a message that her home had burned down?

They started walking toward her home, or what was left of it.

"You can stay with me. I mean, I have plenty of room. A huge garage, and if you wanted more privacy, I could probably get you into one of the cabins if they're not rented."

"That's very generous, but I couldn't..." She stopped short as they rounded the corner. There, where the fire engines were parked, stood a blackened shell of a building. Only the rear and one side wall still stood. Ash and soot covered the small lot. There wouldn't be much to load in the truck, if anything.

The fire crew was busy with mop up activities. Firefighters were rolling up hoses, sweeping away debris in order to make the scene safe for bystanders.

"Mrs. Moreno!" Miranda ran over to the woman who must have been her neighbor. "Oh I'm so glad to see you. Are you all right? What happened? You're not hurt, are you?"

"I am fine. I am fine. Just a silly old woman." The two women hugged, each of them doing their best to comfort the other. "I burned down our home. I am so sorry. I was baking and it got too warm in the kitchen. So I turn on the fan, the one my Miguel put in for me, only silly boy, he must have made a mistake when he connect the wires. I touch the switch. A loud pop. And boom. Lights go out. I run upstairs to see if your lights go out, but you not home. Thank the lord you not home since I smell smoke. I go downstairs, but my door, it is locked."

The woman was explaining all this with her hands flying in the air, her face animated with emotion.

"I so sorry. So sorry I burn down the house. And all your beautiful things you bring home from your travels." The woman started weeping.

"Oh no, Mrs. Moreno. It's not your fault." Miranda hugged the woman tighter. "Those are just things. I'm just so glad you're not hurt. Do you have somewhere to go?"

"Yes. My Rosabella. She come to get me when Carlos get home from work. He feed the children, put them to bed, and my baby girl will come take care of her Mama."

"Good. I'm glad." Miranda wiped tears from her eyes. "I'm sure you'll be well taken care of."

"It should be Miguel who is stuck with an old lady, but he don't have room in his tiny place."

While the two women made sure they were each okay, Cody approached a fireman to confirm what he'd feared, that the structure was unsafe for gathering personal belongings.

* * * *

It wasn't until Mrs. Moreno was safely off with her daughter that Miranda was able to give more than a passing glance at the building that had been her home. Six years. Longer than any other home she'd inhabited. And now it was gone. Just a burnt-out shell of a structure. Like the hope she'd had this morning of perhaps building a real family life for her unborn child.

Well, she'd picked up and moved on before. If there was one thing her mother had taught her it was that life would go on. It might be in a new apartment, in a new town, but the one constant of her childhood had been change. There had been times when they'd left in the night, with only what they could cram into the back of the Jeep Cherokee that would be sold at the next town, where they would blend in with a Subaru wagon when they'd lived in the Pacific Northwest, a used Toyota sedan in the southwestern states.

When they'd moved, they'd made a big change. Never just across town, but several states over. She'd lived in Idaho, Arizona, Utah, Colorado, South Dakota, New Mexico, Oregon, and Nevada. It wasn't until she'd left on her own that she'd made her way to California.

Now she'd be on the road again. Only this time, she had more than just herself to think about. A sudden wave of nausea overtook her, and Miranda sank to the curb. She was currently homeless. Homeless and pregnant and alone.

She dropped her head into her hands, wishing, not for the first time, that she could just call up her mother, and let her take care of her, tell her everything was going to be all right. If only she knew where her mother was this month.

"Is there anything I can do for you?" Cody placed a gentle hand on her shoulder.

She glanced back at the house. "I guess you didn't need to bring your truck. It doesn't look like there's much to salvage."

"No. The firefighter I talked to said that no one would be allowed inside until they've completed their investigation. And even then, the most likely scenario would be that the building's owner would hire a company to tear everything down and haul most of it off to the dump."

"I imagine anything that wasn't burnt up would be damaged by smoke or water." Miranda felt like she was somehow detached from the situation. Almost as if she was watching a video. One with a filter on the lens that made it seem somewhat faded or fuzzy. "I hope my landlord had insurance. Most of the furniture came with the place. All I had were a few souvenirs from my travels."

"That's too bad. It must be hard to lose the sentimental things."

"Yeah, I guess." She did have a souvenir from her last adventure. One she would carry with her for nine months, but keep in her heart the rest of her life.

Miranda shivered as the fog started to roll in. Within seconds someone had draped a sweatshirt over her shoulders. Not someone. Cody. He really was too good to her.

"Thank you." She stood, slipped her arms into the sleeves, and pulled up the zipper. She recognized the Swift River Adventures logo, yet it fit her just right. "This can't be your sweatshirt?"

"I grabbed it from the store. I figured it might get chilly here and I thought you could use it."

"Thank you. That was very thoughtful." She was oddly touched by the gesture.

"That's me. Mr. Thoughtful." He gave a shrug, as if he was somewhat embarrassed by the compliment. "What do you say we go grab something to eat? Think about what your next move is?"

"Sure." She could use a bite to eat, not because she had any appetite, but because... "Do your cabins have Wi-Fi?"

"No. There is no Wi-Fi at the campground, but I do have internet at my house you are more than welcome to use."

"That would be great. It might take a day or two for me to find someplace to live." She looked around for his truck, but couldn't remember where they'd parked.

"Take your time. You can stay with me as long as you need."

"You don't have to do that." She looked up at him and there was a big part of her who wanted to take him up on his offer. But that was crazy. They didn't know each other. She'd stay with him tonight, but only because her car was there and she was too tired to go anywhere else.

"I don't mind."

"But you don't even know me. Why would you invite a stranger into your home, offer her Wi-Fi and a place to stay? Oh. I guess I know why..." Maybe the easiest thing would be to go ahead and sleep with him. Then she could just slip out the next morning before he had a chance to offer her coffee. Or worse, breakfast.

"First of all, you're not a stranger." He stopped walking and turned so that she could get a good look at his face. "I know we haven't known each other all that long, but something happens when you run the river with someone. You become bonded in a way that doesn't happen anywhere else. It's like the river runs through you—through us. Connecting us in a way that is hard to explain until you've experienced it."

He took her hand, and she was surprised by the gentleness of his touch.

She wanted to believe him. To believe in him. But this was the same man who'd listed all the corny ways he'd propose. At the time, he'd been merely trying to get her into his bed.

Now he was offering something else. His home. For as long as she needed. A place to rest. Regroup. Recover from the devastating events that had shaken her.

"Good news!" A firefighter approached with a bright smile on his soot-covered face. "We were able to catch your cat. It kept trying to get back into the house. I think it was searching for you."

The man held a squirming ball of fur toward her and the critter leaped into her arms. A squirrely thing, black and white and covered in ash. It wasn't a kitten, but it wasn't fully grown either. It snuggled against her neck and immediately began to purr.

"Thanks." She barely got the word out before the young firefighter strode back toward his rig and hopped into the big red engine.

"It's cute." Cody reached out to stroke the cat's fur. "What's its name?"

"I... I don't know. It's not my cat." Yet she had a hard time letting it go. The kitty's purr and steady heartbeat managed to soothe her frazzled nerves.

"I hate to break it to you, but I think you've just been adopted." Cody's voice held a note of teasing, but she still couldn't manage to let go of the cat. "See, people don't choose cats. Cats choose people."

"And you're an expert on this?"

"I've been adopted by a cat or two in my time." He dropped his hand. "Well, maybe it was my brother who'd been chosen, but back in the day we were a package deal."

Miranda wondered if that included fatherhood, but she shoved that thought into the farthest reaches of her mind. Back to where she'd buried her longing for a pet of her own. A permanent home. A real family.

"Bring it along. We'll stop off at a pet store on the way home. Pick up some cat food, maybe a little mouse toy."

"But it's not my cat." Miranda stooped down and set the cat on the sidewalk. The furball mewed at her, obviously not happy with her decision. Then it rubbed up against her and flicked its tail, as if it was daring her to just leave the poor creature on the sidewalk.

"Fine." She picked it up again. "But if some kid ends up crying himself to sleep because Fluffy is missing, it's on you, cat. Not me."

Chapter 7

"So here's the spare room. It was my brother's. But the sheets and everything are clean. There are towels in the bathroom. Everything you could need." Well, for the night. She'd need a few things in the morning. Clothes. A place to live. Worldly possessions. "I brought you one of my T-shirts to sleep in, if you want."

Yeah. He couldn't even let his mind go toward the idea of her sleeping in the nude. At least she wouldn't be alone. The black and white cat would snuggle up against her. The cat she claimed wasn't hers, but try telling the cat that.

"Do you want a glass of wine or beer or something to help you sleep?" He would offer her more, but it didn't feel right. He didn't want to just be a source of comfort. Like the cat. He wanted to be something more, but he was afraid that if he did get close to her, he would end up freaking her out even more.

"No. Thank you." She sat on the bed and the cat had jumped into her lap, purring as she stroked its sooty fur. "I'm pretty wiped out."

"Okay." He stood in the doorway, knowing he should get out of her hair. "If you change your mind, help yourself to anything I've got. The kitchen is all yours. And I'm right down the hall if you need…anything."

"Thanks." She yawned and the cat hopped off her lap. "Oh, should I take it for a walk?"

"How 'bout I let her out, and I'll bring her back in when she's done." Cody wasn't sure if it was a female cat, but he didn't like the idea of any other male sleeping with Miranda. Ever.

The cat slipped out the door, and Cody followed. It sure seemed to feel at home in his house, bouncing down the stairs as if it had been born in the mudroom off the kitchen. He wondered if it was used to a litter box. But it meowed at the door, so he opened it and watched the cat explore its new environment.

It bounded off the deck and found a spot under a nearby oak tree. The cat cocked its head, giving Cody a look that said, "Do you mind?" So Cody turned away to give the cat some privacy. Within minutes, the cat had raced up the deck and twined itself around his legs. He reached down and scooped it up, carrying it back inside. The cat leaped from his grasp the minute he closed the door and raced upstairs. Back to Miranda.

Well, the cat did have good taste.

As much as he wanted to check on her again, he figured she could use some space. It had been a hell of a day.

After weeks of dreaming of Miranda, wishing to see her one more time, here she was in his house. But she wasn't in his bed.

She was in his brother's room.

He wondered if she thought of him. The guy she'd met almost two months ago. The guy she thought had been named Carson.

Frustration churned inside him like the gnarliest hole on the river. He grabbed a beer and walked out onto his deck. The moon wasn't quite full, but it was still bright out. The reflection on the river was beautiful. Something he wished he could share with Miranda, but he had the feeling she was more out of reach than ever.

But maybe he needed to let go of the fantasy. What they'd shared wasn't real. It was a vacation fling. Two people escaping from reality under the desert sky. It had been magical. Mystical. A myth.

There was something about being out on a river in the middle of nowhere. No phones, no lights, no motor cars. Just the luxury of peace and quiet and the simple act of being. The outside world couldn't intrude so it was only natural to look inward. To contemplate. To romanticize the moment.

Cody looked at his empty beer bottle, almost expecting to find he'd been drinking a double or triple IPA instead of his usual pale ale. He wasn't some romantic. Hell, he was the exact opposite. The only feelings he'd ever had were of the "oh, that feels good" variety.

It must have been the altitude and dry desert air that had convinced him that what he and Miranda had shared was something special. But for all he knew, she'd been pretending just as much as he had. She'd talked about her world travels. All the exotic places she'd been, but maybe she was playing a role. Maybe that trip had been her first assignment and she'd made all that up to give her credibility.

The woman he spent today with wasn't quite as bold. Wasn't quite as fearless as the woman he remembered. She was every bit as beautiful, but there was something different. This woman was more reserved, like she was keeping something to herself.

Yeah, dumbass. She was hiding the fact that she'd spent almost a week with a guy who was supposedly on his honeymoon. And even if she was attracted to Cody now, she wouldn't act on it. No, she was enough of a lady to not hook up with two brothers.

Well, he'd have to think of something by morning. He couldn't let her get away without coming clean. Maybe over coffee he could say something about how the coffee is different on each river. How he liked to use regional brews. If only he remembered what kind of coffee they'd used on that trip. Too bad the only thing he remembered about that trip was her.

* * * *

Miranda awoke with a start, her heart racing from the nightmare that had haunted her dreams for years. Once again she found herself down a long and unknown road. Bumping over obstacles as her mother ran from whatever demons chased her. In Miranda's dreams, the menace had been shadowy, dark, and mysterious.

But her mother had never wanted to talk about where she'd come from, why she'd run, and continued to run. Instead, she'd made up stories—more like fables—to explain why sometimes a woman couldn't just sit in one place.

The only consistency about the stories was that they were each followed by a sudden move. To the next town. The next state.

The question now was where her next move would be. Did she stay in California? With the rising rents she didn't see how she'd be able to stay in San Francisco. Technically she could do her job from just about anywhere. But she'd need to check in at the magazine once or twice a month at least. So Northern California made the most sense. But she'd need to factor in school districts. Day care centers. Pediatricians.

And she'd have to make these decisions completely on her own. For the past eight years, she'd been more than fine by herself. She enjoyed her own company. Had no problem with eating alone in a restaurant. She could hike or bike or go for a drive without the need check in with anyone else.

But tonight felt different. She was scared. Not because she truly thought someone was out to get her and do her harm. But she just felt overwhelmed by everything. The pregnancy. The fire. Finding out that she'd had an affair with a nearly married man. Then there was his brother. He obviously had no idea about her previous encounter with his twin. He'd been so sweet, and strong, and kind.

What would he do if she tiptoed into his room? Would he understand that she just couldn't be alone right now? Or would he read something into it? And would that be the worst thing that happened to her today?

The loneliness surrounded her. Threatened to drown her. She searched for the cat, but the little furball was curled up at the foot of the bed, looking so tiny, so helpless. No, what Miranda needed was strength. She needed a man.

What she needed was a cold drink of water.

A cold beer would be even better, but that would have to wait several months.

She made her way down to the kitchen and poured herself a tall glass of water. A few bottles or red wine stood in a rustic hand carved wine rack on the counter. If she wasn't pregnant she could have enjoyed a bottle with the sexy stud upstairs. Who was she kidding? If she wasn't pregnant she wouldn't be here. She would have had no reason to seek out the serious, somewhat reserved guy she'd met several weeks back. Yeah, he was fun, but she'd sensed he was holding something back. Oh, that's right, the fact that he was engaged. Maybe that was the reason he hadn't quite been able to completely let go when they'd been together.

Miranda took a long drink of water. She had to be strong. Couldn't let her emotions get the better of her.

She just wondered why she was so easy to lie to. Did she have a big tattoo on her forehead that read "sucker?"

She finished her water and set the glass in the sink. In the morning, she'd be sure to do the dishes. For now, she just needed to sleep.

Wearily she made her way up the stairs. She hesitated at the top, as she couldn't remember which direction the bedroom she occupied was in.

Turning right, she took a few steps before turning and heading the opposite direction. She carefully pushed open the door and tiptoed across the floor. A soft purr coming from the bed convinced her she'd made the right decision. Maybe her luck would start to change. It certainly couldn't get much worse.

Quietly, she slipped into bed and snuggled up next to the cat.

Only, that wasn't a cat in the bed.

She should go. Slip out before Cody noticed she was there. But all the energy drained from her body. Her limbs felt like lead and before she could stop herself, a sob escaped her lips.

Strong arms came around her, and Cody whispered "Don't cry."

His words only made the sobbing worse.

"Hey. Forget what I said." He held her, gently, yet firmly. "Cry all you want. If anyone has a good reason, it's you."

Miranda buried her face in his chest and cried even harder.

He held her close, not saying another word, but she could feel his strength, feel his warmth. And she could feel his arousal pressed against her.

A new emotion flooded her. Desire. Need. She didn't want to feel sad or scared or numb. She wanted to feel pleasure. Passion. Physical contact that had nothing to do with pity.

Miranda let him stroke her face, her hair, her arms. She squeezed the last of her tears from her eyes. The hair on his chest was dampened from her crying. She licked his skin, tasting the salt from her tears, and maybe his sweat.

He moaned and his grip tightened around her shoulders.

She licked him again and rubbed up against his growing erection.

"Oh God, are you sure?" his voice was strained, thick with need.

"Yes." She pushed him onto his back and straddled him. She could feel his thick ridge and she rubbed against him. He felt so good. She tugged her T-shirt over her head. Technically it was Cody's shirt; either way, it needed to be gone.

She leaned closer, ready to take what she needed from him.

"Look, Miranda, before we go any further—"

Placing her finger over his lips, she shushed him. "You don't have to give me the speech. I'm not looking for a relationship either."

"That's not—"

"Honey, you have a sexy mouth. I'm sure you could think of a better use for it than just talking." To prove it, she pressed her lips against his and thrust her tongue into his mouth.

With a groan, he finally gave up on the needless chatter.

His lips were soft, sensuous. A nice contrast to the rough texture of his beard. But the overall vibe she got from him was pure strength. She would have laughed at how she'd been afraid for him when he fell in the river, but he was pulling her panties down her hips, and the fear she'd felt evaporated as a cool breeze blew across her bare ass.

She reached down and tugged at his boxers. It took some maneuvering to keep the elastic from catching on his quite impressive erection.

"Wait." He panted and then reached for the drawer of the bedside table. He tore open the familiar square packet and removed a condom. She held her breath while he put it on, trying not to think about how the last one she'd used had failed.

Cody turned her onto her side and kissed her, his hand sliding between her thighs. "You feel so good."

Okay, so maybe she could handle some talking on his part. And yeah, she did feel pretty good. Especially with the way he stroked her, touched her, and found just the right way to drive her over the edge.

"Mmmmm." She moaned as he found her sweet spot. But it wasn't enough. She needed more. She needed him. His strength. His hardness. She flung her leg over him, and slid down on top of him. That's better. If she could control the pace, the movement. Oh…oh… oh dear sweet….

Waves of pleasure came crashing over her. Sudden. Intense. Almost overwhelming. Her body shook, shimmied, and shuddered. She was utterly spent.

Sweaty, shaky, and slightly lightheaded, she collapsed against him.

"Wow." He let out a satisfied sigh. "That was…"

"Yeah." Miranda couldn't say anything more; she was too overcome with everything. She squeezed her eyes shut so she wouldn't cry. Again.

Cody held her until she fell into a deep and dreamless sleep.

Chapter 8

Wow. That was quite a vivid dream. Cody had finally fallen asleep and a vision of Miranda crawling into bed with him seemed so real. Even her tears felt real. And then she was kissing him and stroking him and riding him. It had been a hell of a dream, until he realized that he hadn't been dreaming. She had come to him in the night. In need of comfort, she'd cried on his shoulder.

Then she'd had her way with him. After she'd fallen asleep, Cody cleaned himself up and crawled back into bed with her.

He'd tried to tell her that they'd met before. But she wouldn't have it. With a determined passion, she took what she wanted. What she needed. And he'd been more than willing to give it to her.

He'd make her breakfast, and they could figure out where to go from there.

But for now, he was content to watch her sleep. She was so beautiful. And he wasn't going to let her get away this time.

Miranda opened her eyes and smiled, but then she jumped up as if she was horrified at what they'd done. She reached for the T-shirt that she'd tossed to the floor.

"I'm so sorry. Last night was…"

"Amazing." Cody sat up, watching as she slipped his shirt over her head.

"No. I shouldn't have done that." She pulled the hem down, covering herself in shame. "I shouldn't have crawled into bed with you. I'd had a nightmare and…" She looked away.

"You have nothing to apologize for. You needed comforting. I like to think I was able to help."

"Yes. No. I mean…" She blushed, her skin darkening slightly. "I'm not usually like that. I mean, I'm not usually so needy."

"I didn't mind." Cody smiled, hoping to ease her discomfort. "I thought you were pretty fantastic."

She glanced around as if she wanted to find an escape. Or maybe just find her panties, since she snatched them off the floor and stepped into them.

"Hey, why don't I make us some breakfast? We can figure out the rest of our day from there."

"Look, I really should get going." She backed toward the door. "You've done enough."

"Miranda, do you have a boyfriend? A husband?"

"No. That's not…"

"Then what's wrong?"

"I just… Things are complicated for me right now."

"Yeah. But that doesn't mean you can't have a little fun." Cody pushed himself off the bed and approached her, but cautiously. "You could definitely use a little fun."

"But I have a lot on my plate."

"How 'bout I add some pancakes and bacon to that plate?"

"You don't take no for an answer, do you?"

"Not very often." He gently touched her shoulders. "But, honey, you were the one who wasn't about to take no for an answer last night."

"Oh my God." She covered her face with both hands. "I was a little demanding."

"I like that about you." Cody dropped a kiss on her forehead. "It's pretty damn hot. I like a woman who knows what she wants and goes after it. Especially if what she wants is me."

She sighed and let him put his arms around her. Not so bold in the light of day, but she'd come around.

"Why don't you hop in the shower? I'll dig up a clean T-shirt and maybe I can find some shorts that will fit you. I think I have a pair with a drawstring. Then I'll toss your clothes in the wash when you get out of the shower."

"Why are you being so good to me?"

"Because I like you." He lifted her hair off her neck and placed a small kiss on her soft skin. "And I'm just a really great guy. Ask anyone."

He sent her off to the bathroom with a soft swat on the ass. And boy, did she have a nice ass.

He made it to the kitchen only to find the cat sitting on the counter, staring at him. The animal looked at him like it knew what he'd been up to and wasn't too pleased about it.

"Do you need to go out?"

It meowed at him. And yeah, he could hear the sarcasm in its voice. They'd have to come up with a name. Maybe that would make the critter feel less judgmental.

Cody opened the back door and the cat darted out. For good measure, he grabbed some leftover salmon and put it into a bowl. If the cat didn't return in a timely manner, he'd put it out on the deck. But if kitty had any sense at all, it would come back for Miranda.

Now, back to breakfast. It couldn't be too hard to make pancakes. He'd just grab the mix and do something really bold, like read the directions. How many times had Carson told him it was as simple as that? It wasn't that he hadn't known how to make a woman breakfast. It was just that Cody had never really cared about a woman enough to make the effort.

Yeah, that probably made him a first class ass. But he was working on that. Starting today. He would make a nice breakfast for Miranda. Then he'd somehow convince her to stay long enough to figure out how to make this work.

After gathering the ingredients, the mixing bowl, and measuring cups, Cody got to work on mixing the pancake batter. He opened a package of bacon and started frying that up. Coffee. He almost forgot the coffee, but he added a little extra to the basket. Hopefully, she didn't take cream, since all he had was some low-fat milk.

Things were starting to come together when he heard a knock on the glass door. It was quickly followed by the slider opening and a cheerful "Good morning, sunshine."

Fisher. With the cat darting between her legs as she entered. "When did you get a cat?"

"It's not my cat." He wasn't exactly in the mood to deal with Fisher right now. "It's, um…"

Fisher looked up. Apparently she could hear the shower running upstairs.

"You slept with her? Of course you did. It's what you do." She crossed the kitchen and reached for a coffee cup. "So, do you need me to finish up with the breakfast, you know, so you can sneak out the back door? I know Carson used to entertain your guests for you the morning after."

"I think I can handle breakfast."

"Sure. Like you handled the equipment and putting everything away after your private trip yesterday. I heard Tyler and Ross had to pick up your slack. She must really be something."

He couldn't help but hear the hurt in her voice. She tried to hide it with her little judgmental attitude.

"It's complicated." Cody took the mug out of her hand and poured her some coffee. "Miranda had an emergency. I asked Tyler to cover for me so I could help her out."

Fisher accepted the steaming brew. Whether or not she accepted his story was another matter.

"What kind of emergency? She couldn't keep her hands off you?"

He ignored her sarcasm, figuring it would be best to give it to her straight.

"Miranda's house burned down while we were on the river. She lost everything she didn't bring with her."

"No shit?" Fisher's eyes widened in disbelief. "Everything?"

"Yeah. Everything but the clothes on her back, and this cat." He pointed to the black and white feline who was currently licking itself, with no sense of modesty. "Only, she says it's not her cat."

"But they both followed you home." Fisher shook her head and then took a sip of her coffee.

"Did you come over here to give me grief?" Cody asked. "Or is there something I can do for you?"

"I'm here to pick up the tuxes and return them to Beverly's Bridal."

"Right." He'd pretty much forgotten all about the wedding. "They're in the laundry room."

"Great. I'll just finish my coffee and then get out of your way."

He should probably invite her to stay for breakfast, but he really wanted to be alone with Miranda.

"Oh, hi." Speak of the devilish vixen. Miranda entered the kitchen wearing one of his shirts and a pair of athletic shorts that hung down below her knees. "Good morning." She glanced at Fisher and he hoped he wouldn't have to explain once again that they were just friends.

"Good morning." Fisher offered her a friendly smile. "Can I get you some coffee?"

"No thanks." Miranda looked a little uncomfortable with the offer.

"I'll get started on the pancakes." Cody wondered how much longer Fisher was going to hang around.

"Yeah, I'll grab the tuxes and head into town." Fisher eyed Miranda suspiciously. "Hey, would you be interested in going with me? Maybe do a little shopping? There's not a lot to choose from, but it's better than raiding Cody's closet. There's a sporting goods store on Main Street where you could pick up some yoga pants and stuff, and the consignment store usually has a pretty good selection of jeans and sundresses. We could even go into Placerville where there's a Walmart and a TJ Maxx."

"Actually, that's probably a good idea. All I've got with me is my swimsuit and the shorts I was wearing yesterday." Miranda jumped at the chance to go shopping. "I could use a few essentials."

"Great." Fisher seemed genuinely pleased with the idea of having Miranda along. "But you need to have your breakfast first. I'll just... Do you want me to come back in a little while?"

"No. Sit. I have plenty of pancakes." Cody didn't want to seem like he wanted to get rid of her, but his head guide was kind of in the way. "The more the merrier."

Not.

Cody turned his attention to the stove. The bacon was nice and crispy so he placed the pieces on a paper-towel-covered plate. Then he slapped a pat of butter on the hot griddle. Once it melted he poured DVD-sized dollops of batter onto the pan.

"So, Cody told me your house burned down. That's so intense." Fisher acted like she and Miranda were old friends. "Were you totally freaked out?"

"No. I mean, once I found out Mrs. Moreno—that's my neighbor—once I found out she was okay, the whole thing was just kind of surreal."

"I'll bet." Fisher sounded fascinated. Sympathetic, but fascinated. "I mean, to see your home just...gone."

"Yeah. It's gone. Just charred wood and ashes."

"But no one was hurt?"

"No. That's the good news." Miranda pushed off from the table and turned toward him. "Could I get a glass of water?"

"Sure. Help yourself to anything." Cody indicated with the spatula which cabinet held the glasses. "I really want you to make yourself at home."

"Thank you," Miranda took a glass and filled it with water. "But I really will get out of your hair after breakfast. I'll follow Fisher into town to pick up a few things, and then I'll be off."

"Where do you plan on going?" Panic began to rise. He couldn't let her take off. Not before he had a chance to set things straight. And he couldn't do that with Fisher there.

"I don't know. I guess I'll find a motel somewhere."

"What about the cat?" Fisher asked. "What's its name, again?"

"I don't have a cat." Miranda sighed.

"That seems like a lot to put on a collar." Fisher helped herself to more coffee. "You really should name it."

"And you'll be better off here, than trying to find a motel that takes pets." Cody reasoned. "I really don't mind having you."

Miranda's cheeks darkened and she turned her back to him. Good thing, too, since he needed to flip the pancakes.

"I don't want to impose."

"Miranda." After making sure breakfast was safe from disaster, he turned around to look Miranda in the eye. "I wouldn't ask you to stay if I didn't want you."

If Fisher wasn't there, he'd show Miranda just how much he wanted her. Again and again.

"Sorry. I guess I'm just not used to people who would take in a near-stranger." Miranda gave him a weak smile.

"No one stays a stranger for long around here." Fisher just had to jump into the conversation. "It's one of the things that makes Swift River so special."

"Can I use that as a quote?" Miranda asked.

Fisher looked a bit surprised. So Cody reminded her, "Miranda writes for *Adventure Chix* magazine."

"That's right." Fisher set her coffee mug on the granite counter. "I love that magazine, by the way. Of course, I mostly read it online, but I'll have to pick up a copy. What was the last article you wrote?"

"I did a piece on the desolate desert paradise of the Yampa River." Miranda said.

"The Yampa, huh?" Fisher looked at him as if she realized that they had met before, but when she saw his slight shake of the head, she put on a fake smile. "I've always wanted to check it out. But they keep me pretty busy around here."

"If you're too busy to go shopping, I totally understand." Miranda said.

"No. Not unless Cody wants to swap me for his trip this morning. There's a group of fifteen coming in about an hour." Fisher made him an offer he couldn't refuse.

"Actually, I think I will have you take that trip." The fact that he'd forgotten all about it wasn't a good sign for how he was going to manage a couple of weeks without Carson or Lily there to keep track of details, like having a three boat trip that completely slipped his mind. "I need to pick up a few things."

"Sure. No problem." Fisher placed her empty coffee cup in the sink. "I'll see you guys later, then."

And finally, he was alone with Miranda. With the whole day ahead of them.

* * * *

Miranda wasn't sure if she was up to a whole day alone with Cody. But she needed to pick up a few things and didn't know her way around

Prospector Springs. Sure, she could head down to Sacramento and find a mall, but she didn't want to hurt Cody's feelings. He had been awfully sweet.

And she'd been the one to crawl into his bed last night. Not that he'd complained. Still, if the situation were reversed, she wouldn't want the guy to go sprinting out the door the next morning, so she would do the right thing and stick around at least through lunch. She'd buy, just to keep them on an even footing.

Cody placed a plate of steaming hot pancakes, perfectly browned, with butter and real maple syrup on the side.

"Looks good enough to eat." Miranda smiled as he added three slices of crispy bacon to her plate.

"Would you like some cider?" He went to the fridge and pulled out a plastic jug. "It's from a family farm up in Apple Hill. It's like nothing you've ever tasted."

"Sure." She smiled. "Sounds great."

"This is good," Miranda said after taking a drink. "Is this the same stuff you sell in your store?"

"Yeah. We do sell it by the pint."

"Then I have tasted it. Yesterday before our trip down the river." Miranda set the glass down. "Oh, that reminds me. I should e-mail my editor and let her know I may need an extra day to get my story in."

"Sure." Cody dug into his own pancakes as she grabbed her phone and sent a quick e-mail to her boss explaining the circumstances behind her delay. It shouldn't be a problem since it was basically a bonus feature anyway. Miranda had come up with the idea and her boss agreed that doing more local adventures held a certain appeal. With summer coming to a close, it was a great time to throw in some last-minute trip ideas for those wanting to get in one more adventure before the back-to-school craziness started up.

One of the things Miranda like most about her job at the magazine was that she never knew from month to month where she'd end up. Sure, there were some stories that were scheduled months in advance, but often there were trips that came up unexpectedly. Sometimes it was because other reporters had to cancel, and being single, without a family to tie her down, she'd always been the go-to person for last-minute itineraries. Other times, it was that an opportunity arose and she couldn't pass up the chance to fly off on a moment's notice to locations she'd never been to, and often times had never even heard of before doing her research on the way.

At some point, Miranda would have to let her bosses know that she wouldn't have the travel flexibility they'd all become accustomed to. As a single parent, she wouldn't be able to fly off with only enough time to pack a suitcase and update her vaccinations.

"These pancakes are delicious." Miranda took another bite, hoping to calm her nervous stomach. She really didn't need to think about how her pregnancy would affect her job. Her ability to travel would become restricted in just a few months. And then? Would she be relegated to product testing and reviews? Would she be reporting on which brand of sport sandal was most comfortable in late pregnancy? Or maybe she could rate baby carriers that would enable her to travel anywhere with an infant strapped to her.

"Thank you." Cody seemed pleased with her compliment. "I'm usually more of a cereal and coffee kind of guy."

"I would have been fine with cereal."

"No. You deserve something special." There was that look again. The one that said he was into her. Maybe more than either of them expected. "But you'll have to settle for my limited expertise when it comes to cooking."

She couldn't help but laugh at his aw-shucks, I'm-just-a-simple-guy demeanor.

"I'm sure this isn't the first time you've had a sleepover." He had certain skills that could more than make up for his lack of culinary skills. Even half asleep, he could more than satisfy, and dropping a couple of Pop Tarts in the toaster would be more than enough to sustain a girl the next morning.

"I've been known to leave the cooking to others. Namely, my brother. But that's all behind me, now." He looked like he wanted to say something more, but Miranda's phone buzzed. Thinking it was a reply from her editor, she picked up. "Sorry. Part of having a flexible, work-from-anywhere kind of job is that you have to pretty much work from everywhere."

"It's like how it is to own your own business. The first few years I don't think I had a day off during the season. Or much of a salary. Every dime we made went back into the business."

"And now?"

"Now we've built up enough business that we can at least budget for most things." He leaned on the counter, relaxing into the conversation. "And we've got employees we know we can count on."

"Like Fisher?" She hated the slight twinge of jealousy she felt about the woman. The one who he'd insisted was just a friend, but the two of them had a closeness that Miranda couldn't help but envy.

"Yeah. She's a great team member." Cody popped a piece of bacon into his mouth, and she wondered if he was trying to cover for something or if he was just hungry. "Most of our long-term crew are pretty loyal, and trustworthy."

"That's great." She opened her email. "Hmm. Weird. The message I sent to my editor was returned undeliverable."

"Try logging into my Wi-Fi." He came around the end of the counter, leaning close, and making her remember things she'd be better off forgetting. Like how he made her feel safe. And sexy. And like a woman who didn't have a care in the world. Yet she did. She had too many cares to think about. But damn, he smelled good. "Just search for networks. That's it, the first one."

She clicked on the network named "SwiftStuds2" and held back a smile at the over-the-top name. Then the password prompt popped up on her phone and he leaned in.

"C-O-D-S-O-N-5-5," he said just above a whisper.

She typed in the password and connected to the Wi-Fi. Then she resent the e-mail.

"Hopefully that will go through." She turned her phone over and tried to turn her attention to her breakfast, but Cody stood so close. He smelled of coffee, bacon, and…sex. The musky scent of their midnight encounter lingered.

"Look, last night was…"

"The greatest night of your life?" He nuzzled her neck and it would have been so easy to succumb to his seduction. "Mine, too."

"It was great, but…" She pulled away, needing to break contact. "I was half asleep and…"

"Sometimes your subconscious knows what you need more than your conscious mind." Cody's voice was low, soothing. "But in the bright light of day, you start thinking about chores, errands, responsibilities."

"Yes. And I have many responsibilities." Miranda couldn't forget that. "Now is not the right time to get involved."

She finished the last few bites of her breakfast and then walked toward the sink.

"Or you could go with the flow." Cody offered. "When I first started rafting, I thought I had to control every movement on the river. And the more I tried to think, the more trouble I got into. But with experience, I learned that sometimes the wisest course was to go with the river. To let the current take me where I need to go."

"You make it sound so easy." A part of her wanted to just let go and take the time to just be. All too soon, she wouldn't have the luxury of following her heart. Or maybe it was just her hormones. Either way, she had to admit there was something about Cody that appealed to her subconscious self. He was the kind of guy who could just exist in nature. He could wake up, smell the coffee, and explore the possibilities. A guy who could follow the wind or the current or the gravitational pull of an exotic stranger.

"What have you got to lose?" He came up behind her, but didn't touch her. He was so close she could almost hear his heartbeat. Almost feel his breath. And in some ways, it was so much hotter than if he were touching her.

Good question. She'd already slept with him. She couldn't get any more pregnant. And it's not like either of them were going to fall in love.

"Can you teach me how to go with the flow?"

"No. I can't teach you that." He stepped even closer. "I'm a guide, not an instructor."

"What's the difference?" She wanted to lean against his broad chest. She wanted to let him guide her, at least for a few more days.

"An instructor can show you that seven plus three equals ten, or c-a-t spells cat." He stepped back, leaning against the cool granite.

"Meow." The cat jumped up on the counter and made her opinion known. She rubbed up against Cody, flipping her tail in his face as if she didn't appreciate the fact that she was just "cat."

"Maybe we should give it a name." He gave her a quick pet.

"Yeah. She deserves that much."

Cody picked her up and lifted her tail. "Yeah, I guess she's a girl."

"Meow." Then she flopped on her side and offered her tummy to Cody.

Cat... Catastrophe... Sophie... No. Too ladylike for a creature who was now licking herself in the middle of the kitchen in broad daylight.

"What about Smoky?" Cody offered. "She did rise from the ashes of your apartment."

"Maybe." She supposed it was better than Oreo. "I don't know."

"Ashley?"

Miranda shrugged. If she was having this much trouble coming up with a name for a cat, how was she going to name her baby?

Turning her attention back to the sink, she grabbed the dish soap. Dawn?

"You don't have to do the dishes." Cody said. "I can take care of it."

"I don't mind. You made breakfast. Let me do my part to earn my keep around here?"

"Does that mean you'll stay?"

"For now." It's not like she or the nameless cat had anywhere else to go.

Chapter 9

After a quick shower, Cody dressed and made his way downstairs. Miranda was wiping down the counters and he was surprised by how much he liked the sight of a woman in his kitchen. Well, maybe it was only this woman.

How many times had he avoided even sharing a cup of coffee with a woman the next morning? Try all of them. He'd let his brother serve up breakfast and the excuse that Cody had to get to work early to prepare for the next trip.

Truth was, he'd never known what to say to a woman once he'd accomplished his goal. Flirting, he was good at. The verbal back and forth, using his words to charm a pretty stranger. He'd enjoyed the chase almost as much as the catch.

But even the chase had gotten old. Maybe it was seeing his brother settled and happy with Lily. No. When Carson and Lily had first hooked up, Cody was pissed. And it wasn't just because she'd chosen his twin over him.

He didn't think he was ready to grow up finally.

Then he'd met Miranda.

Now he knew what he wanted. But he had no idea how to go about it. He'd spent most of his adult years sweet-talking women into his bed. Now he wanted to talk her into being a part of his life.

He'd start by showing her around Prospector Springs.

"You ready to hit the town?" Cody grabbed the tuxedoes to return to the bridal shop on Main Street.

"Sure." Miranda grabbed her purse and pocketed her phone.

"I have to warn you; the shopping isn't exactly what you'd call world class." He didn't think she was too into high fashion, but he'd only really seen her on the river. Outdoor gear, swimsuits, and maybe a fleece jacket were all that was required. She'd probably need more than that. His own wardrobe consisted mostly of Swift River Adventures T-shirts and swim trunks or cargo shorts he ordered online. Two or three pairs of jeans got him through the rare times where shorts weren't going to cut it.

"I'm sure I'll manage. I just need a few basics."

He'd suggest heading down to Folsom if it came down to it, but he really hoped she'd find the charm of downtown Prospector Springs worth the reduced selection.

Cody opened the passenger door to his truck and she jumped up into the seat. Then he set the tuxes in the backseat and came around to the driver's side.

"Wouldn't you rather be on the river, than running errands with me?"

"Nah. I don't mind. Besides, Fisher just got a hefty raise. She'd rather be on the river, earning it."

"Whereas you're perfectly happy slacking off?" Miranda had a teasing note in her voice. "Entertaining your overnight guests."

"I'm not slacking off." It seemed like he'd had that conversation with Carson enough times over the last year or so. But the argument had been that Cody spent all his time on the river, and not enough doing all the other little chores that kept not only the rafting business afloat, but the campground, cabins, and store operating efficiently. "I'll find plenty to do when we get back. I'll stop by the office, check in at the store, and make sure the campground is in tip-top shape. There's more to running the business than just taking passengers down the river."

"So, you're going to give me an inside look at the rest of it?"

"Something like that," he said. "I also want to show you all that we have to offer for those who might want to make a weekend of it. We can check out the local shops, restaurants, and touristy spots."

"Oh, sounds like fun."

"Yeah, did you know the Carriage House Hotel is supposed to be haunted?"

"No. I did not know that."

"Yeah, it's been featured on one of those reality shows about ghost hunting."

"Interesting."

"I've never really believed in all that stuff, but some people really get into it."

"I might have to check it out at some point."

"There's a lot of history in this town. Dating back to the gold rush." He backed the truck out of the driveway and headed toward town. "Like the hardware store is one of the oldest continuously operating businesses in California."

"I'll keep that in mind next time I need a box of nails or a hammer."

"They have all kinds of stuff there. Gold panning supplies, birdfeeders, cookware. Just about anything you could need."

"Considering I need just about everything, I may have to check it out. But most of that kind of stuff will have to wait."

"Yeah, I suppose you'll need clothes more than you need a cast iron frying pan."

"Those tend to only be useful if you have a stove."

He liked the fact that she kept her sense of humor throughout her ordeal. Most people would be curled up in a ball, freaking out, or expecting to be taken care of.

So she'd had one minor breakdown in the middle of the night. But he liked to think he'd done a good job of comforting her.

The drive into town didn't take long. He was able to find a parking spot along the street not far from the bridal shop. Perfect, he didn't want to have to drive around the block or resort to using the city lot with only two hours free parking. This way, he wouldn't have to worry about what time they'd parked or rush to come back and try to figure out how much longer they'd be.

"It will just take a few minutes to drop these off, then we can find you something other than my basketball shorts to wear. Although…" He couldn't help but notice the baggy nylon fabric did nothing to hide her shapely figure. "You look pretty good in my old basketball shorts."

"Please." She shook her head and started walking toward the store entrance.

"What? You're a beautiful woman. You should be used to hearing it by now."

"Are you always this way?"

"Charming? Sweet? Delightful"

"Obnoxious."

"Yeah, I guess so. But you have to admit, you like me." He flashed his most irresistible grin.

"Hold on just a second." She stood in front of the store, with its big window display of poufy white satin gowns. "Just so we're clear. We're just dropping off the tuxedos. The whole joke about proposing when we were on the river. That was just a joke, right? Otherwise, I'll wait in the truck."

"I'm not going to propose. But on a scale of one to ten, how romantic would that be?"

"Proposing in a bridal shop?" She shrugged. "I guess it would depend. I kind of think there needs to be some history behind the proposal. Renting out a ballpark just because you can isn't nearly as romantic as the die-hard fans who met in the beer line and then when the time is right, he proposes in that very same beer line."

"You are a romantic." Cody held the door open for her.

"I'm not looking for romance. Seriously."

"Hi, Cody." Emily, the granddaughter of the store's owner, greeted him from behind the counter. "I see you survived the festivities. I hear it was a beautiful wedding."

"Yes. It was." He handed the rental tuxes over to her.

"Lily promised to send pictures for our wall of fame." She pointed at the large wall filled with framed wedding photos.

"I'm sure she'll send them in as soon as they get the pictures back." Cody rested his forearms on the counter. He wondered if Emily would know where he could take Miranda shopping. "Hey, this is my friend Miranda."

He couldn't help but smile as he introduced his "friend."

"Hi. Nice to meet you." Miranda offered her hand. "And your name?"

"Emily. I went to high school with Cody and Carson." Emily shook hands and smiled.

"So, Miranda needs to do a little shopping, see she—"

"The airline lost my luggage, which is why I'm stuck wearing this." Miranda indicated the T-shirt and shorts.

"Well, you're probably not going to need a ball gown, but I do have a decent selection of essentials." She pointed Miranda toward the lingerie section. "Here, I'll show you."

"I'm sure I can find what I need, thanks." Miranda wandered off toward the back of the store.

"So, she's a 'friend,' huh?" Emily gave him a knowing look.

"It's complicated."

"Oooh. I can't tell you how many complicated relationships end up needing my services." Emily checked in the tuxes and placed them on a rack behind the counter.

"What I really need is some advice on where to take a girl shopping." Cody had gotten the hint that Miranda didn't want strangers to know all her stuff was burned in a fire. "In case she wants to wear something other than a bathing suit and a Swift River Adventures shirt. She might need some jeans. Maybe some dressier shorts."

"Well, The General Store does have some jeans, mostly Levi's and Wranglers, and Good Sports across from Prospector Café will have shorts, shoes, workout wear. They probably have some cute camp shirts, too."

"Camp shirts?" He just wore his company tees while camping. Maybe women wore something more specialized. Like that long-sleeved soft pullover hoodie kind of thing he remembered Miranda wearing on those cool desert nights.

"You know, short-sleeved, cotton, button up. Kind of like Hawaiian shirts but without the print."

"Oh." Not quite what he was picturing, but he'd bet Miranda would look great in anything. He just needed to try to picture camp shirts instead of the lingerie she was trying on.

"Did you find what you needed?" Emily asked as Miranda came out of the dressing room.

"Yeah." She tucked a dark curl behind her ear. A slight blush crept across her cheeks, so Cody pretended to check out the wall of fame. He had no interest in looking at strangers' wedding photos, but he didn't want Miranda to feel uncomfortable as she rang up her purchases. But he hoped he'd be able to inspect the items when they got back to his place later tonight.

"So where to next?" She held up a light purple bag with dark purple tissue hiding its contents. Oh, if only they'd come here last.

"The hardware store." Cody suggested. Yeah, he needed to look at drill bits or light bulbs or hacksaw blades. Anything to keep from picturing the smooth satin and lace against Miranda's soft skin.

"You need to pick up something for your work?"

He kept staring at the bag. "Um. No. But Emily said they have jeans there."

"At a hardware store?"

"Yeah, nothing fancy, but we could take a look. It's down the street."

"Sure, why not." Miranda swung the purple bag casually at her side as they walked down the street. Was she doing it on purpose, or did she not know how worked up it was getting him?

He had to get his focus back. "Hey, here's the hotel I was telling you about."

"The one that's haunted?" She peered into the window. "Oh look, they have ghost tours the first and third Fridays of the month."

Sure enough, there was a flyer advertising the event. "Looks like we just missed it."

"Well, you were busy with the wedding." She sighed and then moved on down the street.

Right. She still thought it was Carson she'd met weeks ago on the Yampa. Carson, whose groom's tuxedo they'd just returned.

He knew he needed to come clean. Sooner, rather than later, but he just didn't know how to bring it up. But maybe it wasn't that big of a deal. She'd crawled into bed with him last night, even though she thought she'd also been with his brother. And she'd been kind of weird about it afterward. Maybe she worried he'd think badly about her if he knew. Or maybe she had always wanted to sleep with twins and now that she'd crossed that item off her list, she could move on.

She stopped in front of The General Store. "Hmm. Not very creative name."

"What can I say, when they first opened in 1860, they didn't have any competition. So they just called it what it was."

"Like 'Cat?'" She pushed open the heavy wood and glass doors, making the ancient bell chime overhead.

"We could head over to the bookstore next. Maybe they have a section on cat naming books."

"Let me guess. It's called The Bookstore?"

"No. It's A Good Read." He liked that she challenged him. Teased him. And he kind of liked that she mocked some of the same things about his town that he'd mocked as a kid, growing up here. Like the fact that if he'd wanted skinny jeans or Vans, he had to go down the hill to buy them. And they didn't have a Barnes and Noble or a Starbucks or even a Burger King.

"Creative."

"They don't have an espresso bar, or five-dollar pastries, but they do have an old yellow Lab named Tucker."

"A bookstore with an old dog?" She pretended to browse the display just inside the door. The one with the Prospector Springs magnets and postcards and bumper stickers. "Does he help you find books about new tricks?"

"Maybe in the adults-only section." He never thought he'd find shopping on Main Street to be anything but torture. But he was actually having a good time.

"You said they have jeans here?" She moved away from the touristy crap to examine the gold mining supplies.

"They've been selling Levis here since the 1870s." He was starting to sound like a tour guide.

"I'm not sure I want jeans that are a hundred and forty years old." She picked up a gold pan, turned it over, then set it down. "I was thinking something a little more modern, like a boot cut."

"I bet you rock a pair of boot cut jeans." He pointed her toward the jeans in the back of the store. "But then again, you'd rock a flour sack."

"Let me guess, they've sold those here since 1860?" Miranda headed for the shelves with the handwritten sign offering women's jeans in a selection of boot cut, slim fit, and 501 original fit.

"No, I think they stopped selling flour about the time Raley's opened in Placerville." At this point, he could be telling an accurate account of gold country history. Or he could be full of shit. Either way, he was having a good time.

"And when was that Professor Swift?"

"1935." That, he did know was true.

"You know you should advertise your historical expertise on your website." She was buying it. Or at least she was playing along. "You might attract more history buffs."

"I'm no more an expert than anyone else who went through elementary school around here." He watched her select a couple pairs of jeans to take to the fitting room between the display of pick axes and weather stations. "We took a field trip to downtown Placerville in third grade. Learned all about the Hangman's Tree, the bell tower, and the Ketchup and Mustard building."

"The Ketchup and Mustard building?" She stood just outside the dressing room, intrigued by his knowledge?

"It was originally a firehouse, then it was City Hall, and now I think it's a real estate office." If he'd known he'd want to impress someone with his historical knowledge, he would have paid more attention in school. "But it's always been painted red and yellow."

"Ah. Ketchup and Mustard." She smiled and stepped behind the curtain.

He let out a sigh and leaned against the shelves of bird houses, hummingbird feeders, and those goofy faces people put on the trees in their yards. He couldn't wait to see her in a pair of well-fitting jeans.

What was it about this woman that got to him? She was hot, but he couldn't quite explain why. She was neither tall nor short. Not too thin or too curvy. She was just right. Her green eyes stood out against her tanned skin. Her long, dark hair was curly, but not too much. In other words, she was perfect. But not too perfect.

She stepped out of the dressing room wearing jeans that had been made just for her.

"I guess these will do." She looked at herself in the mirror, giving a small shrug as if she wasn't sure of the fit.

"Oh they'll do." Cody had to work at getting his tongue back into his mouth. "Of course, up until 1907, it would have been illegal for a woman to look that good in a pair of jeans."

"Really?" She turned to face him, her hands resting defiantly on her hips.

"No. I completely made that up." He hoped she'd find him charming and not utterly full of shit.

"So is anything you told me today, true? Or were you going to let me go looking for the Ketchup and Mustard building only to be laughed out of town?" She was smiling. Mostly.

"You're beautiful. That's the truth."

She sighed, shook her head, and ducked back into the dressing room.

Great. She must think he was a total imbecile. He'd seen it before, on some of the trips he'd done with teen groups. Overeager doofuses, with their raging hormones, trying so hard to impress the girls in their group that is was a miracle they hadn't hurt themselves. And these past twenty-four hours, Cody was no better than the nervous teenagers out on their first co-ed trip.

For years, since middle school, Cody had had a way with the ladies. Getting their attention had been easy. Part of it was being a twin. That in itself garnered attention. But he'd found that making girls laugh, and later, making them purr, had been as natural as swimming. He'd just jump right in, make a splash, and get good and wet.

So go figure that the one woman he truly wanted to impress had come along, and he was as overeager as a Lab puppy chasing a stick into the river.

She came back out, wearing his shorts and T-shirt, with the jeans tucked under her arm. She walked toward the register, stopping along the way to check out various displays. She picked up a bottle of lavender-scented body wash.

After making her purchase, they left the store.

"I thought we could check out the sporting goods store, see if you can pick up a couple pairs of shorts, maybe some yoga pants?"

"Sure. That's fine."

"Then I thought I'd take you to Prospector Café for lunch." Cody hadn't been there since coming back from Utah, but the food was excellent. "They have gourmet burgers, salads, and more."

"So do you work for the tourist board on your days off?"

"Our little town does have a lot to offer." He tried not to get too defensive. "Isn't that what you're looking for in your article? Come for the rafting, but make a weekend of it with shopping, restaurants, and local history."

"No. That's great. Thank you." She sighed. "I almost forgot about the article."

Right. She had a lot on her mind right now. He reached out and took her hand. Just a small gesture, but he wanted to let her know that she wasn't alone.

"Hey, I'm sure your editor will understand."

"Yeah. I'm sure she will." Miranda kept her hand in his and Cody decided he'd be grateful for the little things.

Chapter 10

Apparently some women found spending the day clothes shopping to be an enjoyable experience. Miranda wasn't one of those women. It hadn't been terrible. But just a little awkward with Cody along, practically drooling over the bag of lingerie she'd purchased at the bridal store. Then he nearly broke out in hives when she'd modeled the jeans she picked up at the General Store. Otherwise known as the second oldest continuously operating store west of the Mississippi. So by the time they got to A Good Sport, the sporting goods store where she'd picked up some hiking shorts, tank tops, and a couple of sundresses, she'd figured, the sooner they got out of there the better.

She was looking forward to a nice lunch of, what had he called it? Gourmet burgers, salads, and more?

They walked across the street to the café. It was the kind of place where you ordered at the counter. They had your basic burgers, each named after gold rush terms like the Mother Lode, which was a double patty, loaded with everything, extra cheese, extra bacon, crispy onion straws, sautéed mushrooms, on a sourdough roll. The 49er featured a special sauce of mustard and garlic aioli, arugula, and thinly sliced shallots, and melted gorgonzola. The Claim Jumper had lettuce, cheese, pickles, onions, and a sesame-ginger sauce. The veggie burger was called Pyrite, the real name of fool's gold.

They also had Bison burgers, grilled chicken sandwiches, and salads that would make the swankiest San Francisco eatery look like a pre-packaged convenience store offering. They had a choice of regular thick cut fries, sweet potato planks, and waffle-cut garlic fries, called Snowshoe Thompsons.

Everything sounded so good, but she wasn't sure what her stomach could handle.

Cody ordered a bacon cheeseburger, the Studebaker, with regular fries, and a root beer. Miranda was tempted to just order a thick, old-fashioned milkshake, but instead settled for a Sourdough Sammie. Two thick slices of sourdough, three kinds of cheese and bacon, grilled to perfection with a side salad of mixed spring greens and balsamic vinegar. She ordered a lemonade, freshly squeezed, of course.

When their orders arrived in plastic gold pans, Miranda couldn't help but snap a few pictures from her phone. Yes, this place had atmosphere. And the mural of the town from the 1850s only added to it. When she bit into her sandwich, she seriously considered becoming a food critic. It was that good.

Cody chuckled as she dug into her sandwich.

"What?"

"You're moaning." He dropped his gaze, to remind her that he had indeed seen her naked. And he was well aware of how he'd induced similar vocalizations of satisfaction.

"It's very good." She wiped her mouth with a napkin, not sure if she needed it or not, but she was feeling a little self-conscious. Had she really crawled into his bed and had her way with him last night?

She had. And ninety percent of her was very satisfied with the results.

But then there was that ten percent that realized what a huge mistake that had been.

Suddenly, her sandwich wasn't sitting so well with her. She excused herself to the restroom. Thankfully, she didn't lose her lunch. She took the time to wet a paper towel, dab her forehead and the back of her neck, and return to her lunch companion.

Cody was looking at his phone, a frown creasing his brow.

"Everything okay?" she asked as she slid into her seat to resume eating her sandwich.

"Yeah. I got a text from Ross, at the store." Cody pocketed his phone. "Apparently, the soda and sports drink delivery didn't come, and we're running low on stock. Would you mind if we took a detour to Costco?"

"No. Not at all." A small twinge of guilt swept through her at how much time she'd taken him away from his business already. "Whatever you have to do."

"This could work out to your advantage." He finished his burger and popped the last fry into his mouth. "There's an outlet mall just across the road. So if you want to do some real shopping, while I get supplies, that would be cool."

"You know, I'm kind of shopped out." She took another bite of her sandwich and a sip of her lemonade. "But I can probably pick up a package of socks at Costco."

"Sorry about dragging you down there." He leaned back in his chair. Finished with his meal, he waited for her to be ready to go.

"Hey, no biggie. I get that you have responsibilities." Miranda wiped her face with her napkin, and then pushed the almost empty plate away. The drink was in a to-go cup, so she picked it up and stood.

His face broke into a wide grin. He rose, ready to walk her to his truck. "Yeah. Sure. But my biggest responsibility is making sure my guests—some would call them customers—are satisfied. As important as it is to have the best equipment, the finest selection of refreshments, and the best value for our service, what keeps people coming back for a Swift River Adventure is the personal touch."

"And do you give all your female guests the 'personal touch?'" For some reason, she felt the need to challenge him. No. She knew why. She liked him. A little too much. Her only defense was to push back.

"Just the beautiful, feisty reporters." He placed his hand along the small of her back.

"Yeah, right." She should have twisted away from him, but Miranda liked the feel of his touch. Again. Too much.

"If you're asking me if I've ever hooked up with a passenger, I think you already know the answer to that." His voice was low, so that only she could hear him as they walked out of the café. "Just like I know the answer to the question of whether or not you've ever become involved with someone while on a story."

Did he know about her encounter with Carson? She was an only child, so she had no idea how much siblings shared. And twins were known to have an extra-special bond.

"I will tell you this." He stopped on the sidewalk and turned to face her. He hadn't yet put his sunglasses on. "As long as I'm with you, there will be no one else. I could take a raft full of Victoria's Secret models down the river, and you'd have nothing to worry about. I want you, Miranda. No one else."

He reached down and grabbed her hand.

She should just tell him the truth. And she would, when she had somewhere else to go.

If a guy could have one last fling before getting married, shouldn't she be allowed one last fling before becoming a single parent? Just as long as she kept things casual. That way it wouldn't be too awkward should Uncle Cody show up at birthday parties or soccer matches a few years down the road.

As they drove down the hill to Costco, Miranda couldn't help but wonder what kind of uncle he would be. Would he give piggyback rides? Teach his niece or nephew how to skip rocks and catch a fish? Would he even want to be involved in her child's life or would he only spend time with the legitimate child?

She couldn't think about all of this now. She had to think about what kind of bulk socks she was going to need. And all the other little things she'd need to pick up. Like a home. A bed. Sheets, towels, blankets, dishes, pots and pans. Then in a few months, she'd need to think about all the things the baby would need. A crib, changing table, car seat, and stroller. Diapers.

Instead, she walked out of Costco with a package of socks, her favorite shampoo, conditioner and styling cream, some energy bars, and toothpaste. Cody was loading the sodas, waters, and sports drinks into the back of his truck. He let Miranda help with the paper products and then he slammed the tailgate shut.

"So where to next?" Cody was more than accommodating in tagging along on the endless shopping trip. "There's a mall just up the street and the outlets are just a few blocks over."

"Why don't we hit the grocery store?" Miranda was tired. It could have been from the shopping or because of the pregnancy, but what she really wanted was a nap. "I'd like to cook dinner, as a thank you for all you've done."

"Sure. Sounds good." He held the door for her and she hopped in, ready to buckle up. Her phone slipped out of her pocket and fell to the floorboard.

She picked it up and saw a text notification from her bank. After fastening her seatbelt, she opened up the messaging app and frowned. It was an alert notifying her that a recent deposit had been returned unpaid. The only check she'd deposited was the check from the magazine, which she'd dropped off at the ATM on her way out of town on Sunday.

"Everything okay?" Cody sat in the driver's seat, watching her carefully.

"I'm sure it's just a mix up." Her paychecks weren't huge, but they had been something she depended upon. "My bank is saying my deposit didn't clear."

A quick check of her balance, and she found that she had enough to cover her shopping trip, but if this wasn't resolved, she wouldn't have enough to cover a deposit on a new apartment. And then there would be rent, utilities, and other moving expenses.

Miranda checked her e-mail, to see if her editor had responded to her earlier note about needing more time for the article. Nope. Instead she had a notification that the message had not been delivered.

Surely someone was still in the office. She pulled up her contacts to call her editor directly. An automated message came on informing her "this number is no longer in service."

"What the…" Miranda bit back the rest of her comment and clenched her jaw. Black specks danced before her eyes and she took a few slow, deep breaths. Throwing up on herself would only make the situation worse.

"Do you think I could get one of those bottles of water?" Her voiced sounded a little shaky, but at least she was able to get the words out. "I can pay for it, of course."

"No. Don't worry about it." He jumped out of the truck and went around back, returning with a bottle of water for each of them. "Are you sure everything is all right?"

"Thanks." She unscrewed the cap and took a long swallow. "It appears that my magazine is having some financial difficulties. My last check from them bounced, and it seems their phone and e-mail have been turned off."

"Wow. Really?"

Miranda swallowed the lump in her throat, and stared out the passenger side window. She couldn't look at Cody right now. Not when her life was falling apart. She didn't need to burden him with her problems. And boy, did she have problems. Homeless, apparently jobless, and pregnant was not where she'd expected to be at any point of her life. Just think, less than two months ago, she'd been sitting on top of a desert cliff, a wave of supreme contentment washing over her as she looked out at the river below her. So when a handsome man had approached her, she'd figured "why not?"

Surely she couldn't blame all her troubles on Cody. Or rather, Carson. This is how mixed up she was, she'd forgotten it was Cody's twin brother she'd met and messed around with first. She really was a mess. How on earth was she going to take care of an innocent baby, when she couldn't even take care of herself? She'd been on her own since the age of seventeen; why would she all of a sudden lose the ability to be a grown-up?

A warm, tender hand rested on her thigh. She wanted to warn Cody away from her. To tell him to run, as fast and as far as he could away from her, but instead she took his hand, and gave a quick squeeze, grateful to have some small comfort.

"So, maybe cooking me dinner can wait?" He was trying to save her some money, but she could afford the ingredients for pasta, salad, and bread. "I've still got a lot of leftovers from the wedding, and I hate to waste food."

"Sure." She turned to offer him a small smile. "That's fine."

They drove home in relative silence. Well, they drove to his home. The trees along the way blurred as Miranda tried to think of her next move.

"So if your magazine is out of business, does that give you the opportunity to write for one of those bigger websites?" He broke the silence when they were almost to the resort.

"Actually, a lot of those well-known blogs don't pay writers for their contributions." She'd been asked to post on a couple big name sites, but had declined. "They say the exposure writers get is worth more than any monetary value."

"Yet, they manage to take in a profit?"

"Yeah. Somehow."

"Doesn't seem fair."

And what part of life actually was fair? Nothing she'd experienced, especially lately.

"Maybe you could work on that book you've always wanted to write." Had she mentioned her desire to write a novel? Had she told her secret to his brother?

"What makes you think I'm writing a book?" Even if she did, she wouldn't see any kind of income for months, if not years. She didn't have the luxury of time.

"I just figured you're a writer. You write. Why not write a book?"

"Well, it looks like the only thing I'm going to be working on in the foreseeable future is my résumé."

"Do you have retail experience?"

"I worked in the campus bookstore in college." Why would he ask that?

"Great. We could use some extra help in our store. Especially with Carson and Lily gone for a couple of weeks. We're really shorthanded."

Wow. Was he offering her a job on top of everything else? "Look, I appreciate the offer, but I'm not a charity case."

"No. Of course not. It's just that the guides are all taking turns working in the store on their days off. It's costing me a lot in overtime pay, and they're having to work basically seven days a week, with only a half-day off to take care of personal stuff, like shopping, banking, getting the oil changed in their cars."

Another lump welled up in her throat. She knew better than to say no. But she couldn't quite bring herself to commit to working for a man she was already too tangled up with.

"I mean, Fisher's probably putting in the most overtime, and she's salary so she doesn't really get paid extra."

"Fisher?" The blonde. The one who was in his kitchen that first morning. Who showed up again this morning offering to take the tuxedo rental back. "The woman you're just friends with?"

"Yeah. Friends." He turned to give her a quizzical look. "Why do you ask?"

"I don't know." A slippery feeling snuck into her belly. Jealousy? "I just get the feeling she's not fully on board with just being friends."

"Look, I know it looks like we're close, but I'm telling you, I have no interest in her as anything other than a friend." Miranda wondered if he was also trying to convince himself of that. "She's more like a sister than anything."

"A sister?"

"Yeah. Sister. Besides, she works for me. So you have nothing to worry about. Seriously."

"You just offered me a job. At least I think you did."

"Yeah. I did."

"Does that mean we're just friends?"

"No." He drove into town. "I'd say we're more than friends."

"And the benefits?"

"That's up to you, sweetheart." He grinned, a slow, sexy, somewhat mischievous grin. "I like you, Miranda. I like spending time with you. And if I can help you out a little, I'd be more than happy to do so."

"And what's in it for you?" She was still a little skeptical.

"I get to spend more time with you. I get to know my store is covered and my employees aren't going to walk out on me while I'm trying to hold things together around here. I get to see you in Swift River Adventure Company T-shirts during the day, and hopefully nothing at all at night."

She felt heat creep across her cheeks at that last statement.

"But do you get that it would only be temporary?" She couldn't exactly say no. Not when her options were so limited.

"Temporary? Sure. I know your talents are on the page, not behind a register."

* * * *

Miranda had agreed to work for him. Temporarily. She'd made it very clear it was only a short-term arrangement.

He'd take it. For now. He had no grand illusions that it would work out as well as hiring Lily had for Carson. But hey, it was a start. The last thing he wanted was for her to take off for parts unknown, looking for a job and a place to live that could be hundreds or even thousands of miles from him. This would buy him some time to figure out how to get her to stay because she wanted to, not because she had nowhere else to go.

He would just need to find a way to get her to want to stay. He knew ringing up sunscreen, snacks, and sports drinks wasn't going to be enough to make her want to make a career change. No. He would have to find a way to make her feel needed, and not just in his bedroom.

Cody approached the Prospector Feed store. Shit. He'd forgotten to pick up some cat food at Costco. Fortunately, he remembered before passing the last chance before turning off the resort.

"One last stop." He announced as he pulled into the parking spot closest to the door. "We need cat food."

"Right. And I suppose she still needs a name." Miranda flashed a quick, but false smile.

"How about Lucky?"

She snorted. "Hardly. I've had nothing but bad luck since that cat showed up. Jinx is more like it."

"Jinx. I like it." He patted her on the knee. "Do you want to stay here? It'll just be a minute to grab a bag of cat food, maybe one of those little mouse toys."

"Thanks." She leaned back against the seat, most likely exhausted from the last twenty-four hours of bad luck.

He walked into the store wishing his good luck at seeing her again hadn't come at such a cost to her.

"What can I help you with?" A kid in a plaid shirt and Wranglers was stacking fifty pound bags of feed near the front of the store.

"Do you have cat food?" Hopefully in a smaller size. He worried that Miranda would be a little intimidated by six months' worth of cat food.

"Yeah, over here." The kid dropped the sack he was holding and led him to the stacks of more reasonable-sized cat food. "We've got feed for kittens, adult cats, senior cats. We have your special formulas for kidney health, gluten-free, and pregnant or nursing mothers."

"Um, it's just a regular cat." Really? Gluten-free cat food? They'd fed it leftover salmon, and he just hoped it didn't get spoiled by it.

"Here's one of our more popular brands. It's low in carbs, all-natural, and reasonably priced." He pointed to a twenty-five pound bag of food with a picture of a cat that looked like Jinx, so Cody figured, why not?

"Is there anything else I might need?" That could be a mistake. Now he'd end up leaving here with hundreds of dollars of cat "essentials."

"Is it an indoor cat? Do you use a litter box?"

"The cat goes outside during the day."

"So then you'll want a collar, flea and tick medication, and a good brush."

"What about toys?"

"You can pick up a little stuffed mouse, but that probably won't prevent an outdoor cat from bringing home the real thing." The kid laughed knowingly. "And you'll want to make sure to feed the cat indoors, unless you want to adopt raccoons and skunks as well."

"Thanks for the tip." Cody picked up a bright orange collar with a bell, a hairbrush, and the flea and tick medication with the hand-written sign proclaiming it to be recommended by local vets. "One more thing, could you recommend a good vet?"

"A lot of our customers come from Prospector Veterinary Clinic. They're on Prospector Drive, across from the dentist offices."

"Great. I appreciate all your help." Cody took out his wallet and paid for his purchases. The clerk put the collar, brush, and medication in a paper sack and Cody grabbed the food off the counter.

He just hoped the cat was still around when he got home.

Chapter 11

When they arrived at the resort, Miranda jumped out and grabbed a case of water. "Do I just stock the shelves, or is there an inventory process?"

"Why don't you set that down, and we'll grab a hand truck." Cody had to give her credit for enthusiasm and her willingness to just jump in and take on the job. "And we'll need to have you fill out some paperwork before you start working."

"Oh, right. I just wanted to do my part."

"Why don't I introduce you to the rest of the crew?" He wanted Miranda to feel comfortable here.

"Sure." She slid the water back into the bed of the truck and wiped her hands on her hips before following him into the store.

Ross was behind the counter, and he gave a quick nod to Cody when he heard the bell ring.

"Ross, I'd like you to meet Miranda."

"Hey." Ross smiled as he looked from Miranda to Cody, as if he was trying to figure out the relationship. *Get in line, buddy.* "Welcome to Swift River. I hope you're enjoying your stay."

"Thanks. I'm actually going to be working here." She cast an uncertain glance toward Cody. "In the store, just while your other boss is away."

"Well great." Ross's grin widened. "Why don't you come around here and I'll show you how the register works? And everything else."

Protective jealousy flared in Cody. "Why don't you go unload the supplies you asked me to pick up and I'll show Miranda around?"

"You're the boss." Ross shrugged and headed toward the driveway behind the store.

"Yes. I am." Cody didn't have to get all hard-assed on his employees very often. "And I shouldn't have to remind you to use the dolly. We don't need any work-related injuries around here. Especially with Lily not here."

"Yeah, yeah." Ross gave Miranda one last longing glance before slipping through the door.

"Look, if my being here is going to cause problems…"

"Nah. It's kind of an inside thing. When Lily first got here, she was pretty quick to point out safety issues. We're pretty laid back about most things around here, but while we were always on top of safety on the river, she noticed we weren't so vigilant when it came to dry land."

"Things like acting all macho and trying to carry too-heavy loads?"

"Exactly. Especially in the presence of a pretty lady. Like the time my brother and I took her rafting and we kept trying to outdo each other. Fortunately, neither of us were ejected from the boat."

"So were you both competing for her attention?"

Cody hesitated for a moment, before admitting the truth. "At first. We were both interested, but it soon became very clear that Lily and Carson were meant for each other. I didn't stand a chance."

"Oh." Miranda sounded a little unsatisfied with the answer. "So do you, I mean, did you and your brother compete for a lot of women?"

"Most of the time, the women we'd meet would come in pairs." Cody wasn't always proud of his wilder days. When the Swift twins were the hottest ticket in town. "I mean, if we met girls on a trip, they usually came with friends or sisters. And at the Argo, well, not many women show up to a bar, even a fun, friendly place like that, without backup."

"What about swapping?" She asked with some hesitation. "Did you and your brother ever switch places with a date?"

"Nah. I mean, we've traded places for other things. Like taking a test or avoiding a chore." Clearly, she was testing him. He should come clean and admit to taking his brother's place on the Yampa. How should he even begin telling her about the one time he'd impersonated his brother for six weeks because he was mad at Carson for falling in love? That he'd been pissed off at him for always treating him like the irresponsible playboy he'd been?

Before he could formulate the words, Ross returned with a load of sodas.

"How's it going?" Ross gave a nod in the direction of the register. "You getting the hang of things?"

"We're just getting started." Cody wanted to tell Ross to get the hell out, but he was supposed to be the boss. "So just keep up the good work."

Ross started stocking the cooler at the back of the store, so Cody turned his attention to showing Miranda how to work the register.

"Everything is already in the system, so you just have to use the scanner." He grabbed an energy bar from the counter and scanned it. "See, it comes right up on the screen here."

"Seems easy enough."

"Now to take an item off, say if you scanned it twice, or a customer changes their mind, you just press here..." He indicated the void button. "And rescan."

The energy bar was voided out of the system with another pass over the scanner.

"Now, if an item doesn't scan, you can override here." He showed her how to manually enter a price and where to look it up in a binder kept under the counter. Not surprisingly, she was a quick learner. When a camper came in for some bug spray and a six pack, she greeted her with a smile and asked to see ID for the beer. The woman, in her forties, smiled and blushed and pulled her license out of her wallet.

"Wow." Miranda gushed. "What is your secret for looking so young?"

"Beer and bug spray?" the woman said with a shrug and a glowing grin. The woman left with an extra spring in her step.

"Nice job." Cody really hoped she would stay on longer than the two weeks Carson and Lily would be gone. "I think you'll fit right in here at Swift River."

"I'd put that in my article, but..." Her voice drifted off with an audible sigh.

"Hey, maybe you could come up with some copy for our website." His heart rate quickened with the idea of letting her use her talents, not just her ability to make a sale, in order to feel at home here. "I bet you could help drive traffic to our website, and eventually to our boats."

"I'm not a website designer." She blushed, as if the idea of using her words was suddenly something that made her uncomfortable. "I wouldn't know where to start."

"Just write what you were going to put in your article," he suggested. "Unless you were planning on slamming us in the press. If you were going to say I'm a horrible guide, then leave that out. But you could write about how great my crew is."

"I'd planned on writing a glowing review, but now I have nowhere to post it." She sounded more defiant than defeated.

"Like I said, you could post it to our website."

"I don't know." She shook her head and sighed.

"I'd pay you, if that's what you're worried about." He knew all about people expecting things for free if they knew you. Like the high school friends who thought they could get a free ride down the river since they'd been his lab partners in tenth grade chemistry.

"Can I think about it?"

"Sure." He took a step back, worried he was pressuring her too much. "I'm sure you'll want to ask around, see what the going rate for website copy is. Then we can negotiate a fair price. Which reminds me, we still haven't done the paperwork for you working in the store. It's a good thing our payroll manager isn't here. She'd have my ass."

"Lily? Your sister-in-law?"

"Yeah. She's a total ball-buster. But that's my brother's problem, not mine." The joke fell flat.

Ross had returned with another load from the truck. "Hey, Ross, can you cover the register for a few minutes? I need to help Miranda with some paperwork."

"Sure. No problem." Ross started unloading some juice, knowing the overhead bell would alert him of any customers.

"I'll have you fill out the tax withholding form, at least." He led her to the office that was just off the back entrance to the store. "I would imagine you don't carry your social security card with you, so I'll just take your word for it."

"I always have my passport with me." Miranda reminded him that she was a world adventurer. "It's in my purse."

"Great. Why don't you go get it, and I'll print out the forms? We'll need to get you paid as soon as possible."

While she went to get her passport, Cody booted up the desktop and turned on the printer. He was glad Lily had taken the time to show him how to run payroll and pay the bills, even before she and Carson were engaged. Originally, he'd been trying to get close to Lily. But her goal all along had been to take some of the pressure off Carson. For too long, the twins had been stuck in the roles assigned in childhood. Carson had always been the responsible one while Cody was the fun-loving life of the party. Even in their business, Cody had been more of the people pleaser, tending to guest satisfaction, while Carson took care of the more mundane details of running a rafting outfit, campground, and resort.

So when Lily fell into their lives—literally, they'd fished her out of the river—Cody was upset at the initial disruption of the status quo. But when he realized that Carson needed someone to take care of him for a change, and Lily was the perfect woman for the job, Cody got over it.

It didn't hurt that he'd met someone, too.

That someone was Miranda. And she had no idea how she'd changed his life.

He'd returned from Utah a different man. A man who realized that there was more to life than hot women and cold beer. For the first time in his life, he could picture spending more than a weekend with a woman. He could picture her in his kitchen, riding shotgun in his truck, and yes, in his business. Not as an employee, though. He really could picture Miranda as his partner. The way Lily was Carson's partner. In the business, sure, but more importantly, in life.

Too bad he'd already screwed it up by lying to her when they first met. And the longer he went without telling her, the harder it was going to be when he finally came clean.

Man, he was a coward. Not worthy of her at all. But he couldn't tell her now. Not with all the shitty things that had happened to her in the last couple of days. No, he'd wait until she felt at home here. When she was happy working by his side, sleeping in his bed, eating the meals he made for her. Maybe he'd soften her up with some of that good Zin from the Lost Mine Winery. He'd raise a glass and toast to new beginnings. Or some such shit.

"So, here's my passport. I'm totally legal." She opened her passport, handed it to him to make a copy for her employment file.

"Wow." Her picture took his breath away. "I thought you were supposed to look bad in a passport photo. Are you sure this isn't fake?"

She glared at him, crossing her arms over her chest.

"You look beautiful. That's all." He signed his part of the official form and slid it across the desk so she could fill out her part.

She started filling out the usual information, name, birthdate, but she looked up when she got to the line that asked for her address.

"Excuse me." She pushed back from the desk and stalked outside.

He gave her a minute before following her. His heart broke when he saw her standing next to his truck, arms wrapped around herself, silently shaking.

"Hey." He put an arm around her and she turned toward him, sobbing without a sound. "It's okay. It's going to be okay. I'll do whatever it takes to make everything work out for you."

"You've done so much already. I can't ask for anything more." Her voice was small, frightened, and he felt a sense of powerlessness rage inside him. She was hurting and he couldn't just laugh it off or make a joke or smile and make her problems go away.

He could offer her his home, a job, but she saw it as a handout, a reminder that she had nothing. He wanted to give her the world, but she'd had her world taken away from her. And he had no fucking clue how to fix it for her.

"Hey. We'll skip the paperwork part for now." He resorted to his fallback mode of a no-worries attitude. "If Ross has the truck unloaded, we can head on out, go back to my place, and throw together some dinner."

"No. I want to finish the shift." She straightened her shoulders and tossed her long dark hair over her shoulders. "Sometimes throwing yourself into work is the best thing."

She marched back toward the store and he found himself admiring her even more. An image of his grandmother flashed into his memory. Whenever she'd been faced with troubles of any kind, she'd simply straighten her spine, strap on an apron, and start cooking. Often making extra for those less fortunate than them. He wondered what Granny would have thought about Miranda. Somehow, he knew she would have loved her.

* * * *

Miranda walked into the store hoping to find a rush of customers. Instead she found Ross sitting on a stool behind the counter, a tattered notebook in his hand, pen scratching over the pages. She'd come in through the back door leading to the office, so the bell didn't alert him to her presences.

"Busy evening?" She tried to make her voice sound like someone who didn't have a care in the world. She could scratch acting as a career alternative.

"Um, no. Not really." Ross quickly closed the notebook and shoved it under the counter.

"So what do you do when it's slow like this?" She looked around, as if she could find something to occupy her time, and more importantly her thoughts. "Are there shelves to straighten, inventory to restock?"

"It's pretty casual around here." Ross was trying to play it cool. She wondered what he was up to on his notepad that he was somewhat embarrassed by. "Yeah, if people pick through the shirts or something, we make sure everything gets put back in order. But it's not like we have to make up jobs to keep busy if we're not."

"So, how do you keep from getting bored?" She asked, looking around for some sort of diversion. She saw the neat racks of T-shirts, the tidy display of river sandals, and the section of all those little items campers might have forgotten to pack. Bug spray, sunscreen, pain relievers, and condoms. Turning from that shelf, she noticed a small selection of magazines. There were the ones she'd expect, *Sports Illustrated, Sunset, Backpacker, Outside,* and *National Geographic*—it had once been her dream job to write for them. But she was more than surprised to see the last issue of *Adventure*

Chix. The one with her article on the magical, mystical tour of the Yampa River. She picked it up, almost afraid to look inside and see her words there for all the world to see. Along with a picture, although not a close-up, of her guide.

"You could look at magazines when we're not busy." Ross was trying to be helpful, but her nerves were so raw, it was all she could do not to run out of the store with the magazine and throw it in the river.

"And what were you doing when I walked in?" She didn't want to be too nosy, but she was curious. She had a feeling it was some sort of creative pursuit. No one did math equations for fun and then hid them under a desk when someone walked in on them.

"Um," He ran a nervous hand through his hair. "I kind of play around with songwriting. You know, lyrics. I mean, the music part comes pretty easily. I just sit outside with my guitar, and the melodies just sort of flow. But when it comes to writing the words… well, that's a lot harder."

"Sure. And of course, the best stuff makes it look so easy." She relaxed a little, feeling a kinship with the songwriting raft guide/store clerk. "But writing is hard. Really hard. Especially when it's good."

"Yeah. It is hard." Ross smiled, relaxing a bit himself. "But sometimes I can't help myself. You know, I get off the river, and there's just something that speaks to me and I have to get it out. That probably sounds totally weird, right?"

"No. Not at all." Miranda placed the magazine—her magazine—back on the shelf. "Not to a writer. We totally get it."

"You're a writer?" He sounded almost impressed. "Like books?"

"No. Not books. Magazine articles. Blog posts." Potentially, web copy. If she dared. But lately, her confidence had been shaken. She was afraid she wouldn't be able to produce anything worth reading. With everything going on in her life, she wasn't sure she could write. Hell, she couldn't even fill out a W-4 form. Okay, so maybe it wasn't exactly writer's block that kept her from being able to come up with a home address.

Ever since the positive pregnancy test, she'd been unable to put words to the page. She'd had to request the trip here in person; she couldn't even compose a freaking e-mail.

The funny thing was, she'd always used her writing to get through all the little shitstorms life had thrown at her. From the time she was a teenager—no, even younger, maybe fourth or fifth grade—she'd used words to comfort herself. Whether it was pouring her soul out onto the pages of a journal, composing awful poetry about the boys who broke her heart, or starting dozens of novels where the heroine would take control of her own life and not have to rely on the whims of fate or flaky caregivers, she'd found solace in the written word.

And then she'd found a way to make a living with her words. Oh, that had been empowering, almost intoxicating at first. People actually gave her money to put her ideas on paper. Or a hard drive, whatever. She was a real writer.

"Cool." Ross bobbed his head in appreciation. "Magazines, huh?"

"Yeah. Well, until recently. My magazine just went out of business." She couldn't bring herself to show him her last published piece. Maybe after he left, she'd ring up a sale for herself. One last souvenir of her former life.

"That sucks." Ross gave her a look, like *what-are-you-gonna-do?* "But we're glad you're here. You'll like being a part of the Swift River team. It's not just a job…"

"It's an adventure?"

"No. Well, yeah, it is. But what I meant to say was it's like a family." Ross grinned, he was sweet. A little young, but sweet. "And you're with Cody, huh?"

Her cheeks flamed. Oh, Cody. What was she going to do about that man? He'd been so good to her. It would destroy him if he ever found out that she'd slept with his twin brother. And the baby. Oh, God.

A tingling sensation started in her extremities. Her fingers, toes, and lips started to go numb. She leaned against the counter, hoping the swirling black specks that danced before her eyes would somehow disappear as she sucked in deep gulps of air.

Breathe. Please. Just. Breathe. She could not, she would not faint. Not here. Not now.

"You okay?" Ross rushed around from behind the register. "You look a little woozy."

"Sorry. It's been a long day." She shook off the dizziness, and amazingly it seemed to work. "Thanks for all your help."

"No problem." Ross put his arm around her, to steady her. "Hey, just so you know, Cody's a good guy. No matter what you might hear, he really is. And I think he's lucky to have you."

"Thanks. I think." Miranda wasn't sure what he meant by *no matter what you might hear.*

Chapter 12

"Get your hands off her." Cody came into the store to find Ross with his arm around Miranda. The mild flash of jealousy he'd felt earlier was nothing compared to the storm that raged inside him now.

"Whoa." Ross glared at him. "Take it easy. She wasn't feeling well; I was just making sure she didn't fall."

Cody looked at Miranda's pale skin, frightened eyes, and shaky hands, and he felt like even more of a jackass. He rushed to her side, giving Ross a look that told him that his services were no longer needed in the caring-for-Miranda department.

"What's wrong?"

"I just got a little dizzy, that's all." Miranda leaned against the counter.

"You're not diabetic or anything, are you?"

"No. No, I'm…" She looked up at him, tears and absolute agony swimming in her green eyes. "I'm so embarrassed. I'm such a hot mess lately."

"Hey, no. It's cool." She was still shaking. "Hey, Ross, bring that stool around here, would you?"

Ross appeared with the stool from behind the counter and Miranda sat down.

"What else do you need? Do you need something to eat? A cool drink?"

"Maybe some water." She gave a wan smile. "Or some of that fresh apple juice."

"Ross!" Cody tilted his head toward the cooler and Ross went and grabbed a bottle of juice.

"Thank you." She twisted the cap off and took a small sip. "Mmm. This is good."

"Yeah. I'll have to take you up to Apple Hill in the fall." He said it without thinking she might not be here, but the look of horror on her face told him everything. She wasn't planning on being here that long.

"Yeah, it can be crowded, if you go on a weekend in October." He pretended that it was the mass of tourists that had her balking at wanting to spend time with him in the future. "But midweek in September, you get a better experience. Get to pick your own apples if you want. Have a slice of fresh apple pie. Or apple donuts. The apple donuts are to die for."

"That sounds nice." She was trying not to let him down; he could hear it in her voice.

"It is. This area has a lot to offer." He wasn't going to let her get away. Not without doing everything he can to make her want to stay in Prospector Springs.

She took another sip of juice. "I'm feeling much better. I guess I should have had the cheeseburger for lunch instead of a sandwich and salad."

"I'll make you a nice steak for dinner. With all the trimmings."

"That sounds good. What time does the store close?"

"Seven, but I think Ross can close up."

"Yeah, it's kind of slow today. But Mondays usually are pretty quiet." Ross was being cooperative, despite Cody's initial attack when he first came into the store.

"So what's the schedule for tomorrow?" Cody wanted to get Miranda home, but knew she wouldn't leave until she had a plan for the next day.

"I think Jake was going to pull a double shift, but Brooke said she'd cover the early morning hours before she hits the river. Then Fisher was going to come in once they get off."

"See?" Cody grinned at how perfect Ross's statement fit his plans. "I told you we were short-handed. You can take the second shift, and I'll let Jake know he can open."

"That sounds great." Miranda had perked up quite a bit after drinking half the juice. "What time should I come in, then?"

"How about noon? I'll have Jake hang around about an hour, just to make sure you're comfortable," Cody added. "Then I'll come in the last hour to help you close."

"Sure. But on one condition," Miranda warned. "I'll make dinner after work. You do like pasta, right?"

"Right." He could let her cook for him. As long as she let him be in charge of dessert.

Slow down, cowboy. He needed to chill. She'd given him plenty of signals that he was moving too fast. It was almost as if he'd strapped an outboard motor on the back of a raft. He'd forgotten that the destination wasn't the most important part. It was all about the journey. And the adventure along the way.

"So, Ross, you got this?" Cody held his hand out for Miranda.

"Sure, Boss." Ross chuckled and Cody couldn't help but join him.

"What's so funny?" Miranda asked.

"It's kind of an inside joke. A lot of the guys had a hard time telling me and my brother apart, so they would just call us 'Boss.' It's sort of a thing, now."

He held the door open for her to head to the parking lot.

"So does that mean the women didn't have trouble telling you two apart?" She tossed a playful grin his way.

"Um. Well, Fisher has always been able to tell us apart." He needed to be careful here. "But she's got a Master's degree."

"Wow. Impressive." Did he detect a hint of jealousy in her voice? Not that it mattered. He wasn't interested in Fisher. As he'd explained more than once. But still, if Miranda was jealous, that meant she was interested in him. He could use that to his advantage.

"We only hire the finest people." He hoped she understood that she was included in that statement. "Because it's not just a job, or an adventure, but here at Swift River, we're family."

"Please tell me it doesn't say that on your website." She rolled her eyes, but couldn't keep a smile from escaping her lips. "Because, oh my gawd, that is corny."

"See, I need you." He said it playfully, but deep down he meant it. Funny, a few months ago he didn't even know he had a deep down. "Otherwise, I might end up writing something about how big and stiff our oars are."

"Please don't."

"So you'll help me?" Hope bubbled up like a small freshwater spring.

"I said I'd think about it."

"Great. No pressure."

"No. Pressure is being homeless, jobless, and pre…" Her voice caught. "Present company excluded, alone."

"What about your family?"

"It was just me and my mom." Miranda had a note of melancholy in her voice. "And I haven't seen her in over a year."

"So, what's up with that?" Cody had a hard time thinking about having a mother but not seeing her. What he wouldn't give to have even met his own mother.

"My mom got pregnant with me when she was barely seventeen." Miranda sounded a little too matter of fact about it. "And her parents basically disowned her. So we spent my childhood roaming from place to place, looking for work as a waitress or housekeeper or both."

"Sounds like she was a hard worker." He opened the passenger door for her.

"Yeah. But she was—still is—a wanderer." Miranda heaved a sigh. "Last I heard she was living in Costa Rica. Before that, on a sailboat somewhere in the Caribbean."

"So is that where you get your sense of adventure from?"

"Adventure?" She shook her head. "More like survival."

"Yeah, but you've been to some amazing places in your travels. I grew up with people who've never crossed the county line."

"And you never wander far from home?"

"It's not that I haven't been anywhere else," Cody chose his words carefully. "It's just that there's nowhere else I'd rather be than right here on this river. I know it's not exactly the most exotic or extreme location. But it's kind of what I like about it. It's adventure that's accessible to anyone. You don't have to be rich or train for years to enjoy all that nature has to offer."

"I've been on more technical rivers," Cody continued. "But then I'm more worried about technique than ensuring a satisfying guest experience. I've been on more desolate rivers. But one medical emergency could become tragic. Like this one trip I was on, we had a passenger who was severely overweight. So much so that he got winded just bringing his gear from the parking lot to the van. The first three nights I worried he'd have a heart attack just getting out of the raft, and we didn't have any dry bags big enough to carry the body out of the canyon."

"There's a cheerful thought."

"Exactly. I like the fact that I can take kids as young as eight down the river, and we've had passengers in their eighties enjoy our trips as well." He sounded like a salesman, except he was only telling the way he felt. "You don't have to be a hard-core adventurer to enjoy the river, but experienced outdoorsmen and women still get a thrill when facing the more challenging rapids."

"I don't think you need help coming up with what to put on your website, just write down what you feel."

"Some of it's personal, too." He truly wanted Miranda to understand why his home meant so much to him, and why he wanted to share it with her. "My mother lived here. She learned how to fish and skip rocks and swim on this river. She hiked the trails, picked blackberries, and…"

"So you feel connected to her through the river?"

"Huh? I never really thought of it that way, but yeah, I guess so." A sudden lump rose in his throat. How was it possible to miss someone he'd never even met? "I mean...this was the last place she ever lived. So, I guess there is a connection."

"Hmm." Miranda looked out the window, almost wistfully.

"Is your love of travel a way of connecting with your mother?" Cody wondered aloud.

"No." Miranda sounded a bit defensive. "I hated always moving. Always being the new kid in town."

"You moved a lot as a kid?"

"Let's see, seven elementary schools, three middle schools, and two high schools?" There was a bitterness in her voice. "Does that count as moving a lot?"

"I went to Marshall Elementary, kindergarten through eighth grade, and then Prospector High."

"Wow. Only two schools?"

"And college." Cody said. "But I lived here, and commuted to Sac State. I guess that sounds pretty boring, compared to traveling all over the world."

* * * *

"Traveling can get boring." Miranda didn't want to complain, but... "Especially when it's just work. After a while, one airport is the same as the next, one hotel room blurs into another, and even the scenery starts to blend together."

"So how did you get started with travel writing?" Cody didn't seem to pick up on her dissatisfaction with her lifestyle. Or at least he was polite enough not to dwell on it with her.

"My editor was a guest lecturer for one of my journalism classes." Miranda had only taken the class because she knew making a living as a novelist wasn't something that came with a guarantee. She'd need a way to support herself until she got her first break, so she thought she'd look into journalism. "Then I took a summer internship, and the rest, as they say, is history."

"So was it the writing that appealed to you?" It sounded like genuine curiosity. "Have you always wanted to be a writer?"

"I've always written." But there were times when she still didn't think of herself as a writer. Maybe when she got around to writing a book. But that was looking more like something she'd have to put off a little longer since she'd need a steady income for, oh, at least the next eighteen years.

"Well, then, you'll figure out a way to bounce back." He turned onto the bridge that would lead them back to his house. Miranda looked upriver and she could just barely make out the ruins of the original sawmill where the Gold Rush had all started. An image, faded like an old photograph, formed in her mind. A woman, stepping off the boat in San Francisco. Her chaperone had not survived the voyage around the horn. Her choices were limited as a young woman, alone in the wild west. A brothel caught her eye across the street. No, she'd turned down an offer of marriage because she couldn't sell herself to a man she didn't love or even respect.

Scene after scene filled her mind. A man helping her carry her trunk to the hotel, and pretending to be her chaperone so she could get a room next to his. Sneaking into his room in the early morning hours to steal a pair of trousers and an overcoat. Posing as a young man and staking a claim in the gold fields. Reuniting with the man who assisted her in San Francisco, only to have to hide her identity.

Her fingers itched with the need to open her laptop. She was afraid she would lose the story if she didn't write it down sooner rather than later.

"So, you still up for a steak dinner?" Cody asked when they pulled into his driveway. "I can get the grill going and whip up a salad and some potatoes."

"Actually, I'm kind of wiped out." She didn't want to hurt his feelings, but she really needed some time alone with her book. Or what could be a book, if she could keep the excitement for this new story from getting waylaid by all her other distractions. She'd need to do some research, but she had a feeling there were plenty of resources locally. Besides, it could be fun. "Maybe I'll just make a sandwich and call it a night."

"Sure. I guess it's been a long day for you." He sounded disappointed, but understanding at the same time. "Maybe you should take a nice, long bath, relax."

"That sounds nice, but I really need to break out my laptop." She didn't want to admit that she was suddenly inspired. Not until she was sure she really had something. "I have a lot of research to do. I need to find a place to live…"

"I hope you will take a look around here." Cody sounded like he was trying to play it cool, but there was something in his voice that made her think he really did want her to stay. "I think you'll find that Prospector Springs is a great place to call home."

She found the idea somewhat tempting. But too complicated for her to actually consider it. Yet, she couldn't go too far. At some point, she would need to allow her child to get to know his or her father.

And uncle.

Why did the uncle have to be so damned adorable?

A part of her wanted to pack up and head for Maine or Florida or even Hawaii. But she didn't have anything to pack. And she knew all too well what it was like to be dragged along as a parent resisted any sense of permanence.

"Sure. I'd like to grab a quick bite and then head up to the room with my laptop."

"You are a wild woman." Cody flashed an adorable grin. He was definitely a complication, but he was also a lifesaver. She had to be strong. Focused.

"You have no idea." She sighed.

Cody started pulling food out of the fridge, more of the sliced tri-tip, lettuce, tomatoes, and all the trimming. He grabbed a loaf of bread and a knife to slice thick slabs of sourdough.

"You want to grab a couple of plates?" He pointed to the cabinet next to the sink.

"Sure." Miranda wanted to help.

"And maybe a couple of wine glasses." His request was somewhat hopeful.

"I'll pass on the wine, but I'll be happy to get a glass down for you."

"Nah." Disappointment sounded in his voice. "Wine always tastes sweeter when shared."

"I'm fine with just water." She didn't want to make a big deal about why she wasn't interested in sharing a glass of wine with him. "And you?"

"Yeah, water is good." He went back to making sandwiches, just like he did that first day. Had it only been yesterday? Already, she felt like she'd been here a week. But that would mean Carson would return sooner. She still had time. Not much, but she wouldn't have to make any rash decisions. She wouldn't be taking the first crappy apartment she could find, or a cheap motel because she had no other options.

If only her option wasn't so closely related.

Chapter 13

After helping with the cleanup, which was minimal with only sandwiches, Miranda made her way up to the room she was staying in. She grabbed her laptop and made herself comfortable on the king-sized bed.

With only slight flutters in her stomach, she opened a new document and began typing.

Chapter One

Sarah Matthews stepped off the boat in the bustling city of San Francisco. After several months aboard the ship, she should be grateful to finally be standing on solid ground. But her stomach pitched and rolled more than it ever had on even the roughest seas. She was all alone in the world. Her father had died, leaving his business partner to believe that she would accept his proposal of marriage. After all, he was now the sole proprietor of the horse ranch and stables. But Sarah would not be property. So she'd made up her mind to join the rest of the '49ers and make her way to the gold fields of California.

Clifford Bradley, her father's most trusted friend and unofficial butler, had insisted on making the journey with her, fearful of the hardships a young woman without a chaperone would face in the wilds of California.

But Bradley had not survived the voyage. A disease of the intestines caused him to be wrapped in canvas and buried at sea only a week before they had arrived in San Francisco. The men had mostly left her alone, but she'd overheard discussion about what fate might befall her once they hit land. The word "entertainer" was passed about in harsh whispers. But Sarah was worldly enough, having grown up in a household of just her father and Bradley, to know that an entertainer in the gold fields would not be known for her singing voice or ability to waltz.

She'd already turned down the "opportunity" to prostitute herself in marriage. She would not trade one man's unwelcome advances for those of many. She would just have to come up with an alternative plan in order to survive.

If only she had skills as a seamstress, or baker, or some other such feminine attribute. But she had been raised almost like a boy from the time of her mother's death when she was six. Sarah knew more about riding a horse than baking a pie.

She dragged her heavy trunk down the pier, passing more saloons and brothels than trees back home. Somehow, she would find a respectable place to sleep for the night. And tomorrow she would make her way to the hills. She would find gold. She could work as hard as any man. She'd just need to keep her wits about her.

"Pardon me, ma'am, but that seems an awfully heavy trunk, for a delicate young woman such as yourself." She turned to find a man, startlingly handsome, with his hat tipped in a gesture of politeness she hadn't seen since her father's funeral. "Could I lend a hand?"

Miranda knew it wasn't perfect, but it was a start. Her fingers flew over the keyboard, and the hours disappeared as she immersed herself into the world of 1850s California Gold Rush. Sarah had transformed into Matty, a young man making his claim like several other gold-seekers who'd traveled by wagon train or boat from the East Coast to California. It wasn't until her heroine had been reunited with the man she'd met in San Francisco, the man who had helped her obtain lodging that wasn't as a brothel worker, the man she had stolen from, that Miranda realized the stiffness in her fingers, and the ache in her wrists.

She glanced at the clock. It was nearly one in the morning. Had she really been writing for six hours straight? With a kink in her neck and a strong sense of satisfaction, she realized she had.

After saving her work, she closed her laptop and set it aside. Stretching her arms, neck, and back, she made her way to the bathroom to wash her face, brush her teeth, and take care of other needs.

Even though it was late, Miranda was restless. She'd started several books, in different genres, but somehow this one felt different. Like this one had enough substance to actually carry it through all the way to the happy ending. Sure there would be obstacles along the way. But her characters would take each of them head on, and overcome even the most difficult challenges.

Something she wasn't sure of being able to do in her own life.

Lying down on the bed, Miranda tried to get comfortable. The mattress had the right balance of softness and firmness. The pillow was neither too full or too flat. And the quilt added just the right amount of warmth as a slight breeze blew through the partially open window.

Still, she was restless. The complications in her book and in her own life combined in such a way that she knew she'd never get any sleep this way. But she knew that if she continued typing, her hands would be useless tomorrow. She'd be unable to work the cash register in Cody's store.

She didn't want to let him down. Not after all he'd done to help her.

With a sigh, she got out of bed and headed downstairs. Maybe a glass of water or a snack would settle her nerves. Or some fresh air. The moonlight through the French doors made the deck seem so inviting.

Stepping out on the deck, Miranda made her way to the edge overlooking the river. It was so beautiful here. The moon and stars shining down on the river below. The slight breeze whispering through the trees above. There was something grounding about this place. Something that invited one to put down roots, like the giant oak that looked like it had been there at least a century.

She'd always felt more like a tumbleweed. But maybe her child would have a chance to grow roots. To live in one place—or more realistically— two households. One school from kindergarten through eighth grade. And then on to high school with the same kids who had learned how to read and write and get along together since they were five.

Miranda placed a shaky hand on her belly. It was too soon to be able to feel the baby move, but already she could feel the life inside. A life that deserved so much more than she'd been given. It wasn't that her mother hadn't loved her, because deep down, Miranda knew she had. It was just that parenting was too big of a job for just one person. A child needed a mother and a father. In some cases, a stepmother, siblings, and yes, an uncle.

She'd already complicated things with her child's uncle, so Miranda wasn't surprised to find her feet carrying her up to his bedroom. It wasn't sex she was looking for, though. It was just that she was so tired of being alone. Sure, she'd had friends, lovers, and many people who'd passed through her life. But she'd basically been alone since she was seventeen. No. Before that.

Not tonight.

Tonight she wanted to feel the warmth of another person, sleeping beside her.

Quietly, she slipped into Cody's room, into his bed, and into his arms. He was still asleep, and she didn't mind. She simply snuggled up against him and let her mind shut off, if only for a short while.

Tomorrow, she'd start worrying all over again.

* * * *

Once again, Cody had found his bed occupied by Miranda. She had slipped in beside him in the middle of the night. Only this time, she hadn't demanded sex. Not that he would have denied her, but a part of him was perfectly content with just holding her throughout the night.

That same part of him that was perfectly content just watching her sleep.

Until a soft moan escaped her lips, and he was rock hard.

Rolling over on his back, he tried to think about anything other than waking her up. Like bills. Septic tanks. Game six of the 2002 World Series. Even all these years later, that game was a punch in the gut. And just what he needed to relax enough to keep from exploding before the sun was even up.

Finally, she opened her eyes.

"Good morning." He couldn't breathe. She was so beautiful, her hair sticking up in every direction, her eyes sleepy, and her mouth... Oh her mouth, plump and moist, turned up ever so slightly at the corners.

"Morning." A blush crept across her cheeks.

"Sleep well?" His heart hammered in his chest.

"Yes, actually." She smiled as if she had some sort of secret. One she wasn't going to let him in on.

"So, is the bed in the other room terribly uncomfortable?" He was trying to play it cool, but he was curious as to why she was in his bed, and she hadn't attacked him during the night. "Is there a skunk or annoying woodpecker outside the window?"

"No. Why?"

"Well, you crawled into my bed two nights in a row." He tried to calm his heart rate. "And if the accommodations of the other room are acceptable, I guess it must be me."

"Yeah. I guess so." A wide grin spread across her face.

"Cool." He was anything but. "I mean, I've never spent the night with a woman that didn't involve, well, you know?"

Somehow, the morning after not having sex was becoming more awkward than any other morning after.

"Yeah. Me neither."

"You've never spent the night with a woman without...?"

"That's not what I meant." She sat up, running a hand through her hair, trying to smooth it into some semblance of order. "I just…"

"Hey, it's cool." Cody propped himself up on his elbow. "I actually liked waking up next to you knowing that we'd just slept. It's weird."

"Why, did I snore?"

"No. It's just that it's weird for me." How did he explain that he used to be the kind of guy who only looked out for himself and his own needs? He used to be kind of an ass. "I mean I've never known anyone I enjoyed just being with."

"What about your brother?"

"I'd rather spend the day with you." Cody wasn't just bullshitting her to try to get her into bed. She'd found her way there on her own. "And especially the night."

"Even if we're just sleeping?"

"Honey, I went shopping with you. And I liked it."

"You liked shopping with me?"

"Yeah, especially when you were buying fancy underwear." He was still dying to know what was in that bag. "But you haven't shown it to me. It's like you're trying to torture me."

"I'm not trying to torture you." She smiled and rolled on top of him. "But I may try to seduce you sometime."

"Oh really?" He pretended to be offended. "You think you can just crawl into my bed and have your wicked way with me?"

"Well, yeah." She ran her hands down his body, fully aware of his response. "Unless you don't want me."

"Oh, I want you." He let out a breath. "Miranda, you have no idea how much I want you."

"I think I have a pretty good idea," she said as she stroked his almost painful erection.

"And what are you going to do about it?" His voice came out strained.

"Let me think." She was such a tease.

"While you're thinking about it…" Cody reached into the drawer next to the bed. "I'll just make sure I'm prepared for anything."

She took the package from him and ripped it open with her teeth. Then she unrolled the condom over his shaft.

Cody rolled her over onto her back. He could easily just dive into her, he was sheathed and ready, but things were moving too fast.

Physically, he knew how to slow things down. Take his time. Prolong the moment.

But this wasn't a physical thing. Not just a physical thing, at least. He felt it in every cell in his body, but one organ was affected more than any other. It was the one centered in his chest. And Cody had no idea how to slow down his beating heart.

Man, he wished his brother was here. Not, here, in the bedroom with them, but nearby. So he could talk to him about all that he was feeling. Get his advice. But the one person who understood him the most was off with his new bride. Living the dream. A dream Cody hadn't even thought about dreaming for himself, at least not until he'd walked a few thousand feet in his brother's sandals. But he wasn't Carson. Wasn't ready for the whole marriage, kids, commitment.

But he was no longer the guy who was perfectly content with random hookups with nameless strangers.

There had to be something else.

What did they call it? Dating? Could he convince Miranda to be his girlfriend? Sure, it was complicated by the fact that she was basically living with him.

And they were naked.

So what was he doing thinking so much?

He kissed her forehead.

"Mmmm." She sighed as he dropped tiny little kisses from her head to her shoulders. She relaxed beneath him.

"Oh, Miranda." He caressed her breast, lifting her nipple to his mouth. He wanted to taste, to tease, to tantalize her. "You're so beautiful. So …"

She ran her hands up his back, down his shoulders. Kneading, Squeezing. Loving him.

"So good." Cody trailed more kisses down her belly. Lower, heading toward that sweet spot between her thighs.

"Cody." Moaning his name, she writhed beneath him as he coaxed a slow, sweet orgasm from her. "Oh God, Cody."

After dropping a quick kiss on each of her thighs, he moved up so he could look into her beautiful green eyes. He wanted to see her expression when he entered her. Wanted to see if she felt it, too.

Her eyes widened as he slipped inside and then her lashes fluttered shut. He began slow, smooth strokes. Each movement bringing them both closer to the edge. She fell first, and he followed soon after.

"Wow." Miranda was breathless. Flushed. Glowing. "Just. Wow."

"Yeah." Cody reluctantly withdrew and rested his head on her chest. Her heart beat as rapidly as his and he wondered what would happen next. After they got cleaned up and had breakfast and went about their day.

"It's like…" She seemed as confused by the intensity as he was.

"Yeah. It sure is." Cody had so many thoughts racing through his head. So many feelings.

Stay. Be mine. Don't toss me aside.

"I can't move." Miranda spread her arms wide and sighed.

"You could go back to sleep if you want." He would give anything to be able to spend the day in bed with her. But he had responsibilities. "I could come back for you right before noon."

"I think I can find my way to the store." She propped herself up on one elbow. "It's just across the river."

"I could come back for… um, brunch." He licked his lips, suggesting that actual food would not be a part of the menu.

"I'm not sure if I'll be able to walk as it is." She laughed and the sound filled the spaces inside him he didn't even know existed.

"I could bring you some coffee," he offered. "And breakfast in bed."

"That's okay." She snuggled into the mattress. "Maybe I will go back to sleep. I'll grab something later. And then I'll be at the store by noon."

"Sure. Sounds like a plan." And that would give him a couple of hours to figure out how to bring up the subject of them being an official couple. Not a proposal, but something more than just, "Hey, you wanna hang out and get naked some more?"

Cody went downstairs, glanced at the coffee pot, but hated to go to the trouble for just one cup. He'd thought about one of those single serving coffee setups, but the plastic cups seemed like such a waste and an environmental nightmare. So was using enough water to brew six to eight cups when he'd only drink one and a half. And Miranda didn't seem into coffee. Or wine. Or much of anything except sneaking into his bed and having her way with him.

He was more than okay with that.

But he knew there would be many things to negotiate. Beyond morning beverage choices.

Carson and Lily made it look so easy. By the time Cody had returned from his trip to the Yampa, the two of them had worked out all the details. The only thing left for them to do had been to pick a date and get Cody fitted for a tuxedo.

He had a feeling Miranda would need to move a little slower. Lily had been married before and Carson had practically been born an adult, so a quick move to the altar seemed only natural. They had both been ready.

But Cody knew that if he moved too fast, he'd end up in big time trouble. On the river, if he screwed up, he'd end up wrapping against a rock or flipping his boat. Both situations often came about when a guide was in too much of a hurry. Or wasn't paying attention to the little warning signs. Cody didn't want to screw up with Miranda. But he also knew there was no way he could just let her go.

Chapter 14

Miranda did go back to sleep, after a quick cleanup and taking care of a few personal needs. She slept in until almost eight and woke with a clear picture of the next few scenes in her book. With her laptop in hand, she made a quick pass through the sunny kitchen, grabbing some yogurt, a banana, and a tall glass of that addictive apple cider to take out on the deck.

No need for noise-canceling head phones or background music to drown out the constant noise of the city. This morning, she sat down to the sounds of the river, a few birds, and the whisper of a slight breeze caressing the treetops.

Not a bad view, either, from her temporary "office."

It didn't take long before she was immersed in the world she'd only recently created. Poor "Matty" found herself with the misfortune of finding her claim was across the river from the one man she hoped to never see again. Not that she minded looking at him. He was quite a handsome specimen of man. But he was the last person to have seen Sarah Matthews, and he probably wouldn't be too pleased to find out that she was the one who had absconded with his trousers. And apparently, he didn't have any spare shirts, as he often worked bare-chested in the warm California sunshine.

It was nearly eleven when the cat jumped on Miranda's lap, pulling her attention back to the present century. What had she named the thing? Smoky? Trouble? Nope. That was Cody. He was trouble for sure. Damn, if her heart didn't start beating a little bit faster just thinking about the man. And a not so small part of her wished she'd met him first.

Yes, he was most certainly trouble. It would be so easy to fall for him. He'd been so good to her. Kind, helpful, generous. He'd made it very clear that he wanted her, yet he'd let her take the lead in the bedroom.

Now, she had hoped to take over his kitchen. Make him a nice dinner as a way of thanking him for everything. But she wouldn't have time to go into town for groceries. She'd just have to pull something together from what she could purchase at the store.

Jinx. That's what they'd named the cat. How could she forget? Too much on her mind, maybe.

After a quick shower, she dressed and braided her hair. It would still be damp when she got home, but at least it would be out of the way.

Miranda threw her purse in the Prius and drove across the river to the store. How fortunate for Cody to be able to find a home so close to his work. Or maybe it had all been one big piece of property, spanning both sides of the river. How did a man so young end up with so much land? That's right, he bought the company from the man whose fence he crashed into. Maybe this land had been part of the package. Or else it had already been in the family. Maybe they had arrived during the gold rush and instead of getting rich in gold, they'd prospered from the land.

Did her child have roots that ran so deep? She would have to find out more about Cody—and Carson's family. And maybe someday, her own mother would share the true story of where she'd come from. Did she have grandparents? And if so, why had her mother run from them? What could have been so awful that her mother would chose a life of being alone, just her and her child, with no one for support? When things got hard, her mom simply packed up and moved on.

Miranda wished she had a mother she could just call up on the phone. Share her news about the baby. Ask for advice on what to do next. But chances were, by the time she'd track her mother down, the child would be able to make the call.

At the bottom of the hill, Miranda hit a speed bump. No. It was a tree root forcing the pavement up into a road hazard. So maybe roots could sometimes be a problem.

Hopefully, the store would be busy enough that she wouldn't have to think too much. She arrived only ten minutes before her scheduled start time. She was usually more punctual than that, but she couldn't turn back time.

"You must be Miranda." A young man with long hair and a slight beard stood behind the register with a ready smile and a laid-back tone in his voice. "I'm Jake. Cody said you'd be coming in today and that I should take good care of you. But not too good. And that was an exact quote."

He chuckled and came around the counter to welcome her.

"Nice to meet you, Jake." Miranda shook his extended hand. "I went over the basics yesterday, but I'm glad you'll stick around a little while, at least until I get through a few customers."

"It's been fairly steady today. We should get a bit of a rush here now that it's lunchtime." Jake stepped aside so she could get settled behind the counter. "Then it picks up again as folks get off the river looking for a cold one or something to tide them over until dinner."

He gave her a quick review of the procedures and made sure she knew where to find the binder that had a copy of the price list, general opening and closing instructions, and numbers for who to call if she needed help.

She settled her nerves by tidying up the counter display of postcards, maps, and decals with the Swift River Adventures logo. That took all of thirty seconds. The T-shirts were all hanging neatly on a rack. Candy and gum was lined up on the shelves in front of the register. There wasn't much for one person to keep busy with, let alone two.

Finally, a couple of people wandered inside the store. One went straight to the coolers for something to drink, while the other browsed the T-shirt display.

Miranda rang up a sports drink, a bag of chips, and an energy bar for the first customer and a T-shirt and decal for the second. Jake hung back, ready to jump in if she needed help, but none was necessary.

After a few more customers, sales of everything from sunscreen and sodas to sandals and sunglasses straps, Jake offered to restock the essentials before leaving her on her own.

The early part of the afternoon was a steady stream of campers and picnickers. As the day wore on and rafters started getting off the river, business picked up. She sold more beer, wine, and heartier snacks like sourdough bread, sausages, and the makings for simple supper like spaghetti with marinara.

There were also a few people who stopped by just to grab a quick drink and welcome her to the river. They seemed to know the people who worked here, name-dropping the few people she'd already met and mentioning a couple more she hadn't even heard of. But they all eventually got around to saying something about Cody. And while none of them came right out and said anything, it was pretty clear they were checking out his new girlfriend.

"Hey, Miranda, how's it going?" Fisher came in. With her still-damp hair and sun-kissed glow, she'd obviously just come off the river. "If you're ready for a break, I can take over for you."

"I'm fine. Jake spelled me a little while ago. But thanks." While most of the others regarded her with curiosity, Miranda got the feeling Fisher didn't want her around.

"So, you're working here now?" Definitely didn't want her there. "And you're living with Cody?"

"I wouldn't call it living with him." Miranda didn't want to have to defend herself. Especially not to the woman who was supposedly just friends with Cody. "I'm staying there temporarily. And I'm helping out in the store while I'm here."

"Of course." Fisher picked up a map near the register, flipped it over, and then replaced it in its holder. "Just, be careful. Cody's a great guy and everything. He's just… he's never had a relationship that has lasted a whole weekend. Yet, until recently, he's never lived alone either. So I'm not sure what to think about him all of a sudden inviting someone to live with him."

"Again, we're not living together." Miranda was trying to stay calm. "But even if we were, it's really not your concern. Unless there's something going on between you two that I should know about."

"No. It's not like that." Fisher's cheeks darkened. "Cody and I are just friends."

"I see." Miranda wasn't buying it. "Funny. You both say the exact same words, but when he says it, I believe it. You say it like you're not quite convinced."

Fisher sighed, leaning against the counter. "Is it that obvious?"

"Afraid so."

"Does he know?"

"I couldn't tell you that."

"I'm not trying to get all in your business. It's just…"

"You're in love with him?"

"No. That's not. No." Fisher looked mortified. "He is my friend. And I just worry about him. You know how you shouldn't get involved with someone right after you end a long-term relationship?"

"I thought you said none of Cody's relationships ever lasted a full weekend?"

"Well, that's true. Except for his relationship with his brother. I mean, they were close. They're twins, but I think they're especially close even for twins. And I worry about how Cody is handling his brother moving out."

"I think he's doing just fine."

"You don't understand. There's something different about him." The woman truly did sound concerned. "And it's not just because he was interested in Lily, too."

"So she dated both of them?"

"Well, no. Not exactly. I mean, she went out with Cody first, but I think Lily had her eye on Carson the whole time. She even tried to get me and Cody together, but nothing happened. Really."

As uncomfortable as this conversation had started out, Miranda was actually somewhat relieved to find out she wasn't the first woman the twins had both been involved with. If Carson's wife had hooked up with Cody first, then she couldn't judge Miranda. At least, not too much.

She'd still be judged. Because that's what women did to each other. Kind of like how she was judging Fisher for having a crush on Cody.

"Look, I can see that you mean well, but if you're worried Cody is going to break my heart, I think I can handle myself."

"That's good, but…" Fisher twisted a strand of her long blond hair around her finger. "I think he's trying to fill the space Carson left behind with you."

Miranda still couldn't figure Fisher out. She obviously cared about Cody. Maybe she was even in love with him. Yeah, there was some jealousy going on. But there was more. "Are you worried I'm going to break Cody's heart?"

"What? No. I don't know why I'm even here." Miranda was starting to feel sorry for the poor woman. "It's just that Cody's changed. He's not himself."

"I get the impression he's known as a bit of a ladies' man." Suddenly the numerous visits from his friends and acquaintances made more sense. As did the feeling that she was somewhat of an oddity. Like an exotic zoo animal or a freak show exhibit. "No one has ever seen him settle down with one woman, especially one who is 'living with him.'" Miranda resisted the urge to put air quotes around that last phrase.

"That's part of it, I guess." Fisher squeezed her eyes tight. "It's just that from the minute you walked through his door—I don't know. It's like he's in love with you or something."

Miranda burst out laughing. Then Fisher started laughing. And then they couldn't stop laughing. Fisher was laughing so hard, tears streamed down her face.

* * * *

Cody wasn't sure what to think when he found Fisher and Miranda laughing together in the store. They weren't quite hugging each other, but he was pretty sure he had been the subject of conversation that had them in stitches.

"Hello, ladies." He figured if he made his presence known, they might get it together, but for some reason, they both looked at each other and laughed even harder.

"So, how did it go today?" He stepped closer to Miranda. How did he get rid of Fisher without hurting her feelings? "The store is still standing, and since you didn't call for backup, I figure it must have been okay."

"Yeah. No. it was good." She glanced at him, an expression of wonder or something on her face. Probably had something to do with her conversation with Fisher.

"So, you think you'll come back tomorrow?" Why did he worry she might decline? Not really, but there was that little something that made him wonder if she wasn't two steps from bolting from his life forever.

"Sure. But, there's one thing no one showed me." Miranda came around the counter and made a beeline for the shelf that had the dinner staples. She grabbed a box of spaghetti and a jar of organic marinara sauce. "How do I ring up employee purchases? Is it just like a normal transaction or do I need to do something special?"

"There is a discount. Twenty percent." Fisher jumped in before he could respond.

"Good, then I'll get some bread, too." Miranda grabbed a loaf of the locally made sourdough. They had finally gone through most of the leftovers from the wedding. And she had said she wanted to make him dinner. "I would've bought it earlier, but I wanted to make sure I did it by the book."

"Honey, I don't think you need to worry about anyone accusing you of stealing anything."

Miranda put her purchases on the counter and tossed him a sly smile. "I don't know. Fisher did accuse me of stealing your heart. But I think we have come to an understanding."

"Is that because most people think I don't have a heart?" The initial trepidation he felt when walking in on them was quickly becoming something more like panic.

"No, Cody." Fisher put her hand on his shoulder, making him even more uncomfortable. "Everyone knows you have a very big...heart. It goes with your big...smile."

The girls started laughing again, but he found it far from amusing. It was one thing for Fisher to think he was a joke. But he didn't find it funny at all that Miranda was laughing at him.

At least the two women were becoming friends. That could only be a good thing. Hopefully. Unless Fisher told Miranda how much of a scoundrel he'd been in recent years. Okay, since puberty. But Fisher couldn't hate him too much, since she'd hinted recently that she wouldn't mind taking their friendship to another level. Unless she'd planned on leading him on and then throwing his past at him.

But Fisher wasn't that kind of woman. And he didn't think Miranda was either. Even more reason to get to know her better.

Miranda purchased the makings for a simple spaghetti dinner. His stomach started grumbling just thinking about something other than the tri-tip he'd had the last three nights. Who would have thought he'd get tired of his favorite meal? But his hunger for Miranda wouldn't be satiated.

She tucked the paper sack under the counter and after checking the time, went about the business of closing the store for the day. She flipped the sign to closed, locked the door, and made her way back to the register to run a final tape for the day. Then she counted the cash and stored it in the bank bag to carry back to the office where it would be locked in the safe overnight.

Fisher let herself out and Cody made sure the money was locked in the safe. He returned to find Miranda gathering her purse and her grocery sack.

"I meant to make the sauce from scratch, or at least canned tomatoes, fresh garlic and basil." Miranda didn't need to apologize. "But I kind of got sidetracked this morning and didn't make it to the supermarket."

"Any luck with apartment hunting?" He hoped his disappointment at the thought of her leaving wasn't too obvious.

"Actually…" She gave him an apologetic grin. "I was kind of working on a different project. I didn't get a chance to look for rentals. Sorry."

"I'm in no hurry to get rid of you." That sounded like a cheap line, one he may have used over the years, only to slip away early the next morning hoping the woman would have gotten the hint. But with Miranda he meant it. "You can stay as long as you want. What kind of project were you working on?"

"It's just in the early stages, but I think I may be onto something. Something that can turn into something." She sounded excited, but also a little unsure.

"Something like?"

"Well…" She blushed as she stood next to her car. "You know how you've been sharing all this history about the gold rush? I kind of was inspired, and I've started a historical…novel…set in this area"

"Really? That's great."

"I'll need to do a ton of research, but right now, I'm just getting the bare bones of the story down. I know some writers need to have all the research in place beforehand, but I want to get the main scenes out there while they're still so fresh in my mind."

"That's really cool. I hope you'll let me read it sometime." He didn't want to ask if it was a romance. Especially if he'd somehow inspired it.

"Well, I don't usually let anyone read my work until it's finished. And I've had a chance to clean it up." She shifted the bag to her other hand. "Besides, it's probably not the kind of book you'd read."

"So, it is a romance." Cody's heart rate shot up a notch. "Cool."

"Yes. It's a romance."

Don't offer to help her with research. Just. Don't.

"Well, I guess I'll just have to wait until you finish the book."

Chapter 15

Over the next week and a half, Miranda settled into a comfortable routine. She worked about six hours in the store, wrote either before or after her shift, and often shared breakfast with Cody. She spent the nights in his bed, sometimes just sleeping, but more often making sweet, tender, and passionate love.

"So I was thinking, since you're working the later shift tonight, I'll take you out to dinner." Cody scooped up the breakfast dishes and loaded them into the dishwasher. "I thought I'd take you to The Majestic. The food is as good as anything you'd find in San Francisco."

"I don't know that I have anything nice enough to wear." And it sounded like a place where they'd expect to order wine.

"Well, that's the beauty of Prospector Springs." Cody leaned against the counter with a grin on his face. "At the finest restaurant in town you'll find anything from a little black dress to cargo shorts and everything in between. You could wear jeans and be perfectly comfortable."

"What will you be wearing?"

"Stilettos, a feather boa, and leather chaps." He managed to keep a straight face.

"In that case, I think I'll pass." But she loved his understated sense of humor. He was playful even when he was serious, and something told her that the things he joked about were also serious to him.

"Maybe I could get the tuxedo I returned to the bridal shop?" He moved toward her, putting his arms around her waist. "Or I could just wear jeans, a shirt with a collar…"

He pressed a small, sweet kiss along her neck, just below her ear.

"So you really want to take me out on the town?" She couldn't help but melt into his kiss. "Aren't you afraid people will try to warn me about you?"

"I'm guessing they already have." He paused just long enough for her to think he was almost embarrassed about his reputation. "So what have you heard about me? And why haven't you run off yet?"

"Let's see." She pulled away, just enough to make him squirm. "You've never had a relationship last a whole weekend. You made your brother make breakfast for your overnight guests. One girl tried to run you over with her car..."

"I'm going to kill Fisher."

"She wasn't the only one who told tales." Miranda had to laugh. "That first day, it was almost like being a freak in a carnival. People kept coming in and gawking. And then they told stories, about what a wild one you are. I guess they figured I must have some sort of superpower."

"Superpower?"

"They seem to think I've tamed you."

"Would you say I'm 'tame'?"

"Hardly." He was still a wild man. Wild about her, or so it seemed. "But, what exactly is happening here?"

"You want to know where we're going?" He hesitated. Just long enough for her to think she'd gone too far. He'd make some excuse about how it had been fun, but maybe it was time for her to move on.

"Well, I'm going into the office this morning. There are bills to pay, and I need to check on a leaky toilet in one of the cabins."

"A life of adventure?" Miranda braced herself.

He smiled, but it wasn't the kind of smile she'd expect from a man about to blow her off. It was more of a satisfied, comfortable smile.

"It all comes with the territory." He moved closer, pulling her against her. "Who would have thought having breakfast with you would be the highlight of my day?"

"Compared to leaky toilets and bill paying? Anyone."

"No. I mean every day." He wrapped his arms around her, making her feel so secure. Maybe even loved.

"That's because you haven't been on the river since you took me down." He'd been busy running the business.

"Even on the river, the best part is seeing your smile. Hearing your laugh."

"I bet you say that to all the girls."

"If I've said something like that before, I've never meant it." He lifted her chin, so he could look her in the eye. "This is all new to me. I've always been a catch and release kind of guy. But I don't want to let you go. I know that scares you. It sure as hell scares me. But here we are."

"Here we are." The words almost caught in her throat. She was already in too deep, there was no way she could back paddle now.

"I feel a little like John Wesley Powell, exploring the Colorado River for the first time. I might not know exactly where we'll end up, or what will happen along the way, but what do you say we enjoy the ride?" He caressed her cheek, then ran his hand through her hair as he pulled her into a kiss. Slow, deep, sweet, and hot at the same time. Miranda was flooded with emotions. Beyond desire, beyond passion. For the first time in her life, she felt as if she was where she belonged. She was home.

"It could be fun." She said when she finally came up for air.

"It could be a lot of fun." There was a hint of uncertainty in his voice. "It's not exactly swimming with sharks, but I'll try to make it as interesting as possible."

"What do you mean?"

"I've read some of your articles." He sounded almost embarrassed. "While you were working on your book, I looked up your work. You've been to some amazing places."

"Yeah." Now it was her turn to sound embarrassed. "But you grew up in a pretty amazing place. It's just as beautiful here as anywhere."

"So it's growing on you?" He tucked a strand of her hair behind her ear. "You're not bored without bright lights, a big city?"

"I don't think boredom is going to be a problem." No, boredom was the least of her worries. How could she get bored with a man who was so thoughtful, generous, and kind? She was falling for Cody. Hard and fast, and while that might be a good thing in the bedroom, she couldn't imagine a scenario where it wasn't going to end in a disaster as far as her heart was concerned.

The worst part was that she knew it was going to hurt Cody, too. Hell, everyone around them would be hurt when the truth came out.

She would tell him. Tonight. Over dinner.

* * * *

"Let me finish the dishes, so you can get to work." Miranda grabbed a dish brush to clean out the pan Cody had left soaking in the sink. God she was beautiful, with the sunlight streaming through the kitchen window he could see the shape of her legs through the little sundress she wore.

He couldn't help himself. Cody slid his hands up underneath her dress. Just a touch. That's all he meant to do, but she was so warm, so wet, beneath his fingers that he slid them deeper. And she moved against him, searching for that sensation. The buildup of pleasure that he'd given her time and time again.

He loved how easy it was to make her come. Even in his hands, he could feel it rising, pulsing, growing inside her. Finally she jerked against him and groaned, dropping the dish brush with a loud clatter into the sink. They both stood there, perfectly still except for the spasms of her inner muscles pulsating against his fingertips.

Reluctantly, he pulled away. "Well, get back to work, woman. Those dishes aren't going to clean themselves." Yeah, as if playing the sexist jerk was going to protect his heart.

"Nope." She turned around and reached for his fly, dropping to her knees. "Your turn first."

He jumped back. There was no way. First of all, he was about ready to explode and if she got her perfect mouth anywhere near him, he couldn't be held responsible.

"No. Not yet." He forced the words out of his mouth. "I want to look forward to dessert. I want to think about it all day."

"Shouldn't you be focused on your paperwork and your plumbing?" There was just enough disappointment in her voice to make him worry that he'd hurt her feelings.

"Oh, baby, I want to take my time. Make love to you all night long. I want to have the whole day to think about all the ways I can make you come." He'd found there were plenty. "I'll tell you what. You work on a love scene and I'll do everything you write."

"What if I get writer's block?" Her voice was stronger now, more determined as she stepped closer to him. "What if I have to act it out first?"

She pushed him down onto the nearest chair. Miranda slid her panties down and let them drop to the floor. This time, when she reached for his fly he had no power to stop her. She freed his throbbing erection and slid down over his shaft.

She moved slowly, achingly, up and down. It felt like she must have drugged him because every sensation was heightened. Every slip of her skin against his. Every clench of her muscles as she tightened around him. He could feel the pressure building inside her. Inside him.

The taste of her lips pressed against his, the silkiness of her tongue as she slid inside his mouth. The smell of her hair. Everything was more intensified than ever before.

Miranda ground against him, taking for herself what only he could give her. Finally, she shuddered, gripping his shoulders almost painfully, and he couldn't hold out any longer. He filled her. Filled her with everything that he had. All the emotions he kept deep inside spilled into her.

Still, he couldn't move. Couldn't speak. He squeezed his eyes shut before they could fill with tears.

Casually, Miranda slipped off his lap. She stood, smoothed the sundress down her thighs, and strolled toward the bathroom. "Well, I don't think that's going into the book."

Cody looked down, expecting to see a knife sticking out of his chest. But no, he hadn't just been stabbed through the heart.

"Some things can't be described in words." She turned just before the door. The look on her face suggested that she was as shattered by the experience as he was. "Besides, there are some things I don't want to share with the world. Some things that are just between you and me. And no one else."

"Right." A single syllable was about all he could manage. So maybe she wasn't just using him for research. Maybe she was just as scared of what was happening between them as he was.

When they'd first met, he'd known she was different. She made him feel things he'd started to worry he'd never feel. But he'd convinced himself that it hadn't been real. It had been a part he'd played while he'd been playing the part of Carson. He'd thought maybe he'd just pretended to feel what his brother felt for Lily so the thought of coming home and being alone wasn't so scary.

But these last several days with Miranda had shown him that what he'd felt in the desert was real. And as much as the rapids on the Yampa were milder than here on the American, his feelings then were barely a ripple compared to the torrent he felt for her now.

He was in love. Cody Fucking Swift had managed to fall in love. No wonder everyone was gawking at Miranda. They could all see it before he could.

Did she know?

She would soon enough. He would tell her tonight. They'd order the fig, arugula, and prosciutto flatbread, the filet, and a bottle of Lost Mine Zin. Then over wine and fresh baked bread, he'd lay it all out.

But first, he needed a quick shower. No way could he concentrate on paying invoices with her scent on him.

Slowly, he pushed himself up from the chair. Spotting her panties still on the floor, he scooped them up, shoving them into his pocket, and he hobbled up the stairs to his bathroom. Once he got there, he stripped naked and hopped into a warm shower. Quickly, he soaped up, rinsed, and then dried himself off.

Was he an idiot for even thinking about her walking in on him before he could get dressed? Unless he was looking for severe dehydration, he'd better pull himself together and head on in to work.

When he got downstairs, he found Miranda at the kitchen table, one foot curled under her as she typed away on her laptop.

He couldn't help himself. Instead of walking straight to his truck, he stopped to place a small kiss just below her ear.

"Mmmm." She didn't even look up from what she was writing.

"Looks like you found some inspiration after all."

She grabbed his hand and turned to look up at him with a sweet, satisfied smile on her face. "Yeah. But not like you think. When I write an article, it's based on my experiences and I try to get the details exact as much as possible. But when I'm writing a book, it's different. Every story is based on real events in some way. A photograph, a song, something in the news—all these can trigger the idea for a story, but then my characters take over. It's not about something I've done or would have done that shows up in the book. It's my characters' experiences that I have to be true to."

"So your characters wouldn't have sex at the kitchen table?" He tried to keep it light. Fun.

"No." She laughed. "My characters don't have a kitchen table. They don't even have kitchens at this point. Just a fire pit and a Dutch oven. But I'm thinking they'll build a house together. And she'll admire the way his muscles move as he swings a hammer."

"My brother and I did a lot of the work building this house." He pressed her hand against his cheek. "Not the heavy construction or technical stuff like electrical and plumbing, but we did a lot of the finish work. The tile, deck, and floors were done by us. And yes, we often worked with our shirts off."

"Now there's a visual." She raised her eyebrows suggestively.

He needed to tell her the truth. But not before he told her how he felt about her. Tonight. He'd lay everything out. And if she stomped on his heart... Well, he'd just have to be man enough to take it.

Chapter 16

After Cody left, Miranda didn't think she'd be able to get back into her book. She'd said too much about her process, but the look in his eyes when she'd said she couldn't use their lovemaking in her book made her feel like she needed to explain. She wasn't rejecting him. Quite the opposite. It had been amazing. Too amazing to share with the outside world.

But she would have to get Matty a kitchen table. And chairs. Definitely chairs. Even though she was several chapters away from even getting close to a love scene. No, she spent the next few hours building the attraction between Matty and Jonathan, her hunky neighbor who did like to work without a shirt in the hot California sun. And Jonathan was intrigued by his neighbor, a young man who had to be related to the mystery woman who'd vanished from the hotel well before dawn. The boy could even be her twin, but how did he approach the subject? Especially since there was something about the boy, something that wasn't quite typical of a young man seeking his fortune in the wilds of Prospector Springs. For one thing, Jonathan had never seen him drink or swear or use tobacco. And he never took off his hat or shirt on even the hottest July days.

Miranda soon became enmeshed in the world she'd created. The world she could control. For the most part. Her Matty was a feisty heroine, sometimes having a mind of her own. And it was difficult to keep her from just taking what she wanted, when she wanted it. She had to keep her actions suitable for a young lady in 1850, even one disguised as a man.

The alarm on her phone went off, giving Miranda enough time to save her work, grab a quick lunch, and put the cat out.

Even Jinx seemed to be happy here. And why wouldn't she? She had a place to sleep at night, food in her bowl every morning, and people who gave her attention when she wanted it, but left her to explore her world during the day.

Of course the cat didn't have to worry about what would happen when she dropped a dead bird on the doorstep. But Miranda knew her news would go over about as well as a beheaded quail when she finally told Cody the truth.

The store was busy enough in the earlier part of the day that Miranda didn't have to spend too much time thinking about Cody. Young families came in for snacks, with the kids wearing just their swimsuits and flip flops. Teenagers came in trying to buy beer, but walking away disappointed when Miranda had asked for ID. A young woman browsed the racks of T-shirts, sunglasses, and hats before picking up a magazine and a Diet Coke.

"*Adventure Chix*?" Miranda noticed the cover.

"Looks interesting. Not that I've ever been anywhere more exciting than Tahoe." The woman shrugged.

"Tahoe's nice." Miranda rang up the two items. "You might want to hang onto that issue. It's probably going to be their last."

"Oh really? That's too bad." She looked at the cover, with the woman on a bike on a deserted trail in Arches National Park. "I kind of like the idea of a magazine for women, written and produced by women."

"Yeah. I used to write for them." Miranda almost stumbled on the words. "But fewer people are buying magazines these days, they prefer content online. Especially free content."

"Yeah, that's great and all, but sometimes you just want to sit by the water and flip through glossy pages and imagine all the places you could go. It's just not the same on your phone."

"No, it isn't." Miranda smiled, handing over the change. "Enjoy your magazine."

"Thanks. I will." And the woman walked out of the store with the magazine tucked under her arm.

Finally, around late afternoon, the store was empty. She really needed to take a break, so she sent Cody a text but he texted back, telling her he'd had to run over to Placerville to pick up a part for the leaky toilet. He'd get there as soon as he could, but she could close the store and put up the "Gone Fishing" sign.

Eventually, that's just what she did. When she got back, only a few people were waiting outside the door, but they were understanding enough to wait for a family-operated store to have to close on occasion with just one person working there.

The rest of the day went rather quickly, bringing Miranda closer to her planned dinner out with Cody. The normal butterflies of anticipation were warring with birds of prey dive-bombing with anxiety. She would have to tell him everything. How she never meant to fall in love with him. That she was pregnant. And his brother, his own twin, was the father.

Could he forgive her? Could he even possibly love her after this?

Just the thought of having to see the look on his face made her jumpy. A scruffy-looking man came into the store. Early twenties, maybe late teens, but he looked like he hadn't showered or changed his clothes in days. If not longer. He lingered over by the snacks, and kept glancing over at her, making her even more nervous.

She watched him out of the corner of her eye, not wanting to put him on edge, but there was something about the guy that creeped her out. Movement that looked like he might be putting something down his pants made her speak up. "Can I help you with something?"

Sometimes just knowing someone is watching could deter a shoplifter. If that's what he was up to.

"Yeah." He looked up but his eye contact was off, like he was looking behind her. "Are these gluten-free peanuts?"

"Well, without reading the label, I'd have to say the nuts are probably gluten free, but I don't know if some of the trail mixes might contain crackers or pretzels that might have wheat in them." She kept her voice calm, trying to sound helpful while at the same time hoping someone, anyone, would walk through the door.

"So the gluten-free peanuts aren't, you know, free?" Was he high on something? Or just weird?

"No, you'd have to pay for them. We do have free maps and campground brochures." Oh, that was dumb. Get him to approach the counter where she sat. Why did Cody have to be all the way over in Placerville?

"I'd need cash to pay for them." Was that a question?

"We do take debit and credit cards." Her heart hammered in her chest. Something was definitely not right about this guy.

"No. I'll take cash. What's in the register?" He reached down the front of his pants and pulled out a gun. His hands shook and that only made Miranda even more afraid.

"You'll have to purchase something for me to open the register." She was stalling; she knew it. He probably did too, but she couldn't keep her mouth from running. "And there's not much cash since most of the receipts have already been taken to the bank. You know, before they closed."

"Just give me what you got, lady. And some free peanuts." He took a step back toward the snacks, still keeping the gun pointed at her. "Yeah. Not just gluten-free, but free, free."

He laughed and Miranda knew he was high. She ducked behind the counter just as a sound came from the back of the store. It sounded like a moose charging from the hallway that led to the office. But there were no moose in California.

* * * *

Cody was worried that Miranda wouldn't have taken a break so he pulled into the parking lot and came in through the office. His heart almost stopped when he saw a grungy-looking guy a few feet from Miranda. Something wasn't right. When the man stepped back, Cody saw the gun in the guy's hand. Pointed at his woman.

Instinct took over. He charged the man, cold-cocking him in the jaw and knocking him to the ground.

The gun went flying, and the man appeared to be unconscious, but Cody wasn't going to take any chances. Not with Miranda here. He fell on top of the man, pinning him down.

"Grab me a length of that hoopi over there and call 911." Cody could feel the guy breathing, but other than that, he wasn't moving.

"Hoopi?" Miranda must have been terrified.

"Yeah, the nylon webbing in that basket over there by the carabiners." Cody indicated with a nod of his head while he jabbed his knee into the guy's back.

"Right." She stepped out from behind the counter and found the hoopi and even managed to undo it so he could tie the guy's hands and feet. "911. I'll use the store phone."

She made it behind the counter and picked up the receiver. "Um, yes. There's a robbery. No. Attempted robbery at the Swift River Store. He's got a gun, but he's unconscious, I think."

The man groaned just as Cody got the last knot tied securely around his wrists and ankles. Cody jammed his knee into the guy's back, letting him know that if he even tried to move, he'd be in for a world of hurt.

"Well, the owner of the store came in just as he pointed the gun at me. The robber, not the owner. And he knocked him down. Maybe knocked him out. I don't know. But I think the guy might have been on drugs. Yeah. Please hurry, in case he wakes up."

"Oh, Cody…" Miranda started to walk toward him.

"Stay back there. Please. I can't stand the idea of anything happening to you."

"I can't stand the idea of anything happening to you." She didn't seem to understand that if she were hurt in any way it would destroy him.

"Just stay there. The sheriff will be here soon." He hoped. Because he wasn't going to get up off this asshole until he was handcuffed and dragged off to jail. Only then would he allow himself to take her into his arms and never let her go.

The wail of sirens sounded and after what seemed like an eternity, but had really only been ten minutes or less, the sheriff's deputies arrived, along with an ambulance.

One deputy approached, with his handcuffs ready, while the other retrieved the gun.

"Nice handiwork. I'd say those knots aren't coming loose until you say they are." The deputy knelt down beside the scumbag and clasped the handcuffs around the man's wrists. "But his lawyer is going to want us to bring him in by the book."

Cody undid the knots quickly, and out of habit, began winding the hoopi carefully for the next use. Except this particular length would not be used again. Thankfully, hangings were no longer a part of the local justice system.

The first deputy, Officer Lopez, lifted the robber to a sitting position. He was conscious now, muttering curses and thrashing against the handcuffs.

Lopez went through his line of questioning, having to repeat himself several times, as it was obvious the guy was high.

"When was the last time you smoked?" the officer asked in a calm, yet authoritative voice.

"Yesterday. This morning. Last week." The man jerked against the restraints. "Does it matter? I was just getting some gluten-free. You know everyone's gluten-free these days. Cuz that shit's bad for you."

"But meth's not?" Lopez shook his head, as if he'd had this kind of conversation too many times.

"No man. There's none of that gluten shit in there. It's all pure. One hundred percent natural." Officer Lopez helped him to stand so he could lead him to the patrol car once the EMT checked to see if he could be safely transported. "Even pot these days can't be trusted. That shit's not organic anymore."

"There ought to be a law against non-organic pot." The officer deadpanned and shook his head. "Now, do you understand you're being arrested? That you have the right to remain silent…"

He recited the required line, but the dude was so high, he didn't seem to notice.

"Hey, that guy hit me." He turned toward Cody. "Good punch, man. My face hurts."

"Do you understand you're being charged with attempted armed robbery? And that you have the right to remain silent?"

As in, *shut the fuck up, asshole.* Not that El Dorado County's finest would say such things.

"Yeah. Yeah, I've heard it all before. But the gun's not real. It's just an airsoft gun. But the pellets are biodegradable…"

Cody didn't hear the rest of what the guy said as the deputy shoved him out the door.

The other deputy was questioning Miranda.

"I knew something was off when he was asking about the peanuts. A lot of people ask questions about their food. Making healthy choices is a big deal right now. They like the organic, flash-pasteurized, all-natural juices we carry. And we do have nut-free snacks, vegan, non-GMO, all-natural energy bars. But just the way he seemed to not understand that the gluten-free label didn't mean the peanuts were free. And he was twitchy, and I've seen plenty of people on drugs in San Francisco, so…"

"Yeah. Unfortunately, no community is immune from the problems of drugs." The second deputy, Parker was the name on his uniform, shook his head. "But you were smart to trust your instincts."

"I don't know about smart. I started kind of rambling, like I'm doing now. But I was scared, and I thought Cody was still in Placerville, and there was no one else in the store."

"I'm here now, babe. I'm here now." Cody wrapped his arms around Miranda's shoulders, his legs shaking from the adrenaline still coursing through his veins. "I'm here now."

She melted against him, and he rubbed her arms.

"Well, you were very brave," Officer Parker told her.

"Lucky." She shook her head. "I don't know what I would have done if Cody hadn't come along. I didn't know it wasn't a real gun."

"Oh, it's real." Parker informed them. "It's not an airsoft gun. It's not loaded, but it is real."

"Will that make a difference if it goes to trial?" Miranda asked.

"It shouldn't." Parker shook his head, and tried to offer an encouraging smile.

"Thank you, officer." Cody extended a hand and the deputy shook it.

"We've got your contact information and will be in touch if we need to call you as a witness." The deputy offered Miranda his card.

"Take care of this one." He nodded toward Cody and carried the evidence bag with him out the door.

"I will. I most definitely will." Cody wrapped his arms around Miranda, holding on like she was the most precious thing in the world. Because she was the most precious thing in his world.

"Oh, Cody, I was so scared." She trembled in his arms. "I didn't know what to do. At first I thought he was just trying to shoplift. But then he had a gun. But I couldn't think how to open the register without ringing up a sale, so I panicked and just started babbling."

"You did fine. You were brave. And smart. Keeping him talking gave me the opportunity to come after him." He rubbed her back, calming her. "I'd rather lose a bag of peanuts—or all the money in the register—than lose you. I love you, Miranda."

"Really?" Miranda looked up at him, tears still glistening in her eyes. "You love me?"

"Yes. I love you. I love you so much." He pulled her tight against his chest. Then he lifted her chin and kissed her. Kissed her as if she was his last breath. "I thought I could lose you. I wanted to kill that guy..."

"I'm glad you didn't. I'm glad the police were able to take him away." Her voice was shaken. "And I'm so glad you weren't hurt. You weren't hurt, were you?"

She pulled away and picked up his hand, kissing the knuckles that were still numb from the contact and the adrenaline rush. They'd be sore tomorrow. His hands were sore for a few days after his fight with Carson, and he hadn't hit him nearly as hard as he'd hit this scumbag. But then again, the fight with Carson had been about himself. His own selfishness.

This was totally different. This was defending his woman. And he'd do it again.

"No. I'm not hurt."

"Good." She kissed his hand again. "Let's go home."

"Yes. Let's go home." He didn't let go of her hand as he walked to the front door and locked the door. He flipped the closed sign. And led her out the back, to where his truck was parked. "I'm not letting you out of my sight tonight."

"Please, don't." She squeezed his hand. "And Cody?"

He looked down at her, his heart still hammering in his chest. His legs starting to weaken from the adrenaline letdown, and maybe more.

"I love you, too."

Chapter 17

Cody noticed Miranda's hands were still shaking by the time he pulled up to their house. Yes. He thought of it as *their* house, not his. Sure, her name wasn't on the title, or anything official like that, but it felt like she belonged there as much as he did. Besides, she'd given the deputy this address for her contact information. That was enough for him. For now.

"Hey, babe, why don't you take a nice hot bath, and I'll rustle up something to eat," Cody suggested as he turned off the truck's engine.

"I thought you wanted to go out tonight." Miranda put her hand on the door handle to let herself out.

"I did." Cody reached over and covered her hand, shaking his head. "But like I said, I'm not letting you out of my sight. I can protect you here. We've got plenty of time to sample Prospector Springs when we're both feeling a little more up for it."

"I can rally," she offered.

"Not tonight. Tonight I'm going to take care of you."

"I'm fine." Yeah? She still sounded rattled. But he wasn't surprised she was putting on a brave face.

"Wait here." Cody let go of her hand, hopped out of the driver's side, and went around to open her door.

"The gun wasn't even loaded." Miranda accepted his hand as he helped her out of the truck.

"You didn't know that. I didn't know that." Cody's tried not to think about if that hadn't been the case. "Hell, the guy was so high, I'm not even sure if he knew that it wasn't loaded."

"I'm so glad you came when you did." Her voice wavered a tiny bit.

"Me, too, baby. Me, too." He escorted her to the door. A door that he would start locking from now on. As soon as they were inside, he locked the deadbolt. He had to force it, since it hadn't been turned in ages. "You go on, get cleaned up. I'll see what I can scrounge for dinner."

"I'm not hungry." She sounded weary, defeated.

"Me, neither, but we should eat."

Miranda nodded, and walked up the stairs almost as if she was in a trance.

As soon as he heard the water running, he pulled open the pantry door. There was plenty of soup. That was simple. Hearty. If he had any bread, it could be filling. Next he opened the refrigerator. Beer he hadn't touched since Miranda arrived looked really good. He grabbed one, and pulled out the egg carton to see if there were enough for an omelet. Seven eggs. That was plenty.

He cracked open the beer and took a long swallow. The knot in his shoulder relaxed slightly. If he was this tense, what must Miranda be feeling?

If he needed a beer, she needed a glass of wine even more. He pulled a bottle of Zin out of the wine rack, and uncorked it. He poured a generous glassful and took it on up to Miranda.

He knocked softly on the door.

"Yes?" She called and he let himself into the master bath.

"I brought you this." He set the wine on the edge of the tub. "And I wanted to see if you'd prefer soup or scrambled eggs for dinner."

She looked at the wine glass as if it was something she'd never seen before. Then she lifted her gaze to him. "Thanks. Whatever's easiest to make. Soup, I guess."

"Okay. Well, relax. I'll get some soup going, and you take your time. I'll be ready to eat when you come down." He leaned over and kissed the top of her head.

"Thank you." Her eyes glistened and he turned before he could see her get too emotional. It had been a long day for both of them. But if she asked him to stay or join her in the tub, he was more than willing.

She didn't ask, so he went back downstairs to open a can of soup and maybe throw together a salad or something.

With the soup simmering on the back burner, and Miranda still in the tub, Cody cracked open a second beer. He stirred the soup and listened for the drain so he'd know when she was coming downstairs. Since he couldn't hear anything, he covered the pan and turned off the stove. He'd give her time to enjoy her glass of wine. To relax a little. Then they'd eat, sleep, make love. The order didn't matter.

Tomorrow, he'd make some changes around here. He'd grown up in Prospector Springs, always thought of it as a safe place. But today had been a wakeup call. Even in a small town, there were desperate people. No town was safe from the effects of drugs, homelessness, and crime.

But he was going to keep his home, his family, and his company as safe as possible. He'd buy a security system for the house and resort. Surveillance cameras for the store, office, and boat barn. And until Carson returned, he was going to make sure no one was left at the store without someone nearby, either in the office or patrolling the grounds. Maybe they'd need to look into hiring campground security.

Cody stepped out onto his deck, and he heard a truck pulling into the drive. His muscles tensed as he set the beer on the table, and he walked to the edge of the deck to see who was there. Probably one or more of the guides. No doubt word had gotten around about the robbery. The presence of two sheriffs' cars and an ambulance couldn't have gone unnoticed.

Looking down, he recognized the truck. And the two people getting out of it.

"Carson." He'd never been so glad to see his brother in his life. "Lily. I thought you'd be gone a few more days at least."

"Yeah, well, we got homesick." Carson shrugged and went around the front of the truck to help his wife out of the passenger seat, and lead her to the front door.

Cody made his way into the house, to unlock the door for his brother and sister-in-law. "It's good to see you, but why not take the full two weeks? What, you didn't trust me to keep things running around here?"

Funny how with just minutes of being in his brother's presence all the little things came rushing back. How Carson had always been the responsible one, and Cody had been the guy only looking for a good time. Roles they'd established in childhood seemed to find their way back time and again.

"No, man, I missed you." Carson grabbed his brother into a fierce embrace.

"And I don't have as much energy as I'd like." Lily ran her hand over her belly, which was just barely starting to show a baby bump. "I wanted to come home. It has nothing to do with payroll due in a couple of days."

She gave Cody a quick hug and a peck on the cheek. "I know you've been doing just fine without us. But there really is no place like home. Can I use your bathroom?"

"Yeah. You remember where it is?" Cody pointed to the guest bath, mostly because she hadn't spent much time here. Most of the time, Carson had been at her place. Even before he'd officially moved in with her.

As soon as she closed the door, Cody turned to his brother. "What's really going on? Why are you back so soon?"

"I don't know. I just got a feeling." Carson helped himself to a beer. "The last few days, I felt like something was happening. Or going to happen."

"Like that time me and Billy Lewis got stuck in the caves?" They'd been about twelve, exploring an old mining area that they'd been to many times. Someone had brought down a stack of Victoria's Secret catalogs and *Sports Illustrated* swimsuit issues. A bottle of gin had been stashed down there, too, but when they'd opened it, it smelled too much like pine needles, and no one was brave enough to drink it. Especially since no one knew where it had come from.

"Yeah. That was weird." Carson agreed. "Granny was surprised to see me. She thought we had practice that day. But coach had a work emergency and had to cancel."

"And Billy and I thought it would be fun to screw around before heading back to the ballpark in time for our rides to show up at six." Had he really been that reckless? And stupid?

"I kind of freaked out, not knowing where you were. But then I had this feeling. I couldn't explain it then, and I can't explain it now, but I knew I had to get to the caves." Carson took a pull on his beer. "Oh man, haven't had one of these in a while. You know, with Lily being pregnant…"

Carson got a big, goofy grin on his face.

"Yeah. I know what you mean." Cody lifted his eyes toward his bedroom window. Hopefully, Miranda was out of the bath and relaxed enough that he could introduce her to his brother and Lily. "I haven't had a drink since the wedding."

"No shit?" Of course, Carson didn't believe him.

"No. Really." He set his beer down. "There's something you should know. Man, where do I start?"

"Is everything okay?" Carson jumped right into that protective big brother mode, even though Cody was older by almost a half hour.

"Yeah, it is now." Cody placed a steady hand on his brother's shoulder. "There was a robbery at the store today. Well, an attempted robbery."

"No shit?"

"So that's part of your funny feeling." Cody held a hand up, before Carson started lecturing. "Everyone is okay. The tweaker is in jail, unless he was taken to the hospital."

"Why would he be in the hospital?"

"Because he pointed a gun at Miranda. I had to take him out." Cody flexed the fingers in his right hand. The stiffness was starting to settle in.

"What do you mean 'take him out'? Who's Miranda?" Carson set his beer on the outdoor table.

"You'll meet her. Real soon. Miranda is…" How could he even begin to explain? "Miranda is my Lily."

* * * *

Miranda stared at the full glass of wine. After the day she'd had, no one would blame her for indulging. Just this once. But she couldn't. She was worried enough that the stress of being held at gunpoint, loaded or not, would be harmful for the baby.

And Cody had been so wonderful. Showing up when he did. Unarming the bad guy. Then being so careful with her. But not in a condescending way. He loved her. He loved her and he wanted to take care of her. He knew what she needed and did his best to help her calm down after the ordeal of the attempted robbery and the arrest and everything else.

He'd even brought her a glass of wine. His thoughtfulness brought her to tears. So she'd cried. She cried until she was sure she wouldn't be able to cry anymore. Because when she went downstairs, she'd have no choice but to tell him everything.

She toweled off, put on one of Cody's T-shirts, and carefully balanced the still full glass of wine in her hand.

She reached the bottom of the stairs just as a blonde emerged from the downstairs bathroom.

"Oh, hi." *Who in the world?*

"Hi. I'm Lily." The blonde held out her hand and offered a friendly smile. "I'm Cody's sister-in-law."

Just then, the doors to the deck opened, and Cody walked in, followed by a man who looked just like him. Almost.

"You must be Miranda." Cody's twin approached with an equally friendly smile. Then he pulled her into a hug. "I'm so happy to meet you."

He released her quickly and joined his wife's side. Both of them grinning as if she were some prize Cody had brought home from the fair.

"Yes. Thanks." She glanced down at her bare legs, hoping she was the only one who knew she wasn't wearing anything under Cody's T-shirt. Anything at all. "Will you excuse me for a minute? I need to change."

"Sure." Lily smiled at her, and she couldn't tell if it was fake or not. If Lily knew who she was and what she'd done almost two months ago.

Taking the steps two at a time, Miranda couldn't reach her bedroom fast enough. No. Not her bedroom. Cody's bedroom. The place where she'd been the happiest of her life. The place where she'd finally felt at home.

But that would end. Soon. Oh, too soon.

She quickly put on a bra, jeans, and—what the hell—she pulled Cody's T-shirt back on. She twisted her hair into a quick messy bun, and steeled herself to face Cody's family. Her baby's family.

When she got downstairs, she found Cody in his favorite spot on the couch, with room for her right beside him. His half-empty beer and her full wine glass sat on the wooden table in front of him.

Carson was in the armchair, with Lily sitting half on his lap, her arm draped lovingly around his neck. He was nursing a beer and she seemed content with a glass of water.

"There you are." Cody stood, so much love shining in his eyes that Miranda almost turned around and ran back upstairs. Instead, she put one foot in front of the other and managed to make it into the living room.

He took her hand and led her to the couch. The fear she'd felt when that guy attempted to rob the store was nothing compared to how frightened she was right now. The man she loved and the man whose DNA she carried looked at her with admiration. And the genuine warmth in Lily's eyes told her the poor woman didn't have a clue.

But Miranda wasn't going to ruin everyone's night right now. She'd talk to Cody first. As soon as the others left. She'd put it off too long, and it was going to hurt like hell when Carson and Lily left and she would finally confess her biggest regret. Except she couldn't regret the child growing inside her. And she couldn't regret the time she'd spent with Cody—a man she never would have met if she hadn't met his brother first.

"Cody told us what happened today." Lily took her husband's hand and held tight. "I would have been terrified, but Cody says you totally kept your wits about you."

"I wouldn't say that." Miranda swallowed, wishing she could have some of that wine to sooth her dry throat. "I forgot how to open the register, so I rambled on just long enough for Cody to save the day."

"Cody always did like to play the hero." Carson grinned affectionately toward his brother. "Only this time, it sounds like he wasn't playing."

"No. Not when Miranda's life was on the line." Cody hugged her tighter and it would have been so easy to be comforted by him. So easy to be swept up in all the love that was in this room. The love between the two brothers. The love between Carson and Lily. And mostly, the love between her and Cody.

One small, innocent child could destroy all that love. Just by being conceived.

The room became too warm, despite the breeze through the open windows. Her hands started to feel clammy, and her head began to spin.

"Excuse me a moment." Miranda dashed upstairs and made it to the bathroom before she vomited into the sink. Fortunately there wasn't much in her stomach, so she was able to rinse away the mess. She filled the water glass she kept by her side of the bed and drank it down. Then she splashed cool water on her face. When the room stopped spinning, she slowly made her way to the closet to start packing. Only she didn't have anything to put her clothes in.

Sinking down on the bed, she tried to think what to do next. Maybe if she told Cody he was the father, then they could all be one big, happy family.

Except she would know, and she couldn't live that big of a lie. Not even if it meant giving up on the kind of happiness she'd never even allowed herself to dream about.

She needed to think about what was best for her child. Or what would be worse? Growing up without a father or growing up with a stepmother who hated him or her and an uncle…

Her phone rang. Tom Petty's "Refugee" told her that her mother was on the line.

Maybe, just maybe, her mother could tell her what to do. Just this once. "Hello."

"Miranda, baby. I'm at the airport." Her mother's voice was as casual and cheerful as if it hadn't been eighteen months since they'd last spoke.

"Which airport?" Miranda felt a headache coming on. On top of everything else.

"The San Francisco airport, of course." Mom was oblivious to the fact that calling from the airport, bags in hand, would be an inconvenience even if Miranda still lived in the city. "Come pick me up. We'll go have drinks at the Top of the Mark."

"I can't do that." She needed a mother right now, not a flaky former roommate.

"Oh, are you on an assignment? Just tell me where your key is, and I'll take a cab to your apartment and let myself in."

"Mom." She couldn't quite bring herself to call her by her first name, Elizabeth. She sometimes went by Liz, Beth, Betsy, or even Libby. She changed her name the way some women changed handbags. She'd always said it was a nice way to make a fresh start. "I don't live in San Francisco."

"What? Since when?" But before Miranda could supply an answer, her mother started speaking again. "Where are you living? L.A.? San Diego? Please tell me you did not move to Texas. It's so flat there."

"No, Mom, I'm not in Texas. I'm staying at the Swift River Resort. It's in Prospector Springs." A small part of her wished her mother would offer to come there, to make her soup, and stroke her hair, and tell her everything was going to be all right.

"Where in the world is Prospector Springs? It sounds like the set of an old west show."

"It's in the Sierra Nevada foothills. Between Sacramento and Tahoe. Not far from where gold was first discovered in California."

"Well, what in the world are you doing there? Is it for a story?" Miranda had never been sure of how her mother felt about her being a reporter. She'd never really been sure about how her mother had felt about anything. She'd always played at being happy-go-lucky, not letting anything bother her. Even when they'd been kicked out of their last apartment or she'd lost her job and they'd had to pack up and leave in the middle of the night. She'd always acted like whatever happened was just another adventure, another road to travel.

"No." The pounding in her head increased with the length of this conversation. "Look, Mom, I wish I could help but I can't pick you up from the airport. I just can't."

"Well, then I'll come there." Like it was some small detour.

"No. I mean I don't know how much longer I'll be here." The realization hit her that her mother wouldn't make things better.

"You are your mother's daughter." No. She'd only make things worse.

"I have to go." Miranda hung up the phone and fell back on the bed.

A soft tap on the door made her sit up, wipe her eyes, and try to pull herself together.

"Hey, babe, I'm sorry for the intrusion." Cody was carrying a bowl of soup. "I had no idea my brother was going to show up. But don't worry, they went on home."

"No, I'm sorry I was rude." Miranda's stomach grumbled as she smelled the soup.

"You weren't rude. You've had a very rough day. And no dinner on top of it." He sat down on the bed next to her and lifted a stray strand of her hair off her face. "I sent them away. It's just you and me."

"You didn't have to do that." She would have preferred that he'd been angry, or at least annoyed at her behavior. Instead he picked up the bowl of soup and lifted a spoonful to her lips.

"You'll feel better after you have something to eat." He fed her, like a baby, and her heart ached at the notion that he'd make a good father someday. "It's not the filet mignon I'd planned on offering you tonight, but it's something."

She accepted his offer of sustenance, if only for her baby's sake.

If she'd been thinking about her baby all along, she wouldn't have fallen in love with Cody in the first place. She wouldn't have climbed into his bed, at least.

After a few bites, enough to settle her stomach and empower her to speak the truth, she pushed the soup away.

"Cody, we need to talk." Her heart ached with knowledge that in the next few minutes, she'd have the hardest road to travel. And she'd leave nothing but destruction behind her.

"Uh-oh." He set the soup on the nightstand. "What did I do? I'll fix it, whatever it is."

"No." She couldn't look at him. But she couldn't not look at him. "It's not you. It's me."

* * * *

Oh shit. Wasn't that the kiss of death when it came to relationships? There was a reason he'd never let himself get involved with a woman emotionally. Because he couldn't imagine anything more painful than Miranda breaking up with him and walking out of his life forever. No. That wasn't entirely true. Just a few hours ago he could imagine the only thing worse, and he shuddered.

"Oh, Cody. I'm so sorry." The fact that she was crying didn't make it any easier to breathe. "I should have told you sooner. I should have walked away instead of climbing into your bed."

"So you don't love me." He'd never felt such pain. Not when Carson had broken his nose, not the concussion he'd suffered in football his junior year. Not even when his grandparents had died and his father had shown up out of the blue, looking more for an inheritance than a chance to take care of his sons.

"No. I do. I love you. I love you so much." She reached for his hands and looked into his eyes. The agony he saw reflected there was maybe even worse than what he felt. What the hell? If this was love, how did the human race survive?

"You love me, so what's wrong?" He was afraid to ask, but he had to know why. Why was she ripping his heart out? And what could he do to stop it?

"Cody, I'm pregnant." She said the words like she was delivering the worst kind of news.

Wow. That was unexpected. But okay. He could deal with that.

"Are you sure?" Yeah, dumbass. Of course she was sure. Obviously she wouldn't put them both through this if she wasn't.

"Yes. But that's not all." The anguish in her voice was suffocating.

Oh God, what if she was sick? What if she had some sort of disease where—no, he couldn't think about something like that. Not when he'd thought he could lose her once today already.

"Look, whatever it is, we can get through it. Together."

"I wish that were true. But, Cody." Tears pooled into her eyes, her hands trembled. "You're not the father."

"Oh, is that all?" Relief swept through him. She wasn't dying.

"Is that all?" Miranda jumped up, covering her mouth with her hand. "Is that all? Cody, I'm trying to tell you something. Something that will make you hate me. And I don't want you to hate me. Not when I love you."

"I won't hate you." What the hell could possibly make him hate her? Just because she was pregnant with another man's child. Hell, even if she was married, he still couldn't hate her. Especially since this other guy obviously didn't give a shit. Or else he was some kind of bastard who would be worse than no father at all.

Oh fuck.

He caught her arm just before she walked out.

"Miranda, I don't hate you. I won't ever hate you. But you might hate me." He should have told her. Should have told her when she crawled into his bed that first night she was here.

"I'm the father."

"What? No. You aren't." For a brief instant he saw hope flash across her face, but then the agony returned. "God, do you have to be so fucking good? You can't just claim my child as your own. Not when... Not when I slept with your brother."

"No you didn't."

"Cody, I was there."

"Yeah? So was I."

She looked at him, confusion, pain, and hope all swirling in her eyes, like some kind of gnarly hole on the river.

"I was there, Miranda. On the Yampa. You were... You were so beautiful. I think I fell in love with you the minute you stepped into my raft. You wore an orange bikini, with black board shorts and a smile that could melt a thousand glaciers."

"Oh my God." She put her hand to her chest. "He told you? What? Did he brag about his one last fling before he got married?"

"No. Miranda. Carson didn't have a fling with you." He was such a fucking idiot. "I did. I went to Utah and pretended to be Carson. I'll explain it all later, but basically I was selfish and a jerk and I deserved this broken nose."

He hoped she'd at least crack a smile at the reference to his nose. Especially after seeing Carson's perfectly straight one. But she probably had been afraid to look at him, especially with Lily in the room.

"I spent those six weeks trying to find myself by being my brother. But it wasn't until I met you that I realized who I wanted to be."

"Wow. You're covering for him. I heard that twins have a special bond, but…" She started to flee. To walk out of his life forever.

"No. This isn't about me and Carson." He pulled her back into the room. "This is about me and you. And our baby."

Chapter 18

"You lied to me." Miranda felt sick. This whole time she'd been eaten up by having slept with his brother. Cody knew all along. "And you continued to lie to me by not...Did it ever occur to you that it might have been important to tell me that you were the one I'd met on the river? That I had a reason to come find you?"

"I was just so damn happy to see you again." He tried to take her hands. "Miranda, I—"

"NO. Stay away from me." She pulled away, this time making it to the bedroom door.

"Miranda, wait." He followed her to the top of the stairs. "I didn't tell you because I was afraid you'd run. That you'd never want to see me again. I didn't tell you because I love you."

"You love me?" She turned around, placing her hand on his chest. "No you don't. Not when you lied to me. You let me believe...that I was a slut sleeping with both of you."

"I would never—"

"I can't do this right now." She shoved him backward and he fell against the bedroom door. Turning, she ran down the stairs. Maybe she truly was her mother's daughter because the only thing she could think of was getting away. She made it to the kitchen door before she realized her Prius was still at the store, across the river.

Cody's keys were on the counter. In a panic, she grabbed them and ran barefoot to his truck.

She unlocked the door and climbed inside. After shoving the seat forward, she started the ignition. She didn't know where she was going. She just knew she needed space. Time to think without Cody staring at her, with those big blue eyes so filled with desire. And love. She had seen it in his eyes. He wasn't lying about that. But how could she believe him? How could she believe in him when he just… withheld information? Like she'd withheld information that she was pregnant. But she had a good reason. She didn't want to be a homewrecker.

Tears flooded her eyes, blurring her vision. She reached for her purse, to grab a tissue, but realized she'd left it behind. Which meant she didn't have the keys to her car. Which meant wherever she was going, she would have to take Cody's truck.

Where was she going?

Even if she'd had her purse and her car, she had nowhere to go. And no one to turn to for advice. Unless her mother was having a drink at the Top of the Mark. But she would have moved on by the time Miranda could get there in three hours. And what advice would her mother have to offer?

What had been her favorite saying while Miranda was growing up? "If you're going through hell, keep on going before the devil has a chance to catch up with you." Or something like that.

Oh, how she'd hated that saying. Along with "Not all who wander are lost."

But the saying she hated the most was, "I need a change of scenery."

After a while Miranda stopped forming close attachments. All her friendships were superficial. If she never got too close to someone, it didn't hurt to leave them.

This hurt. This hurt more than she could have ever imagined. Which is why she had been so afraid to get involved in the first place. And once she was involved, why she couldn't tell him the truth.

Could that be why he hadn't spoken up? Was he afraid she'd react exactly how she'd reacted, by running away?

How did he know her so well when they'd just met? For the second time.

She tried to think about the man she knew as Carson and the man she'd fallen in love with. Could they really be the same man? Had she dismissed any feelings she may have developed for the man she'd met on the Yampa because of her lifelong habit of not getting too close to anyone? A vacation fling had been perfect for her. Or so she'd thought. And if her birth control hadn't failed, she wouldn't have thought twice about leaving him in the category of fond memories. Just another experience to write about, but in a detached, unemotional way.

The man she'd met before had also been happy with making their time together nothing more than a side excursion. Another memory to be tucked away, like a postcard from the gift shop.

Yet the minute she'd stepped into Cody's kitchen, he'd made it clear that he wanted more. First, he was joking, making quips about how he'd propose. Then he'd showed her kindness after kindness. Driving her to San Francisco. Insisting she stay with him. Offering her a job. Cooking for her. Saving her from an armed gunman.

The only thing he hadn't done was tell her that he had masqueraded as his brother the first time they'd met.

Except, he had tried to tell her. When she'd crawled into his bed and begged him not to waste his sexy mouth on words. There were other times, too, when he'd started to come clean, but either she'd stopped him, or they'd been interrupted.

If she turned around now, would he take her back?

Nothing ventured, nothing gained. That wasn't one of her mother's sayings, but it seemed to fit this situation. If only there was a place to turn around. But the road was narrow. She might have to wait until she got across the river before she could go back to Cody and they could work on forgiving each other.

While lost in thought, she came upon that root at the end of the road. Hitting the brakes, her bare foot slipped. The truck lurched, spun, and slammed sideways into the large oak. The airbag deployed and Miranda saw the life she could have had flash before her eyes, and then her world went dark.

* * * *

Cody watched her race down the driveway like a woman possessed. No. More like a woman who was facing a firestorm of emotions. Being held at gunpoint had probably been the easiest part of her day. He'd confessed his love for her, but failed to mention that they'd met almost two months ago, not nearly two weeks ago. The day she'd lost her home, her job, and been adopted by a cat. Jinx had jumped out at him as he was trying to go after Miranda, demanding to be fed. So he did the right thing, and poured some kibble into her bowl before heading out to the driveway to watch the woman he loved take his truck and tear out of the driveway for who knows where.

If only he hadn't been such a fucking coward. If only he hadn't been so afraid of losing her, he could have manned up instead of making excuses. Who cared if Fisher had been there when Miranda first showed up at his door? And he hadn't been that hungover that he couldn't have said something like, "Hey, Miranda, I'm so glad to see you again. I've been thinking about you ever since that time we spent together, making love beneath sandstone cliffs, exploring the pictographs..."

The fact that she'd seemed too good to be true should have been his first clue to do everything in his power to not let her get away.

Yet there she went. Down the road in his truck. Was he just going to sit back and wait for her return?

Hell no. He would go after her. As soon as he got some shoes on.

Cody shoved his feet into a pair of sandals. He grabbed his wallet and phone and took off down the road at a brisk jog. Fortunately, it was mostly downhill, so he should be able to catch up with her before she got to the bridge.

His lungs were burning, but in a way he welcomed the discomfort as he ran toward the woman he couldn't lose. Not again.

The sun was sinking behind the hills, and it was getting hard to see. Up ahead, there was a shape in the shadows. A red blur beneath the ancient oak just before the bridge.

Instinct made him run faster, his heart lurching as he realized it was his truck slammed against the tree. With Miranda inside.

He pulled out his phone, dialing 911 as he nearly tripped and fell trying to get to her.

"What is your emergency?" the dispatcher asked over the phone.

"There's been an accident." He gave her the exact location as he made his way to the truck. "I don't know about injuries. I'm not quite there yet."

"We'll send an emergency crew out." She sounded so calm. Like it wasn't her life or her loved one's life on the line. "When you get closer to the scene, can you tell me what you see?"

"The airbag has deployed." And his stomach did a flip. "I'll see if she's conscious."

He couldn't feel his feet beneath him, or his arms as he yanked open the door of the cab. There was blood on the window, and Miranda seemed to be unconscious.

He let out a moan. He couldn't lose her.

"Sir. Is the driver conscious?" The dispatcher brought him back to reality.

"No." His head spun. "And there's blood her forehead.

"Can you check for a pulse?"

"Yes." He'd been trained in first aid, whitewater rescue, and CPR. But he'd never had to use his training on someone he loved. But what good was that training if he couldn't draw on it when it mattered most?

He blew out a breath and told himself that this was just some random person, and he was the first responder. He reached down deep, recalling the times he'd saved lives. He had to do it again.

He felt for a pulse and was relieved to find her heart beating. She roused slightly, groaning, and it was all he could do not to drag her out of the vehicle and carry her back to the safety of his home.

"Miranda, baby. I'm here. An ambulance is on its way."

"My head." She groaned.

"You're okay, baby. You're going to be okay." She had to be.

Cody had dropped his phone. He had forgotten about the emergency dispatcher. All he cared about was that Miranda was alive. Nothing else mattered.

Except for their baby.

What if? No, he couldn't think like that. The ambulance would be here soon, and he'd make sure they took good care of her. Of both of them.

Finally, the EMTs arrived and Cody was pushed aside while they assessed the extent of her injuries.

She was conscious, but confused, unable to recall details about the accident.

Finally they were loading her into the ambulance, and Cody tried to follow inside.

"I'm sorry, sir, but you're going to have to stay here." A female EMT informed him.

"I can't." Cody felt utterly helpless. "She's my... She's my life."

"Did you say she's your wife?" she asked.

"No."

"Then you'll have to stay here." The woman pushed him back. She was just trying to do her job, but it pissed him off. He should be with Miranda.

"I can't..." he repeated, his voice rising in frustration. "She's pregnant."

"Calm down, sir." The woman, who was almost a foot shorter than him pushed him again. "Did you say she's pregnant?"

"Yes." Cody ran his right hand over his face.

"How far along?" Her tone was somewhat suspicious, like she didn't believe him or something.

"Let's see, it would have been the last week in June, so two months?"

"And did the two of you have a fight this evening?"

"What? No. I mean, she was upset. There was a misunderstanding."

"And did you strike her during this misunderstanding?" Her voice was laced with suspicion.

"No. Why would you think that?"

"There are abrasions on your right hand, the kind consistent with having struck someone or something." Not suspicion, but accusation.

He looked down at his hand, and sure enough, it was scraped up from when he'd hit the bastard during the robbery.

"This was from earlier. See, there was a robbery."

"A robbery. Sure there was." This woman didn't believe him. And worse, she thought he was some kind of animal who would lay his hands on a woman. That he could hurt Miranda in any way.

"Officer?" She marched past Cody toward the deputy sheriff who had just arrived. "Officer, I think you should follow us to the hospital. Our victim may have been involved in a domestic dispute prior to the accident."

The deputy stepped out of the vehicle.

"No. She wasn't." Cody followed her toward the patrol car.

"You, sir, will stay here." The woman turned on him like a guard dog.

"Like hell, I will." Cody was done with this woman.

"Sir, I'm going to ask you a few questions." It was Officer Parker, the one who'd been dispatched to the robbery. The one who had retrieved the gun.

"Yeah, sure. But tell her how I got this." He held up his hand. "Tell her there was a robbery at my store this afternoon. That Miranda was held at gunpoint and I punched the guy to keep him from hurting the woman I love."

"First, you need to calm down." Officer Parker's tone was calm, yet authoritative. "It's been a rough day, I know. But that incident is separate from this one."

"Ma'am. I'll check in with you at the hospital." He turned to the EMT, acknowledging her concern, while dismissing her to get back to her job. "Don't worry. I've got this."

She climbed into the front of the ambulance and Cody watched them pull away, sirens blaring.

"If anything happens to Miranda because she was too busy accusing me…" Cody's legs gave out. He slumped to the ground near the side of the road.

"Take a minute. I'm going to check out the scene, then I'll be back to get your statement." The deputy walked toward the truck. He took pictures and measurements and did whatever else he needed to do in order to complete his job.

Cody sat on the side of the road, not knowing what Miranda was going through. How badly she was injured. The airbag had deployed, but she'd still hit her head. There was blood on her face, but nowhere else. He was almost afraid to look at the driver's seat.

Resting his elbows on his knees, he cradled his head as if that would keep it from exploding. Keep his heart from shredding into a million pieces.

Officer Parker walked slowly back to where Cody was sitting.

"Good, you're still here." Like he had anywhere else to go.

"Could you take me to the hospital?" Cody didn't care that he sounded desperate.

"I need to ask you some questions about the accident. And what led up to it."

"I need to know if she's okay."

"I understand that, but the EMT crew and the doctors in the emergency room can see to that better than we can. So let's finish up here, okay?" Parker was calm, cool, and only slightly condescending.

"Were you in the vehicle?"

"No. She took the truck. I followed on foot."

"And can you tell me what happened before she took the truck? Did you have an argument? Had she been drinking?"

"No. She wasn't drinking. And we weren't fighting. Not exactly." Cody let out a breath. How did he explain the situation? "She told me she's pregnant. Only she wasn't sure who the father is. But when I told her it didn't matter, that I love her and I'll love the baby…"

"Did you strike her? Threaten her in any way?" Coldness could be heard in his voice, but maybe that was the only way he could continue to do a job like his.

"No. God, no, I'd never… You saw the guy at the store. I thought he was going to kill her. I can't lose her. Or the baby. I just can't."

"So she's not just an employee, then." Parker's tone softened, yet remained detached.

"No. She's more than that."

"And did she tell the medics about her pregnancy?"

"I told that woman, but she got all up in my face. Especially after she saw the scrapes on my hand." Frustration continued to build. "But do I look like a guy who'd beat a woman?"

"You have to understand we see a lot of cases where looks can be deceiving."

"Yeah, I guess I can see that. But please," Cody couldn't stand being away from Miranda another minute. Couldn't stand not knowing if the baby was going to make it. "Please, can you take me to the hospital?"

"Is there someone you can call?" the deputy asked, as if it was some sort of imposition.

"Come on, man, you're going there anyway." Now that Cody knew he was no longer a suspect, he needed the guy to see him as just a guy. A guy who needed to get to his woman.

"Fine, but you should call someone to pick you up."

"Right." Cody grabbed his phone just as the tow truck arrived. He texted Fisher, asking her to meet him at the hospital. And then he climbed into the front seat of the patrol car.

Chapter 19

The drive to Prospector General Hospital seemed to take forever. The longer he went without knowing what was happening with Miranda, the harder it was for him to not freak out.

He'd texted Fisher, instead of Carson. For one thing, she was closer. But he needed his brother. Only he couldn't put this on him until he knew if the baby was okay. Lily would no doubt come and she was also pregnant. No need causing more worry until he could find out what was going on.

Who would have thought both he and Carson would become fathers at the same time? He was going to think positive. The cousins would be the same age, and they could grow up together. Go to Marshall and Prospector High at the same time.

Cody barely waited for the squad car to come to a complete stop. He was out the door and nearly sprinting to the entrance of the emergency room.

"I'm here for Miranda Wilde. She was in an accident. I need to know how she's doing. And the baby."

"Slow down, sir," the receptionist said. "What is your name and your relationship to the patient?"

"I'm Cody Swift. Miranda is my fiancée." He hoped that would be good enough to allow access. "She's carrying my child."

"Okay, you'll have to wait over there. She's still being seen by the doctors."

"Deputy Parker." The receptionist recognized the officer. "Go on in."

"Oh, he can go in, but I can't?" He couldn't stand this. "I have to see her."

"Mr. Swift, I'm going to ask you to sit down only once. After that, I'll have to ask you to leave."

"Fine." He exhaled. "Fine. Just tell me when I can see her."

He sat, gripping the arms of the stiff and uncomfortable chair in the waiting room. The TV was turned to the Giants game, but he couldn't give a damn about baseball right now. There were magazines strewn about. A basket of toys in the corner. A vending machine was just outside in the hallway, and a water cooler stood next to the reception desk.

He couldn't breathe in here. The air was heavy with the smell of disinfectant. People came in and out. Nurses, doctors, patients. An elderly man with a bad cough was brought in by a young woman. Cody wanted to jump up and tell the guy to stay away from Miranda, he could be contagious... But the receptionist handed over a paper mask and the man slipped it on dutifully.

Cody sank back into his chair.

Another patient arrived. This time a young man with a nasty cut above his forehead. Probably needed stitches.

Cody and Carson had been in this very waiting room with their fair share of stitches, concussions, and other minor emergencies. How did Granny do it? How did she sit here and wait for her loved ones to receive medical treatment?

For the first time in a long time, Cody thought about his father. Had he been sitting out here in the waiting room when his mother was dying? Or had he been in the room during the birth? Had he had to stand by and watch as the birth of his sons caused the death of his wife? Seeing Miranda threatened had almost been enough to send Cody through the roof. He almost understood what it might have been like to lose someone so suddenly. What might have made his father lose it.

"Cody, what happened?" Fisher came through the door, all the irritation she may have felt with him gone, replaced by genuine concern. "You said Miranda was in an accident. Is she okay?"

"I don't know. They won't let me see her." He must have looked like hell because Fisher bit her lower lip and turned away from him for a moment before squaring her shoulders and then taking the seat next to him.

"Oh, Cody." She took his hand but wouldn't look at him. "I'm sure she'll be fine."

"She's pregnant." Maybe if he kept saying it, it would still be true.

"How could she know? You've only been together, what, a little more than a week?"

"No. I met her before. When I was gone."

"She's the one." Fisher let out a resigned sigh. "I figured you'd met someone, but then Miranda showed up and just moved right on into your life. Into your heart."

Why did Fisher sound like she was the one afraid of losing someone dear to her?

"You love her." It wasn't a question.

"Yes. I know. No one ever thought I was capable of love."

"No. I knew" She stood up and pretended to check out the score of the game. She sighed and then turned to look at him. "I knew everyone has always underestimated you. But mostly you underestimated yourself. I'm happy for you. I really am."

A "thanks" was on the tip of his tongue when a nurse came through the doors.

"I need to order an ultrasound for the patient in bed number two." The older woman barked orders like the hospital belonged to her.

"Miranda?" Cody jumped to his feet. "The woman they brought in from the accident on Riverside Drive?"

The nurse looked at him as if to ask, "Who the hell are you?"

"Please. I'm the father. I have to know if my baby is okay."

The nurse sized him up. She probably noticed the cuts on his hand and wondered about him. Finally, she nodded and led him to the closed door, but stopped before opening it.

"You have to be strong. No matter what." She narrowed her gaze the way his Granny used to do when she meant business. When she had to be the parent, not the doting grandmother.

Cody felt the color drain from his face. Was this nurse trying to prepare him for one of life's very hard lessons?

"It's always the big ones." Her tone softened, and she smiled. "All indications are that the baby is fine. The ultrasound is just to make sure."

"Okay." Strength returned to his legs. Breath returned to his lungs.

"I need you to be the big, strong man that you are. I need you to take her hand, and reassure her that everything is going to be all right. Can you do that? You're not going to faint if for some reason there is something wrong with the baby?"

"I can do that." He willed his heart rate to slow down. He'd dealt with emergencies before. He'd rescued people from the raging river. He'd been able to keep calm and reassure others that their buddy was going to be okay, even when, once or twice, he'd been lying.

"Good." The nurse slid her card through the slot in the door. "Cause it's a real pain in the ass when guys your size pass out. Knocking machines over, needing twice as much oxygen to revive you. And the tears? Tears in big men are the worst. Except the happy tears. Like when they see their child for the first time. Those are good tears. And yeah, the bigger they are, the harder they cry."

She was good, by putting a visual of a big guy like himself bawling like a baby at the sight of his newborn, she'd gotten him to relax enough to put one foot in front of the other.

*   *   *   *

Miranda's head and neck hurt. Her whole body ached, but overall, she hadn't suffered more than a concussion and some bruising across her shoulder and hips where the seatbelt had restrained her. A cut above her left eye, where she'd hit the side window, was the only visible damage as far as she could see.

It was the invisible damage she was worried about. She wasn't spotting, so the nurse, who was normally the labor and delivery nurse, but she was covering for an ER nurse who'd gone home sick while they waited for her replacement, assured her that all indications were that the baby was just fine. She'd gone to go get the ultrasound herself, and Miranda had a feeling that she thought all the babies in this hospital were her responsibility.

Miranda's heart swelled when she saw Cody walk through the door with the nurse. Tears flooded her eyes and he rushed to her side.

"You're here." Was all she could say.

"Oh, baby, I'm here. I'll be here no matter what."

"You don't hate me?"

"Of course not." He dropped a kiss on the top of her head. "You don't hate me?"

"No. No, I..." She looked over at the nurse. Nurse Meredith was her name. At first glance, she looked like she may have been born shortly after the gold rush, but she had a wise look in her eyes and an agile spring in her step. In other words, she'd been around, but she had no intention of slowing down.

"You don't have to worry about me," Nurse Meredith said. "I've been here over thirty years. I've seen it all."

An orderly wheeled the ultrasound machine in, and then left so they could have their privacy.

"Have you had an ultrasound yet?" The nurse asked, slipping on a pair of gloves.

"No. I haven't even had my first prenatal appointment yet. Maybe you could recommend a doctor here in Prospector Springs."

"Certainly." She pulled out a wand and slipped what looked a little like a condom over the end of it. Cody's grip on her hand tightened.

"Since you're only about two months along, we do the ultrasound internally." Nurse Meredith addressed Miranda directly, but she was also answering Cody's unspoken question. "It's more accurate and it's perfectly safe."

She squirted some gel on the wand and lifted Miranda's gown. "Now you're going to be strong there, big guy? Just like you promised?"

"Yes, ma'am." Cody squeezed Miranda's hand, gently this time. "I promise."

Miranda held her breath as the nurse inserted the ultrasound wand. She was almost afraid to look at the screen as a blurry image took shape. A sound, somewhat like an AM radio signal with interference, but also unlike anything she'd ever heard, came over the speaker.

"And there's the heartbeat." She could hear the joy and wonder in the nurse's voice. All her years of experience couldn't hide the awe of sharing a baby's beating heart for the first time. "And there's another heartbeat."

"Wait? What? My baby has two hearts?" Miranda started to sit up, but the nurse placed a gentle hand on her abdomen.

"No, honey. Your babies each have their own heartbeat. Congratulations. You're having twins. And from what I can see, two perfectly healthy twins."

Miranda looked up at Cody, expecting to see the same joy she felt reflected in his eyes. But instead she saw a look of absolute terror on his face. He was as white as the pillowcase under her head. He stood up. Wobbled, and then staggered toward the door. He grabbed onto the curtain around her bed, but it slipped through his fingers. He shook his head, and then mumbled. "Not twins. Anything but twins."

Miranda's eyes filled with tears. Relief that her baby—rather babies—were just fine, but sorrow that Cody was so freaked out about her having twins.

"He'll come around, dear. Men are funny that way." Nurse Meredith withdrew the wand and discarded the protective covering as well as her gloves. "Once he gets used to the idea, he'll be just fine."

"I always thought twins skipped a generation." Miranda didn't want to think about what would happen if he didn't come around.

"Not always. So, are you the twin, or is he?"

"Cody is a twin. He and his brother Carson are identical."

"Cody and Carson Swift." The nurses tone changed, became somber. "I remember the day they were born."

"You delivered them?"

"No. I got here just afterward. Just after…" She reached for a tissue. "There was no reason for it to go like that. The damn doctor should have known better. But don't you worry dear, he's no longer practicing. I'll hook you up with one of the best. Dr. Wilson is one of the top OBs in the state. She's delivered hundreds of babies. Many sets of twins. You'll love her."

"Thank you, but what happened when?" Then she remembered. Cody had told her his mother died in childbirth. No wonder he was freaked out. "I already know. Tell me, is there anything I can do to make sure…"

Her head started to throb again. She leaned against the pillow, tears leaking down her face. "How do I make sure the same thing doesn't happen again?"

"Make an appointment with Dr. Wilson's office as soon as you check out of here." Nurse Meredith took her hand and patted gently. "I'm going to recommend the doctor admits you tonight. Just for observation and so we can monitor you and your babies more closely."

"Yes. Of course." Miranda was tired. Scared. In pain. And once again, alone.

"Now, I don't want to alarm you, but you should get used to the idea of being closely monitored. Even though you're young, fit, and healthy, twins are always a high-risk pregnancy." Nurse Meredith was like the grandmother she never had. "Prospector General has one of the finest birthing centers in the state. Normally a hospital this size doesn't have the resources to hire the finest doctors and keep up to date with the newest equipment, but after the lawsuit, the board of directors wanted to make certain a tragedy like that never happened again."

"What lawsuit?" Miranda lifted her head, but it hurt to move. Now that she knew her babies had survived, she felt the pain throughout her body from the accident. Only she couldn't ask for any pain medication. She wasn't going to take any chances.

"Of course, he doesn't remember, he was just a baby." The nurse checked the readings on the machines that were hooked up to Miranda. She smiled before asking, "Is there anything else I can get for you, dear, before I go?"

"No." Miranda closed her eyes briefly. "Wait. Could you find Cody? See if he's okay?"

Chapter 20

Cody walked right past Fisher sitting in the waiting room. He needed air. There was not enough oxygen in the hospital. But when he stepped outside, it wasn't any better.

Twins. He'd never wanted to have kids. Always done everything he could to prevent it. Everything short of surgery. But he'd always been cautious. Every time. Even when a woman insisted she was on birth control, he always used a condom.

Except maybe with Miranda. Now he couldn't be sure.

He'd been afraid of something like this happening. And if twins ran in his blood, what about…? Oh God, he couldn't even think about what else could possibly be carried along his genetic line.

Someone lit up a cigarette, even though there were signs posted about the entire hospital being a smoke-free facility.

"Do you mind?" Cody didn't care if he came across as rude. In fact, he was almost itching for a fight. "There are people here."

"What's your problem?" The guy sneered, but he moved a little farther away.

His problem? He wasn't prepared for this. For any of it. He was a fucking coward.

Cody pulled out his phone and dialed his brother's cell.

"Hello?" Carson sounded a little groggy. Like maybe he'd been asleep. But it was only…hell, he had no idea what time it was. It was dark now. That's all he knew.

"Carson." Just knowing his brother was nearby—well, a half hour away, but close enough—was a huge comfort. "Hey, man, sorry to bother you. But can you get away from your bride for a bit? I need you."

"Yeah. I'm on my way." It sounded like Carson was climbing out of bed. Hell, he might not have been sleeping. He was technically still on his honeymoon. "Where are you?"

"Prospector General."

"I'll be there as soon as I can. Are you okay?"

"I don't know." His whole life, Cody had both resented and relied on his brother's constant presence. Right now, he missed him terribly. "Miranda was in an accident. She's going to be fine."

"Okay, so do you need me to drive you both home?"

"She's pregnant." So many emotions were attached to those words. Cody could hear his brother stomping down the stairs to his own truck. "With twins."

"I'm coming. It's going to be all right. Just know that." Carson was always the calm one. The responsible one. Here he was, bailing his brother out again. But Cody was finally mature enough to realize he needed Carson. Needed his steady presence. It wasn't enough to pretend to be like him.

"How can I know anything right now?"

"Let me grab my Bluetooth. So we can keep talking." Carson must be getting into the truck, a model that wasn't new enough to have built-in wireless connections. He'd have to use the earpiece he kept in the center console. "Okay. I'm here. Twins, huh?"

"Twins." He wanted the babies. Deep down, he really did. He could almost picture two little miniature Mirandas. But he didn't deserve them.

"Look, Cody. I know how you feel. Believe me." Carson sounded so fucking calm. How could he know what he was going through? "I know you're scared. I know this because you're man enough to ask for help."

"I can't do this." He couldn't admit that to anyone else.

"Yes, you can."

"It's too hard. What if…"

"I know. I have the same fear." And there was something in his brother's voice that made Cody believe him.

"Yeah?"

"Of course I do. Sometimes, when Lily's sleeping, I'll look over at her. She's so perfect. So beautiful." Cody could hear him exhale. "Then I think about all the things that can go wrong, and I get so scared."

"What if I can't do it? What if I'm…" He couldn't bring himself to say it.

"Like Dad?" Thank God his brother knew him so well. "You won't be."

"What if twins aren't the only thing that runs in the family? What if being a lousy father is somehow genetic?"

"Just the fact that you're asking yourself that question tells me that you'll be a great father." Carson chuckled, as if any of this was some laughing matter. "Just in case you think I'm some sort of Jedi, I'm not. That's Lily's advice. I asked her the same questions you're asking me. She's a wise woman. You should listen to her."

"That's your job." Some of the terror he'd felt dissipated. It was so good to have his brother home. Even if they no longer lived under the same roof.

"Well, yeah. But she is somewhat of an expert on pregnancy. She's been trying for years, remember?"

"Yeah. Maybe she should have gone with her first plan and used a sperm donor. I mean what if the kid looks like you?"

"Same old Cody." Carson's laughter broke the remaining tension. "But yeah, let's just hope our babies take after their mothers, huh?"

"Yeah."

"I also hope that Miranda and Lily can become good friends. I know Lily would love that, but Miranda seemed a little..."

"She thought—oh, shit, you're not going to believe this." Cody leaned against the post outside the hospital entrance. "You know how I took your place on the Yampa?"

"Yeah."

"Well, I took your passport, too."

"What?"

"I was Carson Swift to everyone I met there." It sounded stupid, even for a screw-up like him. "Even Miranda."

"I had a feeling she was the one."

"Did you hear what I said? She thought she'd met you. And she came here to tell you that she's pregnant. Only Fisher got to her first and told her that you had just left for your honeymoon."

"That must have been fun to explain. But obviously you pulled it off. So when's the wedding?"

"You don't understand. She found out it was me, tonight. Right before she smashed my truck into that tree at the bottom of the hill."

"Oh, shit."

"Tell me about it."

"So she freaked out, huh?" Carson sighed. "Why didn't you tell her sooner?"

"Because I'm an idiot."

"Yeah, but she loves you anyway."

"She did. I don't know man, when that nurse said 'You're having twins,' I kind of lost it."

"Then get your ass in there and find it."

Cody didn't say anything because he knew his brother was right. His brother was always right.

"How do I do that?"

"You're going to have to grovel. Big time. Like the most epic grovel a man has ever done." Carson wasn't telling him anything he didn't already know, but now he welcomed, rather than resented, the advice.

"I'll go big or go home."

"No. You'll go big, then you'll go home. With your woman." Carson switched off the phone. Or else they got disconnected. There were still stretches around the county where cell coverage was iffy.

A white Toyota Tacoma pickup pulled into the hospital parking lot. Carson got out and pulled Cody into a hearty embrace. A man's hug, where words weren't necessary. They'd said all that needed to be said.

Cody was just so glad his brother was here. Because he knew Carson wouldn't let him get away with failure. Carson would be there to pick him up, dust him off, and send him back out to try again.

And Cody would do the same for him.

The two men stepped apart. Both of them knowing what the other was thinking. They'd have each other's backs. But it would be different, too. Their women would come first. Always.

"Hey, Cody?" Fisher had come outside, looking for him. He'd totally forgotten about her. "The nurse came out looking for you. They're moving Miranda to a room and she wanted to know if you want them to make sure it has one of those chairs that fold out into a bed so you can stay with her, and I told her of course, so I thought I'd come find you and…Oh, Carson. You're back."

Fisher gave Carson a quick hug. "Well, if you're here, I guess I'm not needed anymore."

"Hey, Fisher. Thanks. For everything." Cody knew she cared for him. And yeah, not just as a friend. But she was also the kind of person who wouldn't let her own hurt or jealousy keep her from doing the right thing.

"Hey, you know me." She shrugged. "Well, I'm going to head back to camp. Someone's got to keep an eye on things."

"Be careful, okay?" Fisher was tough, but after what happened today, well, he didn't want her to take any chances. "If you see or hear anything suspicious, don't hesitate to call the sheriff."

"I'll be fine. The guys are all around. None of them wanted to go out tonight, so, you don't have to worry."

"Good."

"Oh, but wait. I almost forgot." She reached into the pocket of her shorts. "I went into the store, just to make sure everything was put away and all the doors were locked. And the phone rang while I was in there. A lady named Elizabeth Wilde said her daughter was staying there and she wanted to know if we had any more cabins to rent. I told her I couldn't tell her if a Miranda Wilde was there or not, but we did have one last cabin for the night. So I took down her number and credit card information. Then you texted me right after I hung up, so I wrote down her phone number. I figure if she is Miranda's mom, one of you might want to call her and let her know what's going on."

"Thanks, Fisher. You're the best."

"Don't you forget it." She smiled at both of them and then tossed her braid over her shoulder before heading out to her Jeep.

* * * *

Miranda was moved into a private room. Her insurance was paid up through September, so she didn't have to worry about coming up with the money for a huge hospital bill. She had two months before she'd have to renew it.

A soft knock on the door kept her from dwelling too long on problem. "Can I come in?"

It was Cody.

"Yes. Please."

"Oh, Miranda. If I could start all over again. I would do so many things different." He rushed to her side, taking her hand and kissing her palm, her wrist.

"Ooh, stop. That tickles." She shivered.

"I know I screwed up. Big time. I told you I'm new at this. I've never been in love before."

"Neither have I."

"I gotta tell you, when it comes to the river, I'm a pretty confident guy. I know what I'm doing."

"Except when you forget the pump and fall out and…" She couldn't let him completely off the hook.

"Yeah, yeah, yeah. In my defense, I was just so happy to see you again."

Tears welled up in her eyes.

"I know. I should have told you."

"But you thought I'd be mad at you? You thought I'd run away."

"I was stupid."

"I did run away. And I wrecked your truck."

"It's time for me to get a newer one anyway. One with more safety features. That can fit two car seats in the back. Two." His voice was laced with a combination of shock and awe.

"Yeah, I know. It doesn't seem real to me either. Even with these." She reached over to the table next to her bed and pulled out the print copies of the ultrasound. Two little white arrows pointed at two tiny blurred spots that the nurse had shown her were her babies. She took the woman's word for it.

"Wow." He stared at the pictures. "Just, wow."

"Don't worry, the nurse assured me they will look more like something on the next ultrasound."

"Those are the hearts, right?" Pointed at two bright spots on the image. "I remember it pulsing right there when she first brought up the picture. And then she pointed there, at the second heartbeat."

"And then you kind of lost your mind."

"Yeah. But I found it. It's two feet above here." He pounded on his chest, and she noticed he had tears in his eyes. "Promise me you won't ever run out on me like that again. I know I look like a big strong guy, but I can't stand the thought of losing you. Ever."

"Come here." She held her arms open and he carefully crawled into bed with her. "I won't ever run away like that again. I promise. I'm not my mother."

"Oh, hey. That's right. I almost forgot. Fisher gave me this." He reached into his pocket and pulled out a yellow sticky note.

"What is it?"

"It's your Mom's number. At least I think it is. Elizabeth Wilde?"

"Yeah, that's my mom." How would Fisher get her mom's number? She wasn't even sure if she had the right one.

"Anyway, she called and made a reservation at one of our cabins. How did she know to find you here?"

"I told her I was staying there. She called, when I was upstairs changing. But I couldn't deal with her right then."

"Maybe you should call her. I mean, let her know you're okay. And she might want to know she's going to be a grandmother."

"She might want to know that. But there's something you should know about my mom. She's not like other moms. She's always been more of a sister or roommate than a mother. I know she loved me in her own way. But she might not stick around. Even for her grandchildren."

"As long as she doesn't take you with her..." Cody lay back down next to her, and very gently brushed the hair of her face. "Hopefully she'll stick around for the wedding."

"What wedding?"

"Our wedding."

"Wait, did you just propose?"

"When I propose, you'll know it." He lifted his head and tried not to jostle the bed.

"Right, there will be fireworks and skywriting." She remembered that day on the river. His river. When he'd joked about how he'd propose to her if they hadn't just met. "Or was it in a rowboat during a rainstorm?"

"With a dozen swans and a frog choir." He did remember. "I suppose in your condition the hot springs is a bad idea."

"Yeah, and no champagne either."

"So how would you like me to propose?" There was no joking in his voice this time.

"Well, a hospital bed is definitely not the scenario I've always dreamed of." Her heart swelled with possibility. "Maybe a nice stroll down by the river. You could drop down to one knee. Confess your everlasting love for me, ask me to be your wife, the mother of your children."

"My best friend and partner?"

"Isn't your brother your best friend and partner?"

"Nah. You're a much better kisser." He flashed that mischievous grin she'd fallen for. Fallen so hard.

"That's just gross."

"Yeah. Sorry. Sometimes I'm still twelve years old. If we have boys, that's something you'll have to get used to."

"So you're saying you won't act like a twelve-year-old if we have girls?"

"No, I'll still act like a twelve-year-old." He laughed. "Until they start dating. Then I'll be a crotchety old man."

"The kind to sit on the front porch cleaning his shotgun when their dates come to pick them up?" For the first time since she'd gotten the positive pregnancy test, Miranda allowed herself to envision what her family would be like. No picket fences, but she'd definitely make sure there was a gate on the deck so the little ones couldn't get too close to the river. Cody would probably build them a treehouse. And she'd volunteer in their classrooms.

It would be perfect. Too perfect. Fear bubbled up inside her. What if she couldn't be that kind of mom? What if she got restless living in Prospector Springs, where the nurse who'd given Cody and his twin their first shots was the one to give her own twins their first shots?

What if he got bored with her?

She shivered. Most of the time when something seemed too good to be true, it was because it was.

"You okay, babe?" Cody pulled the covers over them.

"I don't think they'll let you sleep in the bed with me."

"Well, I'll stay as long as I can, then."

That's what she was afraid of.

Chapter 21

The hospital had let Cody sleep with her, and his steady presence went a long way toward calming some of her fears. Any man who could sleep through the nurses checking on her throughout the night probably wasn't going to be intimidated by midnight feedings. She would have to figure out a way to wake him up if she wanted help with diapers.

When he'd gone downstairs to get coffee and a bite to eat, she went ahead and called her mother.

"Miranda, what a charming little place you've found here." Mom answered the phone as if they'd just spoken yesterday. Okay. Maybe they had spoken yesterday, but that wasn't the point. "Did you know gold was discovered right up the river from here?"

"Yes, I know all about the gold." She sighed. "I'm sorry I didn't call back last night. I'm okay, but I was in a minor accident."

"You know. I had a feeling. Call it mother's intuition." Mom sighed. "I don't know, these last few weeks, I just felt like you needed me. Only...I know I haven't been much of a mother."

"Please, don't start that." Miranda's headache had eased, but now it felt like it was coming back. "You did the best you could. And I had an interesting childhood."

She hoped Mom wasn't in one of her moods where she'd dwell on all the ways she'd failed as a mother. When she'd make all these grand plans to settle down and become Lois from *Malcolm in the Middle* or Kitty from *That '70s Show.*

"Oh honey, are you sure you're okay?" Mom almost sounded like she was truly worried. "There I was, in the Congo, and I just had this feeling that you needed me."

"I'm fine. I should be released soon." Miranda had no idea her mother had been in Africa. But whatever. "Maybe we could meet for lunch. There's a nice little café that has really good burgers but also salads and pasta and daily specials."

"That would be nice."

Nice. Yeah. Because Miranda didn't have the courage to tell her over the phone.

"The people here are so friendly. I can see why you'd come here from San Francisco."

"I think I'm going to stay around here for a while." Miranda didn't want to seek validation, but the little girl who still wanted her mother's approval couldn't help but hope. "I like it here."

"There is something about this place." Her mother actually sounded supportive. "So have you finally found a home?"

"Yes. I've found a home here."

"And what else have you found here?" Her mother asked. "Have you found love?"

"Yes. I have."

"That's wonderful. I'm happy for you."

"So, where are you off to next?" Miranda tried to play it off like it wasn't a big deal. The Congo, Korea, Katmandu, it didn't matter, her mother would never be there for her.

"Well, if you don't mind, I think I'll stick around here for a little while." Mom sounded almost afraid to ask. As if maybe she was the one who worried about being left behind.

"Do you think you could stick around about nine months?" Maybe they could establish a real mother-daughter relationship.

"Nine months? That is a long time." Or maybe not.

"Well, what about seven months? So you can meet your grandchildren."

"Grandchildren?" Her tone softened.

"Yes, Mom. I'm pregnant. With twins."

"Twins? How wonderful." Her mother sighed. "You know, Miranda, when you chose to do something, you always went all out. Twins."

"Yes, twins." It was still hard for her to wrap her head around the idea. "Look, Mom, we'll talk more when I get out of here. Cody will be back soon and the doctor needs to check on me before they let me come home."

"Cody? Is that your young man? I can't wait to meet him."

"You'll meet him today."

"He's good to you?"

"Yes. He's wonderful. Kind, caring, strong. You'll see."

"Handsome?"

"Very."

"Does he have an older brother?" Mom always liked to joke about the two of them double dating. It wasn't funny when Miranda was a teenager, and it still wasn't amusing.

"No, he has a twin. They own the rafting company and resort where you're staying."

"It's a very nice place. I'm sure he'll take good care of you."

"And I'll take good care of him," Miranda added.

"Those babies, too?" Her mother had a wistful tone in her voice. Maybe her grandchildren would give her a reason to stay in one place for a while. Or maybe her grandchildren would travel to visit her—wherever.

They chatted for a few minutes longer, before the doctor came in and gave Miranda the all clear. She would need to take it easy for a few days. Until she was completely headache free for twenty-four hours. She would need to follow up with the obstetrician Nurse Meredith had recommended and take her prenatal vitamins.

Miranda dressed in the clothes she'd worn last night. There was just a small drop of blood on the left shoulder.

Finally, Cody returned. He had a goofy grin on his face. He must have come to accept the fact that she was carrying his twins.

"How's my girl?" He leaned over and kissed her forehead.

"Ready to go home."

"Yeah? I brought you something." She hadn't noticed he was carrying a paper sack. "I noticed you didn't have any shoes, so I got you some sandals."

She opened the sack and pulled out a pair of blue flip-flops. Perfect.

"Thank you. Did you drive my car here?"

"No, my brother let me borrow his truck. He and Lily dropped it off this morning." He held his hand out to steady her while she slipped her feet into the sandals. "We can keep it for a few days while my truck is in the repair shop."

"So the damage wasn't too bad?" That was a relief.

"Nah. I should be able to get a good price on it. There's a lot of demand for that truck, even with minor damage to the front fender."

"That's good. I'm sorry about—"

"Don't say another word about it." He cut her off. "I'm sorry, too."

"Don't say another word about it."

"Okay. I'll just have to show you, then." He scooped up the discharge paper and led her out of the hospital to his brother's truck.

"I called my mother. She'd like to meet for lunch."

"Are you feeling up to that?" He had a protective note in his voice.

"Yes. I think it will be nice to visit with her. She says she might stick around for a while."

"Did you tell her about the babies?"

"Yes. I think she's excited."

"Are you excited?" Cody reached for her hand. "Because I am."

"You know? I think I am." She squeezed his hand. "More so now that I know they're your babies."

"I'm really sorry I put you through that. I wish I hadn't let you go after getting off the Yampa."

"I'm really glad you didn't let me get away the second time."

"Me too."

* * * *

Cody wanted to stop on the way home, but figured Miranda would like to take a shower and put on some fresh clothes. Besides, she'd need better shoes to walk down to the river with him. Flip flops would get her in and out of the truck, but they weren't great for walking on uneven river rock.

Miranda came downstairs wearing another one of those sexy little sundresses. He couldn't help but think about the last time she'd worn a sundress in his kitchen. Guess it was their kitchen now.

"Let me just call my mom and let her know we're leaving so she can meet us at the café." Miranda reached for her phone.

"Not yet." Cody stood, taking in her beauty. "Let's take a little walk. Down by the river."

"You want to go for a walk down by the river?" Understanding swept over her face, and she smiled knowingly.

"Let's go." He took her hand and led her down the stone steps that had been placed here and there to make the trek easier to navigate and also to mark the path down to the water's edge.

"Did you want to play some volleyball?" Miranda joked when they passed the sand volleyball court. She was like him in that way, making jokes when nervous. He could hear it in her voice. She knew what he was up to. Yet she agreed to come along, so that boosted his courage.

"Maybe later." He was on a mission right now. The ring weighed heavy in his pocket. He figured it would have been harder to find just the right one. But, like with Miranda, he knew the instant he saw it, he'd found the one. Not too fancy, but with an understated elegance.

Carefully, he led her down to one of his favorite spots in the whole world. A flat slab of granite perched out over the river. He used to come out here when he needed to get away from Carson. Sometimes he'd throw rocks in the water, other times he'd just sit. Never in any of his forays out here did he dream of bringing a woman here. Not to propose. But here he was.

After making sure Miranda had steady footing, he dropped down on one knee, reached for her hand, and spoke.

"Miranda," He looked up into her eyes, shining with tears—of joy, he hoped. Suddenly, his throat tightened. His mouth went dry, and for a moment he was afraid he wouldn't be able to say the words. "Miranda. I used to think the river was the most powerful force of nature. It can carve granite, and carry thousands of cubic feet of snowmelt down the mountain. It can overflow its banks and overwhelm you with its beauty. The river can generate power, and sustain lives. It can bring people together. The river brought us together and I found out there's something even more powerful. Love. I love you and I want you to be my best friend and partner, my lover, the mother of my children."

"You forgot shopkeeper." She smiled mischievously.

"I thought that was supposed to be temporary."

"I thought your name was Carson." Her grin widened playfully.

"I guess I deserved that." He loved that he could joke with her. Even in this most serious of moments. "I don't deserve you, though. I hope to, someday, be worthy of the love you've given me. The children you'll give me. And the life we can make together. Miranda, will you marry me?"

"Sounds like a grand adventure." Her smile softened, the tears that pooled in her eyes spilled over. "Yes, Cody, I will marry you."

"Here." He remembered the ring. He took it out of the box, and slipped it on her finger. Perfect fit. Just like they were a perfect fit together.

"Oh Cody. It's beautiful."

"Not as beautiful as you are."

"I love it." She looked down at the diamond glittering on her hand. Tears of joy spilling down her cheeks. "I love you."

"There's just one more question."

"What's that?"

"Where would you like to go on our honeymoon?"

She looked back at the house and smiled. "I don't need to go anywhere else. I have everything I need right here."

In case you missed it, here's a glimpse of the first Swift River novel,

SWEPT AWAY

Carson Swift may look exactly like his twin brother Cody, but they're as different as tie dye and camouflage. Reliable, responsible, and usually the designated driver, Carson is also over being his brother's keeper, but suddenly his plans to break free are complicated by the woman they fish out of Hidden Creek . . .

Lily Price is not your typical damsel in distress. Infidelity, infertility, and downsizing provide a triple threat to her ego, but falling into the swollen river nearly ends her life. If not for the handsome stranger—make that two handsome strangers—she might not have had a chance at having a baby by any means necessary . . .

As Carson helps Lily overcome her fear of the river, she helps him save his rafting business from going under. She also saves him from abandoning all that is important to him in order to get a taste of freedom. Together they find that love is the ultimate adventure.

A Lyrical e-book on sale now.

Learn more about Kristina at
http://www.kensingtonbooks.com/author.aspx/30540

Chapter 1

"Man this water's really pumping." Carson Swift hiked a few steps ahead of his twin brother, Cody. His feet landed firmly on the familiar trail to Hidden Creek, but his thoughts were a million miles away. Make that eight hundred miles, give or take, depending on whether he took Highway 50 or Interstate 80 through Nevada. "With the water this high, I don't think we'll catch a lot of fish."

"Good thing we have steaks in the fridge." You'd think he was nine, not twenty-nine, by the way Cody trotted along excitedly, skittering small bits of gravel along the well-worn path. He was too damn happy with his life. "We're not pulling anything out of the river today."

"At least it's finally warming up." What a coward. Carson had dragged his brother out here to have a serious conversation. Instead, he was discussing water conditions. The weather.

"I thought winter would never end." Cody would probably still catch a fish or two. He had that kind of luck. Women and trout landed at his feet without much effort. "But summer's coming and it's going to be a hot one."

Another summer stretched out in front of them. Long, hot days on the river. Longer, hotter nights at the Argo—throwing back a few beers, shooting pool, picking up pretty strangers. Who wouldn't want the easy life of a whitewater guide?

"June bookings look pretty solid." Carson tried to look at the sunny side of the creek. Business was good. That wasn't why he wanted out.

"We should get quite a few bachelorette parties." Cody had suggested advertising in the regional bridal magazines. His idea was to offer Girls' Weekend trips, complete with a selection of local wines and discounted cabin rentals. It was one of the few times he'd taken an interest in the business itself.

Most of the time Cody was all about the fun. Hot babes and cold beer on a warm summer night were the only things he seemed to care about. Except in winter, when he'd head up to the mountains to ski. Leaving Carson to take care of repairs and maintenance.

"Plenty of family trips too." All those intact families. Smiling. Laughing. Bonding. Being there for each other. Reminding Carson of what he didn't have.

"Don't forget bachelor parties." Cody was always up for a good time. The man lived his life as though it was one big party. A lot of guys would give up their flat screen TVs to walk in his sandals. "Man, we've got the best job in the world."

"Sure. A day's work for us is a vacation for most people." Carson still loved the heart-stopping rapids and Zen-like calm stretches on the river. He still loved helping people connect with nature and discover a little something about themselves along the way. And he still loved the constant, yet ever-changing force of the river.

It was the change that called to him now. He might as well be guiding the jungle boats at Disneyland. He was seeing the same sights, telling the same jokes over and over again until he felt like one of the automated characters. He needed a change of pace. A change of scenery. A change of company.

"Yeah, we've got it made." Cody trotted along like a kid on the first day of summer vacation. He had no idea his brother didn't share his enthusiasm for the status quo. Carson was afraid of becoming stagnant. A breeding ground for bad blood.

It wasn't that Cody was a bad guy. He was just there. Always. They lived together. Worked together. Ate together. The only thing they didn't do was sleep together. Although there had been women who would have been willing to take on them both. Cody probably could have been talked into it, but it was bad enough sharing breakfast and small talk with his brother's dates. Carson wasn't about to share anything more.

He should just get it over with. Say the words. *I'm leaving.* But the lump in his throat rose like the spring runoff, drowning out his voice. If he could think of another way to get Cody to grow up already, he'd take it. But the only way to get him to change would be to force it on him. He had to toss his brother overboard and hope he'd come up swimming.

"What the hell?" Cody skidded to halt. "Is that woman actually swimming? In this high water?"

* * * *

Damn. This water is cold.

Lily came up for air, sputtering and spitting out a mouthful of river water. She grasped for something—anything she could hold onto. But the current was too fast, too strong for her to grab hold of anything. She tried to find her footing, but the force of the river kept her from getting her legs underneath her. Quickly she realized that it was probably for the best. If anything, she could end up breaking a leg if she slammed against a rock. Or worse, her foot could become entrapped and it wouldn't be long before the river pulled her under, drowning her.

She wondered how long it would take to find her body. Would some fisherman stumble upon her days, weeks, or even months from now? Or would the current eventually pull her downstream, where she'd wash up lifeless on the shore?

For the first time in her adult life, Lily was thankful she was childless. There was no baby to leave motherless. Left to be raised by her rat-bastard ex-husband.

Water shot up her nose, and Lily coughed. She tried once again to regain control of her body, but she was caught in a force too powerful to fight.

The movies were all wrong. Her life didn't flash before her eyes. Nothing but water and sky and regret rushed past her as she was carried downstream.

Lily didn't want her last conscious thought to be about her ex. About her failures.

As a wife. A daughter. An employee.

A woman who hadn't been able to conceive.

She tried to think of something positive. Relaxing her body, she willed her last thoughts to be about something beautiful. Like Hidden Creek. She'd always loved it here. The smell of the pines and the whisper of the wind through the trees. How the night sky was so clear and the stars shone so brightly she felt as if she could reach up and touch them. Blackberries that would be ripe in another month. She could bake a pie in the cozy kitchen of her cabin.

Her cabin. The one thing she'd fought for in the divorce. The place where she'd hoped to raise a family.

But now it would go back to Brian.

Over my dead body.

With a new sense of urgency, Lily fought back against the current, flailing about as if her life depended on it.

* * * *

Carson turned his attention to the river. He expected to see the slow, graceful movements of a woman out for an afternoon swim. He expected smooth, easy strokes and efficient flutter kicks as she propelled herself through the water. He expected to pass her by without another thought. Instead, he felt his muscles tighten, his heart rate accelerate, and his vision narrow as the realization that she was in trouble hit him like a flash flood.

Instinct kicked in. He dropped his rod, pulled his keys and phone from his pocket, and raced into the raging river. He dove into the waist-deep water, swimming aggressively toward her. The current was strong. He had to be stronger.

"Just relax. I've got you." He kept his voice steady, projecting strength, confidence, and competence. He couldn't let her panic. *He* knew he was trying to save her, but there was no way of knowing what was going through her mind.

She struggled briefly, mumbling something, as he wrapped his arm around her waist and pulled her against his chest. The buzz of adrenaline flooded his system, blocking out the cold, the current, and everything but the need to keep her head above water and bring her to shore. He kicked hard to propel them away from the strongest part of the current. Working with the flow of the river and not against it was crucial in getting them both out alive.

The river slowed as they approached the eddy. Carson adjusted his grip and his hand slid up over the smooth curve of her breast. He corrected his hold on her, but not before his thumb grazed her nipple.

Focus.

Get her out of the water.

All the hours of training drained from his head. This wasn't the first time he'd rescued someone from the river. It certainly wasn't the first time he'd touched a woman's breast. He should be able to get his mind back on track. Once they made it back to dry land, then he could think about her perfect breasts. When she was safe, he could let his mind wander in the direction his fingers had wanted to go. Not to mention his mouth.

"I've got you." He tried to sound calm, in control. Like someone who knew what he was doing. Her life was still in his hands. "Trust me."

Her body relaxed against his as she wrapped her arms around his neck. Relief flooded him as he realized she wasn't going to panic and try to fight him. He still had to get her out of the water. Then get her somewhere warm. The image of his bed flashed through his mind and he brushed it away like a pesky mosquito.

Cody stood downstream, holding his rod case over the water. A rope would be better, but they'd left the hoopi in the truck. The tubular nylon webbing, often used by climbers, was one of their most valuable pieces of river gear. Almost as versatile as duct tape, and Carson wished he had some with him. He did have his brother. Cody might not remember to pay his cell phone bill on time, but get him on the river and he was one of the most reliable men around.

"Hold tight." Carson reached for the case, and grabbed hold as Cody pulled them toward the shore, reeling them in like a couple of steelhead. Carson got his feet under him and helped the woman stand.

"You're okay. You're going to be just fine." His legs felt like wet beef jerky now that the adrenaline drained from his system. His heart rate should be returning to normal, but he'd just felt her up in the middle of the river and he didn't even know what color her eyes were. Let alone her name.

"Thank you." She shivered.

Hidden Creek would be a very different river in another month. Once the runoff slowed, it would be marked with gentle riffles, calm pools, and some of the best trout fishing in Northern California. Today, it was a surging flow carrying a winter's worth of snowmelt as it merged into the South Fork of the American River. Not as cold as it had been a few weeks ago, but still cold enough that twenty more minutes might have led to a different ending.

Carson tore off his wet shirt and pulled the woman against his bare skin. "I've got to get your core temperature up." He massaged her arms and torso briskly, hoping she wouldn't think he was some kind of perv. But, damn, she felt good pressed against him, soft in all the right places and naked except for her bikini bottoms. The idea was to warm her up, but he was the one on fire.

"Cody. Give me your shirt." His words came out harsh and demanding. His brother obeyed, pulling the dry T-shirt off and tossing it to him in one swift motion. Carson slipped it over her head, breaking the contact but not the impact of her bare skin against his.

"What's your name?" Carson asked.

"Lily Johnson." She held her hand out, but quickly retreated. "Sorry. It's Price. Lily Price."

She shook her head before extending her hand again. Her grip was firm and surprisingly warm. Had she recently changed her name or was her confusion because of injury? He glanced down at her left hand. Bare. But that didn't mean a thing. The river was a thief. She'd been known to take jewelry, sunglasses, and bathing suits. Even lives.

"I'm Carson Swift." Carson dropped her hand, but he still felt the charge as if he'd been struck by lightning, and the water only intensified the conductivity. "This is my brother, Cody."

"Oh, so there are two of you." She let out a sigh of relief. "I thought I was seeing double."

"We're twins." Cody reached out to shake hands. "Identical."

"Nice to meet you both." Lily glanced from one brother to the other. The glazed look in her honey-gold eyes told Carson she'd have to work at telling them apart. They were too much alike. On the outside.

"It's our pleasure." Cody emphasized the last word, letting her know that he was interested. Then again, Cody rarely met a good-looking woman he wasn't interested in.

"Well, thank you both for…" Lily held her breath just long enough for Carson to suspect she was not as calm as she pretended to be. "Saving my life." She flashed them a fake smile to let them know she was fine, thank-you-very-much.

"Hey, no problem." Carson wanted her to believe it was no big deal. All in a day's work.

Except it was a problem. A big problem. He couldn't just walk away from her now.

Physically, she'd recover. She'd be sore for a few days, but the color had already returned to her cheeks. She stretched her arms overhead and rolled her head from side to side. He almost expected her to throw a few jabs in the air just to prove she was a fighter. But she kept casting glances at the river as if it might reach up and swallow her. Carson worried more about her emotional state. Fear could creep in like an unwanted vine and if left unchecked, it would take over, choking the life out of her.

"Let's get you someplace warm." Carson took her arm to lead her back up the path. "My truck is just down the creek."

"Oh, that's okay." Lily eyed the water again with mistrust. "My cabin is right on the river."

"Cedar shingles? Green trim?" Cody asked. They had fished this stretch of the river enough times to know the place she was talking about.

"That's the one." Lily's face lit up with pride. There were only a few residences along the way and hers was by far the most welcoming.

"Trust me," Carson said. "My truck is much closer."

She shrugged and then bent down to pick up his keys and phone.

"You might need these then." She handed the keys to him and their fingers brushed, sending a shiver down his spine.

"Is there someone we should call?" Carson asked as he took the phone.

"No." Lily shook her head. Sadness flickered across her face, disappearing almost instantly. "I'm enjoying the solitude of Hidden Creek."

"So you're all alone out here?" Cody's voice dripped with invitation. Could he be any more obvious? The woman had just been plucked from the river and Cody was trying to get her into bed.

"I'm taking a much-needed vacation." Lily's voice held a hint of defiance. "The first since my honeymoon seven years ago."

"So will your husband be joining you?" Carson's voice cracked like a thirteen-year-old boy. He half-hoped she was still married. Then he could just forget about her.

Yeah. Right.

"My *ex*-husband can go to hell." Lily's voice shook a little. As if she wasn't used to using such strong language. Or maybe she wasn't used to standing up for herself. "Did I say that out loud?"

"You did." She made him laugh, in spite of everything.

"I am so embarrassed." Lily blushed, a deep, dark pink. "I'm not really the bitter ex. I swear."

"What, did the guy cheat on you?" Cody asked. Leave it to his brother to use a woman's divorce as an opener to hit on her.

"Yeah. Among other things." Lily looked down at the trail, as if it was the most interesting thing in the world. Obviously she didn't want to talk about it. She marched forward, but stumbled on an exposed root.

Carson grabbed her arm. Just to steady her. The sooner he got her back to her cabin, the better.

"Let's get you home. Get you warmed up, and we'll be on our way." Carson would sleep better knowing she had no lasting effects of her ordeal. Besides, he already felt responsible for her.

He needed someone else to worry about like he needed another Swift River Adventures T-shirt.

Maybe he could use another shirt. His was dripping wet and covered in dirt. Lily was the only one of them wearing a shirt, dry or otherwise. And damn, if she didn't look really good in it. Her hips swayed ever so slightly as she walked. She wasn't very tall, but her legs stretched long and lean beneath the faded blue shirt. Her damp hair fell just below her shoulders. Carson couldn't tell if it was light brown or dark blonde, but either way it would look great spread across his pillow.

He didn't need to peek at Cody to know he was thinking the same thing. They were way past the age of acting like horny teenagers. Or they should be. Besides, Carson wasn't going to stick around; he had no business lusting after her.

She was just something else he would leave behind.

* * * *

"So, Lily, what were you doing swimming in such high water?" one of the brothers asked. The one who'd pulled them both from the river. He'd also given her the shirt off his back. Literally.

"I wasn't swimming." Lily didn't like the defensive tone in her voice. "I... I fell in."

"Well, it's a good thing we came along when we did," the other brother said. He tried to keep his tone light, but Lily sensed an undercurrent of worry. They all knew what might have happened if the brothers hadn't been there.

Some Mother's Day this turned out to be. Not that she was fortunate enough to be a mother. And instead of being a good daughter, spending an uncomfortable day not talking about her divorce with her mom, she'd decided to relax in the sun, finally diving into that novel she bought for herself last Christmas. With everything that happened to her in the last few months, Lily hadn't had time for small pleasures. Now she had all the time in the world. The next few months, at least. She planned on taking the summer off before looking for another bookkeeping job, or even landing clients of her own.

Lily had felt a little reckless sunbathing on that rock like a teenager. She'd even switched to SPF 15 instead of her usual 50. UV rays had turned out to be the least of her worries. She should have waited for the paperback or gotten an eBook. With the bulk and weight of a hardcover edition, the book had slipped out of her hands and as she reached for it, she'd tumbled head first into Hidden Creek.

She was a strong swimmer, an experienced swimmer, but the swift current had taken her by surprise. She'd tried swimming back toward the rock, but there was no way she could fight the force of all that water. Disoriented and a little ticked off at the twenty-seven dollars she'd spent on that book she'd never get to finish, she'd started flailing about, reaching for something, anything to grab onto so she could get her feet back under her.

She'd been in the water ten minutes, maybe longer, when she'd heard a deep male voice, felt strong arms around her, and realized she wasn't alone in the water.

The rest happened so fast. She was in the water. Then out. Somewhere along the way, she'd lost her bathing suit top and this man was holding her close. There was a second man, identical to the first. He gave up his shirt and flirted with her. The first guy seemed worried about her. But she was fine. Really. They were making too much of a fuss over her. "Sorry to interrupt your fishing trip." Lily tried to steady her voice, to sound like a woman who could take care of herself.

"Hey, it's okay," one of the guys said. "The water's a little high for good fishing, anyway."

"We caught something much better." His brother smiled and spoke with a light-hearted tone. He was definitely flirting with her. She remembered flirting. It's what her ex had done with every woman but her.

"Tell me again who's who." They'd reached the end of the trail. Lily was trying to keep them straight, knowing it must be hard to be constantly mistaken for your twin.

"I'm Cody, the good-looking one." The first brother flashed his dimples and smoothed back his blond hair in an over-the-top, I-know-I'm-good-looking way.

"Yeah? When was the last time you got a haircut, you hippie?" His brother gave him a friendly shove. Lily's gaze strayed to his wet shorts. He'd been the one to jump in the water after her. He'd been the one to really save her life. She shivered at the thought. And at the way the damp fabric clung to his muscular thighs.

"At least I don't look like an escapee from boot camp, like Carson here." Cody snapped to attention and offered a salute.

"I like it short." Carson sounded a little offended. "Besides, my hair's so thick if I go more than four or five weeks without a trim, I have to put stuff in it."

"And it would just run out into the river, poisoning the fish." Cody recited the words like scolded schoolboy. "Lighten up, man."

"So I care about what gets washed into the river." Carson shook his head and chuckled. "You only care about what you pull out."

"Hey, at least I catch something once in a while."

"I'm not talking about the fish."

They teased each other, but there was genuine affection in their banter. Lily envied their closeness. As an only child, she'd envisioned a large family of her own someday. Three, maybe four kids running through the house. Walking down to Fairy Tale Town or the Sacramento Zoo. Baking cookies and hanging their artwork on the refrigerator door. The only thing hanging on her refrigerator now was an appointment card for Foothills Fertility Clinic.

She followed the twins to a white double-cab Toyota truck. Carson clicked open the locks and held the front passenger door for her. He offered his arm to help her climb up into the cab. A jolt, almost as startling as the icy-cold water, shot straight through her.

How long had it been since she'd been touched, really touched, by a man? For the last few years, sex had been entirely clinical. An act of procreation—and desperation—that had nothing to do with intimacy.

But he hadn't really touched her. Not like that. He was only trying to help. Like he'd been trying to help when he pulled her against him. And he was only trying to help when he'd touched her breast. Lily wasn't going to read anything into it. She didn't need a man. She definitely didn't need two of them.

Carson went around to the driver's side and Cody slid into the backseat. Lily clicked her seatbelt in place. If only she could restrain her nerves so easily.

"So tell me." She turned so she could converse with both of them. "What do you two do when you're not rescuing topless women?"

Masculine laughter filled the cab. The deep, rich sound warmed Lily from the inside out. Carson started the ignition and turned the heater on full blast, to warm her on the outside.

"We run Swift River Adventures, a rafting company out of Prospector Springs." Carson's smile showed a man who took pride in his work.

"It's not far from where gold was first discovered in California." Cody leaned forward, inching closer, making her aware that there was entirely too much testosterone in this tiny space. They were big men. Strong men. Very good-looking men.

It took twice as long to drive to the cabin as it had for her to float downstream. At last, she was home. *Home.* Even if it was only temporary.

"Nice place." Carson shut off the engine and turned toward her. His eyes were as warm, and as blue, as a summer's day. "Are you renting for the summer?"

"Nope. It's mine." She was still getting used to the idea. "All mine."

"Is it a vacation cabin?" Cody asked from the backseat.

"Not exactly." Lily turned to find Cody's eyes were just as startling and blue as his brother's. "My house in Sacramento sold a lot quicker than I anticipated. So this is home. Until I figure out where I want to end up."

"Well, I'm glad you're here now." Carson's voice was slightly lower than Cody's, without the teasing note. She just hoped she'd be able to find other ways to tell the two of them apart. They both wore faded khaki shorts, complicated athletic sandals, and nothing else. Carson had tossed his wet shirt in the back of his truck and she was still wearing Cody's.

"So, Lily." Cody didn't seem to want his brother to get the last word in. "What do you do when you're not charming the shirts off a couple of fishermen?"

"I'm an accountant." Or she had been.

"No way." Cody leaned forward again. "You're much too interesting to be an accountant."

"I think that was supposed to be a compliment." Carson shot his brother a disapproving look. "What kind of accounting?"

"I don't have my CPA license." Lily was making excuses again. Focusing on what she lacked, not what she could do. "I do general bookkeeping, payroll, just about anything except income taxes. But my company decided to outsource my duties, so here I am."

She exited the truck and approached the front porch steps. Both men followed her across the wraparound deck and through the front door of the two-story cabin. The place had been built in the 1940s, when things were made to last. The floors were well-worn oak planks, the fireplace had been built with rocks gathered from the area, and a large picture window overlooked the river below. Three bedrooms, plus a loft, would provide plenty of space for the large family Lily still hoped to bring back here someday.

They entered the bright, spacious kitchen, with its knotty-pine cabinets, butcher-block counters, and a large cast iron sink big enough to bathe small children in. Lily had so many dreams for this place. None of them involved being divorced, jobless, and alone.

"Do you have any tea?" Carson eyed the kettle on the back burner of the gas stove. "Or hot chocolate? Something to warm you up?"

"How about some whiskey?" Cody suggested. His grin made her somehow think of those old cartoons with the big St. Bernard lumbering through the snow with a barrel of whiskey on his collar.

"Um, yeah. Tea bags are in the cabinet over the stove. There's beer in the fridge." Lily pointed to the old-fashioned Frigidaire. Not the most energy efficient appliance, but it reminded her of a simpler time. Back then, fresh fruits and vegetables replaced microwave popcorn as a snack. Cupcakes were made at home, not ordered online and delivered to your door. And families were created when a man and a woman loved each other very much and wanted to share that love with a child. It didn't take a credit check or a series of lab tests. "Make yourselves at home while I go change."

"You should take a long, hot shower," Carson suggested. His voice warmed her and made her shiver at the same time.

"Are you offering to wash my back?" The words just slipped out. She wasn't the kind of woman who traded suggestive comments with a man she'd just met. She'd never even made that kind of statement to her ex-husband.

"He doesn't have the skills." Cody stepped closer, invading her space. "But I'm very skilled." He lowered his gaze to her chest and licked his lips subconsciously. Or maybe it was on purpose. He seemed like the kind of man who knew exactly what he was doing when it came to women.

"Sometimes it takes more than skill." Carson shot his brother a disapproving look. Oh dear, they were fighting over her. Not fighting really, just competing for her attention. She should warn them that she'd vowed to go the rest of her life without ever having sex again. She'd spent the last few years with pillows propped under her hips every Tuesday and Friday from 10:15 to approximately 10:27. All for nothing.

Water under the bridge. Over the dam. Spilled out into the ocean by now.

She closed the bathroom door and slipped the oversized T-shirt over her head, catching a glimpse of herself in the mirror. A large bruise bloomed along her left side, stopping just below her breast. More bruises appeared along her hip and back. Tears stung her eyes as she realized just how lucky she was that Carson and Cody had decided to go fishing that day.

"I'm going to fix you a cup of tea," one of the twins said through the door. "Do you need any help in there?"

"No, I got it." Lily tried to make her voice as strong as possible. She didn't want whoever it was to think she was weak.

"Just checking." His voice was strong, steady, and very sexy. "Let me know if you need anything. Despite what Cody says, I'm very good at washing backs."

It was Carson. Her heart fluttered as she remembered the feel of his arms around her. His hand on her breast. The way he'd pressed against her, trying to warm her up. He was so solid, rock hard arms, chest, and well, if that was shrinkage…

She turned on the shower. It would take a few minutes to warm up. The water, that is. She was already warm in all the wrong places. Maybe she should take a cold shower instead. Like that would help get her mind off the two hunks in her house. Either one of them was twice the man Brian was. And put together? She shuddered as she stepped under the hot water.

The warm spray did wonders to release the tension in her body. It wasn't just the day's events, but the last eight months of stress that she needed to wash down the drain. She had turned thirty wondering why it was such a big deal. She had a good job, a nice house in a desirable neighborhood, and a smart, successful husband to share her life with. The only thing missing was a baby. They had been working on that.

But then she'd lost her job. No big deal. They didn't need the money. She was going to quit when she got pregnant anyway. But they had been trying for three years. Two years longer than most people waited to get tested. The results were more than disappointing. It had been the final straw that had broken the overstrained backbone of their marriage.

Damn. She must have gotten shampoo in her eyes. The stinging sensation couldn't possibly be tears. She had nothing to cry about. She was alive. That had to count for something. She still had plenty of time to have a baby. She had options. Maybe even right there in her living room.

Stop. Don't go there.

She wasn't desperate. Gone were the days when only a married couple was given a chance at having children. She could probably even adopt, if it turned out that Brian wasn't the only one with fertility problems.

With a little effort, Lily managed to dress after her shower. A bra was out of the question, considering the bruises on her side. The guys had already seen her girls in all their glory, so she slipped on a dark green T-shirt, hoping she wasn't asking for trouble. She'd just have to go out there and be herself. If only she knew who that was.

That's what she'd come up here for. To live life on her own terms. And that meant taking one step at a time, starting with marching into the kitchen where her rescuers were waiting.

"Oh, good. You're both still here." Lily put on a brave smile. "I'm not sure how to thank you. For everything."

"Don't worry about it." Carson handed her a cup of tea. "We're just glad we could help."

"I could make you dinner. Or something." Lily tried to think if she had enough food for three.

"No. That's okay," Carson was quick to decline. "You should get some rest."

"We could light your fire," Cody offered, and his brother gave him a quick elbow to the ribs. "In the fireplace. To make sure you stay warm."

"Oh, that's not necessary." She wasn't sure if Cody was trying to be funny, but the way Carson glared at him made her suspect that Cody's over-the-top flirtation was a sore subject between them.

"Is there anything else you need?" Carson's concern was a little overwhelming. She needed to get a grip on her emotions. Her hormones. All she had to do was finish her tea and thank them for saving her life. She wasn't looking to create a new life with either of them.

Meet the Author

Kristina Mathews doesn't remember a time when she didn't have a book in her hand. Or in her head. Kristina lives in Northern California with her husband of twenty years, two sons and a black lab. She is a veteran road tripper, amateur renovator, and sports fanatic. She hopes to one day travel all 3,073 miles of Highway 50 from Sacramento, CA, to Ocean City, MD, replace her carpet with hardwood floors, and throw out the first pitch for the San Francisco Giants. Visit her on the web at kristinamathews.com.

www.ingramcontent.com/pod-product-compliance
Lightning Source LLC
Chambersburg PA
CBHW022153260626
47155CB00017B/1856